PRAISE FOR

DIRTY MARTINI

"In *Dirty Martini*, Jacqueline 'Jack' Daniels is back, this time fighting a devious criminal who terrifies the entire city of Chicago . . . Konrath's latest should be taken straight, no chaser needed."

—*Publishers Weekly*

"Mix Konrath's witty repartee with edge-of-the-chair suspense, over-the-top killing devices, and action that never takes a breather, and you have Konrath's latest white-knuckle thriller. Not to be missed."

—*Library Journal*

"Like Jeffrey Deaver, Konrath ratchets up the suspense until readers don't dare stop flipping the pages; the characters are sharply drawn; and the dialogue sounds like real (though funny) people talking . . . Konrath clearly understands the importance of creating a believable, interesting villain."

—*Booklist*

"Filled with suspense, action, and comedy, and will leave you laughing out loud."

—Paul Pessolano,
Borders, Snellville, Georgia

"I have never enjoyed a book more—it had me laughing so hard I was crying."

—Jim Munchel,
Borders Express, Camp Hill, Pennsylvania

"J.A. Konrath's best one yet."

—Heather M. Riley, Borders,
Rockford, Illinois

"Jack is smart, tough, and totally believable. *Dirty Martini* goes down smooth."

—Dave Biemann, Mystery One,
Milwaukee, Wisconsin

DIRTY MARTINI

This book is for Jim Coursey,
who has been there for me since the beginning.
Best friends forever, man!

DIRTY M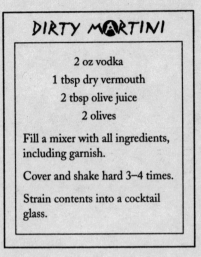RTINI

2 oz vodka

1 tbsp dry vermouth

2 tbsp olive juice

2 olives

Fill a mixer with all ingredients, including garnish.

Cover and shake hard 3–4 times.

Strain contents into a cocktail glass.

DIRTY MARTINI

N o security cameras this time, but he still has to be careful. The smaller the store, the more likely he'll be remembered.

He's dressed for the part. The mustache is fake. So is the shoulder-length hair. His facial jewelry is all clip-on, including the nose ring and the lip ring, and his combat boots have lifts in them, adding almost three inches to his height. He's wearing a Guns N' Roses T-shirt that he picked up at a thrift shop for a quarter, under a red flannel shirt that cost little more. The long sleeves hide the tube.

When they interview witnesses later, they'll remember his costume, but not his features.

He picked a good time of day—the store is busy. The woman behind the counter is speaking German with one of the patrons, three people in line behind her. To the left, an old lady is pushing a small cart, scrutinizing some imported canned goods. In the rear of the store, a fat man is picking up a .5-liter bottle of Weihenstephaner beer.

At the deli section, he finds the cooler with the fresh fruit. Pretending as if he's trying to decide, he eventually picks up a red apple.

He cradles the fruit in his left hand, avoiding the use of his fingertips. Palmed in his right hand, attached to the tube that runs up his sleeve, is the jet injector. It's four inches long, shaped like a miniature hot glue gun. He touches the orifice to the surface of the apple. Pulls the trigger.

There's a brief hissing sound, lasting a fraction of a second. He puts the apple back and selects another, repeating the process.

Pssssssttttt.

After doing four pieces of fruit, some potatoes, and a plastic container of yogurt, the jet injector needs to be armed again—something that will attract attention. He leaves the deli without buying anything, stepping out onto Irving Park Road and into the pedestrian traffic.

Ethnic stores are easy. He's already done a supermarket in Chinatown, contaminating some star fruit and dried fish, and a Polish butcher shop on the West Side, injecting almost the entire stock of kielbasa. In Wrigleyville he visited a large chain grocery store and made quick work of some apples, pears, and packages of ground beef, mindful to keep his head lowered so the security cameras didn't get any good facial shots. Just south of Chicago's Magnificent Mile he paid for admission to the Art Institute and spent thirty minutes in the cafeteria, using his jet injector on practically everything—cartons of milk, juice boxes, fruit, candy bars—and when the clerk turned her head he sprayed a cloud burst into the nozzles of the soda pop machine.

He has two stops left: an all-you-can-eat buffet on

Halsted, and another grocery store on the North Side. Then he's done.

For today.

Tomorrow he has another eight stores picked out, news permitting. The incubation period is anywhere from a few hours to a few days. There's a chance people will get sick sometime tonight. Paralysis is terrifying, and once it begins, the infected will rush to the hospital. Diagnosis isn't easy, but the agent will eventually be discovered. Then the alphabets will be notified—the CDC, WHO, FBI, CPD.

If the panic spreads ahead of schedule, he'll have to move up with the Plan and do the second round in a dif-ferent way.

It will be interesting to see how things turn out.

He heads down Lincoln, stopping in a fast-food chain. In the bathroom he detaches the injector from the tube, placing it in his pocket. He washes his hands with soap and holds them under the air drier, which is labeled *For Your Sanitary Protection*. This prompts a smile. When he's finished, he removes a moistened alcohol towelette and goes over his hands again.

At the counter, he orders a burger and fries, and eats while surreptitiously watching the kids frolic in the in-door playland.

Children's parks are a cesspool of germs. All that openmouthed coughing and sneezing, all those sticky fingers wiping noses and then touching the slides, the ladders, the bin of a thousand plastic balls, each other. It's practically a hot zone.

When he finishes eating, he returns to the bathroom, attaches the jet injector to the tube running up his sleeve, and lightly shakes the cylinder strapped to his waist under his shirt.

There's plenty left.

He arms the injector using the key to torque back the spring, and walks out of the washroom over to the cubby where a dozen pairs of brightly colored kids' shoes lie in wait. Getting down on one knee, he pretends he's tying a lace.

Instead, he injects the rubber soles of five different shoes.

A small child pokes him from behind.

"That's my shoe."

He smiles at the boy. "I know. It fell on the floor. Here you go."

The child takes the shoe, switches it to his other hand, and wipes his nose with his palm.

"Thanks," says the boy.

The man stands up, winks, and heads north on Lincoln to catch the bus to the all-you-can-eat buffet.

CHAPTER 1

IS THAT A REAL GUN?"

The little girl probably wasn't much older than five, but I'm not good with children's ages. She pointed at my shoulder holster, visible as I leaned into my shopping cart to hand a bag of apples to the cashier.

"Yes, it is. I'm a cop."

"You're a girl."

"I am. So are you."

The child frowned. "I know that."

I looked around for her mother, but didn't see anyone nearby who fit the profile.

"Where's Mommy?" I asked her.

She gave me a very serious face. "Over by the coffee."

"Let's go find her."

I told the teenaged cashier I'd be a moment. He shrugged. The little girl held out her hand. I took it, surprised by how small it felt. When was the last time I'd held a child's hand?

"Did you ever shoot anyone?" she asked.

From the mouths of babes.

"Only criminals."

"Did they die?"

"No. I've been lucky."

Her eyebrows crunched up, and she pursed her tiny lips.

"Criminals are bad people."

"Yes, they are."

"Shouldn't they die?"

"Every life is important," I said. "Even the lives of bad people."

A woman, thirties, rushed out into the main aisle and searched left, then right, locking onto the girl.

"Melinda! What did I tell you about wandering off!"

She was on us in three steps. Melinda released my hand and pointed at me.

"I'm okay, Mommy. She's got a gun."

The mother looked at me and turned a shade of white appropriate for snowmen. I dug into my pocket for my badge case.

"Lieutenant Jack Daniels." I showed her the gold star and my ID. "You've got a cute daughter."

Her face went from fraught to relieved. "Thanks. Sometimes I think she needs a leash. Do you have kids?"

"No."

She opened her mouth, then closed it again. I watched her puzzle out what to say next.

"Nice to meet you, ma'am," I said in my cop voice. Then I went back to my groceries. An elderly man, who'd gotten into the checkout line behind me, gave me a look I usually received from felons I'd busted.

"It's about goddamn time," he said.

"Police business," I told him, flashing my star again. Then I made a show of looking into his cart. "Sir, this lane is for ten items or less. I'm counting thirteen items in your cart, including that hemorrhoid cream. And while hemorrhoids might give you a reason to be nasty, they don't give you a reason to be in this lane."

He scowled, used a five-letter word to express his opinion of people with two X chromosomes, and then wheeled his cart away.

Chicago. My kind of town.

I really missed living here.

Shopping in the suburbs was cheaper, less crowded, closer to home, and no one ever called me names. I tried it once, at a three-hundred-thousand-square-foot supermarket that sold forty-seven different varieties of potatoes and had carts with little video monitors that broadcast commercials and spit out coupons. Never again.

You can take the girl out of the city, but you can't take the city out of the girl.

I finished paying for my ten items or less and then left the grocery store. The weather hung in the mid-sixties, cloudy, cool for June. My car, an aging Chevy Nova that didn't befit a woman of my stature or my style, was parked just up the street, next to a fire hydrant. I stuck my bags in the trunk, took a big gulp of wonderfully smoggy city air, and then started the beast and headed for the Eisenhower to battle rush hour traffic.

"Four more dead, bringing the death toll up to nine. Hundreds more botulism cases have been confirmed, and a city-wide panic has . . ."

I switched the radio station to an oldies channel, and let Roger Daltrey serenade me through the stop-and-go.

It took an hour to get to the house. It never took less.

By my rough calculation, I was averaging ten hours a week driving to and from work, so if I retired in ten years, I will have wasted over five thousand hours—two hundred days—in the car.

But, on the bright side, I had a big backyard that demanded to be mowed, trees that needed trimming, a clothes dryer in need of repair, a hole in the driveway, mice in the attic, a loose railing on the stairs, water damage in the basement, and flaking paint in the bedroom.

Lately, my sexual fantasies revolved around once again having a landlord. Looks, age, and hygiene didn't matter, as long as he had a tool belt and said, "Don't worry, I'll fix it."

Being a homeowner sucked. Though officially, I wasn't a homeowner. Chicago cops were required to live within the city limits, so the house was in my mother's name. While far from feeble, Mom had recently had some medical problems, and we decided that it would be best if she moved in with me. She agreed, but insisted we buy a house in the suburbs. "Where it is less hectic," she'd said.

As far as the city knew, I still had my apartment in Wrigleyville. A dangerous game to play, but I wasn't the first cop to play it.

I exited the expressway onto Elmhurst Road, drove past several tiny strip malls—or perhaps it was one giant strip mall—and turned down a side street festooned with eighty-year-old oak and elm trees. There weren't any streetlights, and the cloudy day and abundant foliage made it look like dusk, even though dusk was an hour away. I pulled into the driveway, pressed the garage door opener, pressed it again, pressed it one more time, said some bad words, then got out of the car.

The suburbs smelled different from the city. Woodsy. Secluded. Clean and safe.

I hated the suburbs.

I lugged the groceries to the front door, set them on the porch, reached for my keys, and froze.

The new door I recently had installed—a security door made of reinforced aluminum with the pick-proof dead bolt that I always made sure was locked tight—was yawning wide open.

CHAPTER 2

OP MODE TOOK OVER. My mother, the apple of my eye who'd guilted me into buying this suburban hell-house, was visiting friends in Florida and wouldn't be back for another week. Latham, my boyfriend, had a key, but he also had a car, which wasn't parked in the driveway or on the street.

Several times in my professional past, people had figured out where I lived. Bad people. Which is how I let my mom convince me to move to the middle of a forest preserve.

I set down the bags and opened my purse, removing my .38 Colt Detective Special, using a two-handed grip, elbows bent, barrel pointing skyward. I nudged the door open with my shoulder, holding my breath, trying to listen. The hardwood floor my mother adored squeaked like a tortured squirrel with every step I took. A male voice came from deep inside the bowels of the house.

"Debemos cantar algo más . . ."

I considered my options. My radio was in the car. Cell phone was in my pocket, but 911 would take a few minutes to respond.

"¡Dios mío!"

From behind. I spun, dropping to one knee, hearing and then feeling my Donna Karan skirt tear, drawing a bead on a chubby Mexican man in a full red and gold mariachi uniform, complete with sombrero and oversized guitar.

"Jack!"

I ascertained that the mariachi wasn't an immediate threat, turned toward the other voice, and saw Latham standing in the hallway, wearing a tuxedo.

"Jesus!" I said, hissing out a breath.

Latham smiled. "Don't shoot them until after you've heard them play."

I holstered my gun, Latham came over to help me off my knee, but somehow he wound up on his.

"Latham, what are—"

Guitars began to play, and two more mariachis joined their friend next to the breakfront. Latham dug into his tux jacket, coming out with a jewelry box. His red hair was combed back, but a lock of it curled down his forehead. His green eyes were glinting.

"Jacqueline Daniels, I love you more than I've ever loved anything in my entire life."

Oh my God.

He was proposing.

I had a huge rip in my skirt. I bet my hair was a mess. Did my makeup look okay? I hadn't checked it in hours.

"I want you to be my wife. I promise I'll do everything within my power to make you the happiest woman on the planet. Jacqueline Margaret Daniels, will you marry me?"

He looked so damn cute, his eyes all glassy, a goofy smile on his face, that dumb music playing behind us.

Then he held out the ring, and I started to cry. A solitaire diamond, shining like it had batteries, exactly the kind of ring I'd always dreamed of having.

He took my left hand, went to put the ring on.

I pulled away.

His cute face crumpled.

"I've thought it all out, Jack. I know you've been burned by marriage before. And I know you just moved here, and you aren't going to abandon your mother. We have time to work all of that out. I'm not setting a date. I just want . . . need . . . the commitment."

For some insane reason, I thought about the little girl at the supermarket, and how right it felt to hold her hand. What are you thinking, Jack? You're forty-six years old. You can't possibly . . .

My cell phone rang once. Twice. Three times.

"Are you going to get that?" Latham asked.

Shit. I dug the phone out and slapped it to my face.

"Daniels." I turned to the mariachi band and yelled, "Shhh!"

"This is the superintendent's office. She's called an emergency meeting. You need to get to police headquarters immediately."

The secretary broke the connection. Latham knelt patiently at my feet. To our left, three fat mariachis waited expectantly. I felt like a spotlight had come on and I'd forgotten my lines.

"You have to go," Latham said.

"Latham—"

"It's okay. Go ahead." He smiled, and the smile was so pure, so genuine, it broke my heart.

Then he put the ring back in its little red box, and my heart broke a second time.

"I'll be here when you get back," he said. "Do you mind?"

I reached out a hand and touched his freshly shaven cheek.

"Of course I don't mind. I love you. I just—"

He stood up, kissed me, and the mariachis broke into song. I'd never kissed a guy with a band playing backup music, and I found it incredibly stupidly romantic and more than a little exciting. My hips touched his, and he slipped his hand down the small of my back and pulled me even closer. It had been about a week since I'd had sex, and I moaned a little in my throat, arousal flushing through me like a drug. Then the lovely guitar strumming was replaced by screams of pain and terror.

My unfriendly cat, Mr. Friskers, had wrapped himself around one of the mariachis' heads like a face-hugger from the movie *Alien*. He did this often enough that we kept a loaded squirt gun in the refrigerator. Latham jogged off to get it, and I tried to explain to the mariachis that pulling wasn't going to work, because the cat just dug in harder.

They tried to pull anyway.

Mariachi blood flowed.

Latham came back with the squirt gun and some paper towels, apologizing profusely in bad Spanish. After the first spritz, Mr. Friskers fell to the floor, hissed at Latham, and then bounded off down the hallway.

The mariachi escaped with both eyes still in their sockets, but his mustache was dangling at an odd angle. His bandmates found this amusing enough to spur them into giggling fits.

"Go save the city," Latham said, pressing a paper towel to the bleeding singer's face. "We'll talk later."

"Are you sure?"

He winked at me. "Go on. I have to find the rest of this guy's mustache anyway."

"Thanks," I said, though it felt like spoiled milk in my mouth.

"Call me before you get home. I'm cooking dinner. German."

My favorite kind of food. I felt like a super-jumbo cowardly jerk.

I walked out the door, past the grocery bags I'd left on the porch, and climbed into my car. In the driver's seat, head buzzing, I stared at the large tear in my skirt but found myself unable to go back into the house to change. I couldn't face Latham.

He deserved so much better than me.

I pulled out of the driveway, thinking about my rocky relationship with the world's most adorable accountant, Latham Conger. He was a bit younger, attractive, intelligent, caring, good in bed, and the most patient and forgiving person I'd ever met. In all the fairy princess fantasies I'd die before admitting I had, he perfectly fit the role of Prince Charming.

Unfortunately the fairy princess fantasy didn't mesh well with the veteran city cop reality.

The Ike got me back into Chicago in an hour and some change.

Police headquarters was located in a sprawling 400,000-square-foot building on Thirty-fifth and Michigan. The lobby, like the exterior, was a mixture of orangish brown and off-white. Lots of tile. Lots of fluorescent light. It reminded me of a hospital.

My partner, Sergeant Herb Benedict, was pacing the hallway in front of the super's door. Herb was ten years my senior, and twice my weight, and he sported a walrus mustache and hound dog jowls. Worried wasn't a look that Herb wore often, but at that moment he looked positively distraught.

"Been in there yet?" I asked.

"Waiting for you. What happened to your skirt?"

I resisted the urge to smooth a hand over the tear.

"It's the new look. All the kids are doing it. Know what's going on?"

Herb shook his head, three chins jiggling.

"No. But it's big."

"You okay?" I asked. The bags under his eyes seemed darker than normal.

"Yeah. Why?"

"You seem kind of preoccupied."

"So do you."

We exchanged a look that promised we'd talk later, and went into the office.

There were three people in the room. Superintendent

Terry O'Loughlin—newly appointed by the mayor—was someone whom I hadn't had a chance to meet yet, but whose reputation was well known. Behind her back, cops called her OTB, *one tough broad.* She'd forsaken her public appearance dress blues for a red pantsuit that looked like it came off the rack at Sears, and fit about as well. Subtle makeup, brown hair cropped short, and a wedding ring that looked to be cutting off the circulation to her chubby finger.

Captain Bains, my boss, stood next to her desk. Bains resembled a short, fat, unattractive version of Burt Reynolds, down to the jet-black hairpiece that didn't match the gray in his mustache.

The third man was someone I didn't know. Tall. Blondish. Sort of geeky looking, but dressed sharp. Before anyone had a chance to say word one, geeky guy was crossing the room toward me, his hand out in front of him.

"Lieutenant Daniels." His shake was moist but aggressive, and he repeated it with Herb. "I'm Davy Ellis, of Ellis, Dickler, and Scaramouche. Call me Davy."

"Lawyer?" Herb asked.

"We're a public relations firm currently working with the city of Chicago to boost the image of the police department."

I glanced at Bains, who gave me a curt nod but no explanation. What the hell was going on here?

"Lieutenant Daniels." Superintendent O'Loughlin stood up and extended her hand. She wasn't much taller standing than sitting. We shook, and her grip was stronger than Davy's. "I'm glad you've finally graced us with your presence. It's a pleasure to meet you."

"Car trouble," I lied. "The pleasure is mine, Superintendent."

She did the shaking thing with Herb, and then we were instructed to sit. Bains joined us. Davy remained standing.

The super pushed a piece of paper across her desk. "My office received a letter this afternoon, addressed to me."

Herb and I leaned forward and read.

> *I am the one spreading the botulism toxin. I've visited sixteen places so far. One was a deli on Irving Park. You will agree to pay me two million dollars, or my next target will kill hundreds of people.*
>
> *This isn't terrorism. I'm not some dumb Islamic fundamentalist. I'm a venture capitalist. I'm investing in fear and death. Pay me or I'll branch out.*
>
> *Take out an ad in the Friday Sun-Times in the personals and say "Chemist—the answer is yes."*
>
> *You'll hear from me soon.*
>
> *To prove I am who I say I am, this paper has been coated with BT.*

Even though I could see the photocopy smudges, I suddenly wanted to distance myself from the paper. Botulism had been the top story for the last two days. The quick and deadly effects of the disease were terrifying.

"There was a powdery residue in the envelope with the letter," the super said. "The secretary who opened it is at Rush-Presbyterian. She tested positive for botulism toxin. Three other people at the First District came into contact with the letter. So far they're asymptomatic, but they're being treated with antitoxin and remain under observation."

Herb also seemed uncomfortable being so close to the note.

"I heard on the news there are nine dead so far," he said.

The super's mouth became a grim line. "The number is actually thirty-two, with over six hundred confirmed cases. We haven't released the figures. The CDC, WHO, and USAMRIID have been notified, but everyone else is still under the impression that this is a naturally occurring outbreak, not a terrorist act."

My mind harkened back to the anthrax scares after 9/11. The paranoia. The panic. Having this happen in my city was unfathomable. I thought about the tens of thousands of restaurants, cafés, bakeries, delis, supermarkets, and food stands in Chicago. One person, spreading a deadly toxin, could kill untold numbers before we even caught a lead.

"Has the FBI been contacted?" I asked.

"Yes. The Feds are sending a Hazardous Materials Response Team, which should arrive anytime. I'm sure Homeland Security will have a hand or three in as well."

The super took a deep breath, then hit me with a stare so intense I had to fight to maintain eye contact.

"You and Sergeant Benedict have been on high-profile

cases before, and when this breaks, it will be world news. You've had experience with product tampering. You've also had experience where the perpetrator contacted the police department."

I didn't volunteer that both of those cases were actually the same case, and that the MO was entirely different from this one. Instead I said, "So we're here to consult?"

"No," she said. "This case is yours."

Herb made a tiny gagging sound. I tried to get my head around this. Bains glanced at me like he didn't believe it either.

"We appreciate the vote of confidence, Superintendent O'Loughlin. But if this is simply because I'm a woman—"

"Spare me the kiss-ass and the righteous indignation, Lieutenant. I didn't choose you because you're the best cop in the city, or because you have tits. There were ten people on the list ahead of you. All of them men. The mayor got roasted when he appointed a woman in charge of the CPD. I'm not anxious to commit the same career suicide."

That's what I figured. "So why—"

Davy stood behind the super, the smile on his face so wide, it touched his ears.

"Your approval rating is at eighty-three percent," he said.

"Excuse me?"

Davy sat on the corner of the desk and gave me a friendly Dale Carnegie pat on the shoulder. I could feel his hot, moist palms through the silk of my blouse.

"The people of Chi-Town love you, Lieutenant Jack Daniels. You caught that crazy family last year, that brain tumor guy before that. Plus, the Gingerbread Man. Putting you in charge of this case will counteract some of the negative publicity we'll receive when the story goes public. You'll be giving hope to the hopeless."

Unbelievable. I wasn't the best qualified to run this case, but they picked me because I could smile pretty for the camera.

"Superintendent O'Loughlin—"

"The decision has been made. You have a blank check on this. Unlimited resources. If you aren't competent, find people who are."

The super hit the intercom button, asking the nurse to come in with the botulism toxin vaccines.

I looked at Herb. He was staring into space, either in deep thought, or unable to adequately process the situation.

I could relate. This wasn't just a bad case. This was a career killer. They hadn't caught the anthrax terrorist. Had he continued, he could have crippled the nation. And decades earlier, Chicago had been plagued by another tamperer, the Tylenol Killer, who had laced the pain reliever with cyanide. TK had single-handedly and irreversibly changed the face of over-the-counter drugs. Capsules to tablets. Tamper-proof bottles. Blister packs and double-sealed boxes. Seven dead, and billions of dollars in revenue lost. And he'd never been brought to justice.

Catching bad guys required evidence and eyewitnesses. Poisoners were the hardest perps to catch. A single, organized, motivated individual, with a basic knowledge of chemistry, could wreak more havoc on Chicago than all of the crime in the last fifty years combined.

I felt like hiding under the desk. O'Loughlin read my mind.

"Failure isn't an option, Lieutenant. This is the second-largest police force in the nation. I've got 16,538 people under my command. Fewer than one-quarter of them are women. You fuck this up, you fuck it up for me and for every female who has busted her ass to be treated like an equal in this sexist, chauvinist-pig pen. Catch the guy, you're a hero and we'll give you a parade. Screw up, and your career is over."

The nurse came in, toting a little white case.

"And if I refuse?" I asked.

O'Loughlin didn't blink. "You can pick up your white gloves and whistle down the hall. We'll start you at the intersection of Congress and Michigan. Make sure you brush up on your traffic signals before you report for work tomorrow at five a.m."

She grinned, and it was chilling. "If you want to speak with your union rep, I have him on speed dial. Or I could voice your concerns when I have dinner over at his place tonight."

I looked at Herb again, but he was still spacey. The nurse rolled up the sleeve of my blouse and dabbed my arm with an alcohol pad.

"Okay then," I said. "Let's get started."

CHAPTER 3

THE SUPER HAD a table brought into her office, and Herb and I made a list of cops that we trusted. We picked from different areas so there wouldn't be shortage in any particular district. When we were finished, we had a task force of a hundred cops. O'Loughlin added eight secretaries to the group.

"First thing we need to do," I said, "is close every deli on Irving Park Road."

"Be discreet," Davy suggested. "Panic won't help the situation. This city tends to riot when its sporting teams win a championship. They won't react well to terrorist threats."

Herb folded his arms, but his heart didn't seem into it. "The public needs to know."

Davy shook his head. "Not a good idea. The tourist business in Chicago is a billion-dollar industry." Davy held up his fists and began ticking off fingers. "Hotels. Airlines. Taxis. Restaurants. Museums. Shopping. Who would go out to eat if they knew someone was randomly poisoning the city's food?"

"That's the point," I said.

"We're also talking thousands, tens of thousands, of jobs here. Plus Chicago might never recover from the stigma. Look at Toronto after the SARS scare. Hundreds of millions in lost revenue."

I didn't know who I despised more, the homicidal killers or the bean counters. I gave the super my brightest *us girls need to stick together* smile.

"Second thing we need to do is lose the PR guy." I jerked my thumb at Davy. "There's a shark out there, and he doesn't want to close the beaches."

The super shrugged. "The mayor wants him here. He stays."

Herb looked sour. "Are we going to tell the public?"

"I'll pass along your recommendation to His Honor."

My turn to look sour. "What about the lawsuits that are going to rain down when the public finds out we knew there was a threat and didn't tell them?"

"We weigh that against destroying businesses, ir-revocably hurting the economy, and yelling fire in a crowded movie theater and the resulting panic it would cause."

"But there is a fire," Herb said.

She wouldn't budge. "There's already been a lot of media speculation that a tamperer is involved. People are being careful."

Davy smiled at me like the annoying little brother I never had.

"Not careful enough," I insisted. "Let's confirm the rumors. If everyone is on the lookout, maybe he'll stay in his house and stop poisoning our city."

Now the super folded her arms. "The decision has been made. We sit on it for now."

You can't fight City Hall. I changed gears. "How many other contaminated scenes have we found?"

O'Loughlin picked up one of the folders littering her desk. "None have been verified yet, but there are eleven possibles. The CDC is taking patient histories at area hospitals to pinpoint outbreak epicenters. We're meeting with them later today."

"Any evidence from the scenes?" I asked.

"That's what you're here for."

"Have they been closed? Even the possibles?"

"Yes."

I put Herb in charge of that.

"Also," I told him, "interview the people exposed so far. The sick, and the families of the deceased. Plus the cops and the mail carrier who handled the letter."

The super raised her eyebrow in a question.

"Sometimes big crimes are committed to cover up smaller crimes. Maybe the Chemist had a specific target, and the rest of this is all smoke and mirrors."

"I'll need more cops," Herb said.

"Retirees," I said. "Put them back on limited duty."

The super nodded, then took a phone call.

The extortion letter had gone on ahead to the crime lab, and I dug out my cell and spoke briefly with my guy there, Scott Hajek. He'd confirmed botulism in the envelope and on the letter through the wonder of mass spectrometry. Postmark came from the post office around the corner, mailed yesterday. Stamp and seal on the envelope both self-adhesive, so no saliva. Eleven prints found on the envelope and paper. The letter had been printed on an inkjet, using Arial Black font, available on almost every computer made after 1994. No hairs or fibers or business cards revealing the Chemist's address had yet been found, but Hajek was still on it.

"Priors," Captain Bains said. He'd been silent for so long, I'd forgotten he was there. "I can get a team searching for anyone in our system with a past record of poisoning, product tampering, or extortion."

"Keep it open to women," I said.

O'Loughlin cut off her phone conversation in mid-sentence and gave me the eyebrow.

"Poisoners tend to be women," I said. "It's a crime that doesn't involve physical aggression or personal contact."

"How about the botulism itself?" Herb asked. "Any way to trace that?"

"Maybe I can help with that."

I looked over my shoulder, and in walked . . . a hottie.

While I appreciated a good-looking guy as much as any woman, my days of getting dreamy-eyed and giggly were thirty years behind me.

This man, however, made me feel sixteen again.

He was gorgeous. Early thirties, tall, broad shoulders and narrow hips, a Marlboro profile, and piercing blue eyes that were otherworldly. His suit wasn't as expensive as Davy's, but he filled it out a lot better. It was as if God had taken half of Brad Pitt's genes, mixed them with half of Sean Connery's, and added more muscles and thicker hair.

"Special Agent Rick Reilly, HMRT."

He did a round of hand-shaking. When his fingers

touched mine I felt a shock, then spent the next few seconds wondering if I'd imagined it or not.

"*Clostridium botulinum* is a bacteria that occurs naturally in the soil throughout North America," Rick said. He had a rich baritone, with just a hint of Southern lilt. "It produces a toxin that has the honor of being the most poisonous substance in the world. A single gram could effectively kill a million people. Symptoms of foodborne illness can begin as early as two hours after exposure, or may be delayed for as long as two weeks."

"What are the symptoms?" Herb asked.

Rick sat on the super's desk, facing me and Herb. His crotch was just below eye level, and the very fact that I was even thinking about it meant my mind wasn't in the game. I refused to look.

"Let's say you ate some contaminated seafood. It doesn't matter if it came straight from the freezer, or the microwave. Heat and cold might kill the bacteria, but the poison they produce is still deadly. The next morning, your mouth might be unusually dry. You might also have some abdominal cramps. Maybe even some vomiting. But no fever. It feels like a hangover. What's happening is that your bloodstream is circulating the toxin to your neurological junctions, where it binds irreversibly, blocking acetylcholine release."

"English," O'Loughlin barked.

"It goes where your nerve endings meet your muscle fibers, and paralyzes them. You can't walk or move. Your face droops. You get double vision and lose your gag reflex. And eventually, you can no longer breathe."

I thought about the shots the nurse had administered the hour previously, and wondered if my dry mouth was the result of nerves or the result of a bad batch of vaccine.

"What's the treatment?" I asked, my voice cracking slightly.

"Antitoxin and ventilation. It can take months to fully recover, and there may always be some residual paralysis. With effective treatment, there's less than a twenty-five percent loss of life. If treatment is delayed, or if there's a shortage of adequate equipment, the death toll rises."

"Can people transfer it to each other?" the super asked.

"Normally, no. Botulism isn't contagious. But we seem to be dealing with a weaponized form that may have inhalation properties, so if someone has BT on their hands or clothing, cross-contamination is possible. For example . . ."

He reached over and stroked the back of my hand. I felt another spark.

". . . if I had BT on my fingers, I could have transferred a lethal dose to Lieutenant Daniels. The toxin can enter the body many different ways. The lungs, the stomach, wounds, mucus membranes"—his eyes met mine—"or through sexual contact. The spores will remain on her skin until they're washed off."

"Bleach?" I asked.

Rick smiled at me.

"A bubble bath would be fine."

Then he lowered his eyes, for just a fraction of a second, and eyed the tear in my skirt. I felt my whole body blush.

Thankfully, he hopped off the desk and walked over to the corner of the room, where he'd left his briefcase. He dug around inside and pulled out a syringe, a salt shaker, and a spray bottle.

"I've been with the CDC crew all day, and we've been trying to imagine a delivery system to contaminate food. A syringe would be able to penetrate food products and offer the highest likelihood of spreading the disease. A squirt bottle, used by someone polishing fruit in the fresh produce aisle, would work, but the toxin doesn't last too long when exposed to O2. But if the Chemist is using dry spores, which last longer in an oxygenated environment, a salt or pepper shaker would do the trick."

"Do you know which he's using?" Herb asked.

"We don't know yet. We've found contaminated food, but no needle holes. And we haven't seen spores on the outside of food in quantities that would suggest a shaker. He might be soaking food in the toxin at his home, then bringing it to the stores."

"Where would he get the toxin?" Bains asked. "Can it be ordered online?"

Rick sat on the desk again, his crotch again at eye level. This time I looked. *Ay caramba.* Rick didn't lack in that area either.

"The toxin is available for sale at hundreds of locations throughout Illinois," he said. "Anyone with a few wrinkles will pay big money to get their hands on some."

"Botox." Davy smiled, and I noted that he had no smile lines at all.

"Exactly. In small doses, the same toxin that paralyzes

your diaphragm can paralyze the tiny muscles in the face that cause frown lines and crow's-feet. But pharmaceutical Botox sprayed on food wouldn't cause the kind of epidemic we're seeing here, and because Botox uses the toxin, not the bacteria, it can't be cultured. A much easier source of botulism is honey."

Rick waited for a response. I bit. "Honey?"

"Yes, darling?"

Bains thought this was hilarious. No one else laughed.

"Sorry." Rick gave me an *aw, shucks* look that made my hormones gush. "Serious topic, thought some comedy might help. Honey contains botulism spores. That's why it carries warnings on the label, not to feed to children under the age of one. Their intestinal bacteria aren't mature enough to handle it."

"You can culture botulism from honey?" Herb asked. He didn't look happy.

"It isn't easy, but it's possible. Even from pasteurized honey."

"So there's no way to trace the bacteria strain?" Herb again.

"Anyone with some basic lab equipment and a few biology books could learn to culture botulism. Weaponizing it would be more difficult, but there's a wealth of information on the Internet. This particular toxin has been identified as type E. It's common to this area."

O'Loughlin grunted, then said, "Botulism cases are monitored by the CDC, right?"

"They keep track of all reported cases, and hospitals are required by law to report them."

"Is it possible the Chemist contracted botulism at some point? We could track past cases to find him."

Rick nodded. "Good thinking, but there are fewer than one hundred cases of botulism reported every year in North America, and all have highly detailed patient histories. I'm guessing the Chemist hasn't been infected with botulism. He's probably being extremely careful. You don't develop an immunity to BT, even if you've been exposed before."

"I thought we all got vaccines," Bains said.

"Those are experimental, and it's unlikely that the Chemist has access to the vaccines. So far the public sector can't obtain them."

"What if he works for the government?" I asked.

"It doesn't really matter. The only vaccines in production are for type A and type C strains."

A little alarm went off in my head.

"You said we're dealing with type E."

"Correct."

"So these vaccines won't protect us from this illness?"

I watched Rick's confidence slip a notch. "They may offer some protection."

"Really?"

Rick frowned. "No."

"How about antibiotics?" Bains asked.

"Works on the bacteria, not the toxin. The toxin is what kills you."

Herb asked, "How about that antitoxin you mentioned?"

"That can halt advancing symptoms, but can't reverse

them. Once the nerve ending is paralyzed, it's paralyzed forever. Which is why recovery takes so long—you have to grow new neurological junctions. But right now we've got two pharmaceutical companies working nonstop to supply Chicago with more doses. They should be able to provide us with a thousand by the week's end."

"We've already had three thousand reported cases," I said, my stomach clenching. "What are we supposed to do?"

Rick looked at O'Loughlin.

"The federal government doesn't make deals with terrorists," he said, just as my cell phone buzzed. "But if I were you, I'd give the guy his two million dollars."

I excused myself and answered the phone.

"Hi, Lieut. Hajek here. We've traced a print. It's strange, though."

"Cut the drama and spill."

"Jason Alger, sixty-three years old, lives in Humboldt Park."

"Record?"

"No. He's one of ours. CPD, retired. I'd ask if maybe he came into contact with the envelope somehow, maybe visiting the station. But except for the super's secretary, all of the prints are his, and one is beneath the adhesive stamp. He has to be the one that sent the letter."

"Good work, Officer."

I explained the situation to the room, and we were out the door thirty seconds later, off to interview one of our own.

CHAPTER 4

H<small>E CALLS HIMSELF</small> the Chemist, but he isn't a chemist. He isn't a botanist either, although the extensive greenhouse that takes up his entire backyard makes his neighbors think otherwise.

He's just a simple government employee, unhappy with the system. But unlike the thousands of other government employees, punching their clocks, hating their lives, he's devised a way to make the system pay.

The Plan is still in the first phase. He's been working on it, refining it, modifying it, for six years, three months, and eleven days. Though he is not perfect, the Plan is. In four days, nine hours, and sixteen minutes, it will all be over. He'll be rich, on a bus to Mexico. And Chicago, along with the entire Midwest, will be permanently crippled.

People will die. Many more than anyone could possibly expect. Thousands more.

The apartment is all set. Has been, for over a week. A baited trap, waiting for the mice. It will make the TV news tonight for sure. Possibly even national. He considers setting the TiVo, but quickly dismisses the thought. He isn't going to miss anything. They'll repeat the footage.

The summer air is cool and crisp. It's night, so activity will be minimal, but he puts on the netting just in case.

It's in a sealed plastic bin next to the greenhouse door. He places it over his head, then reaches for the gloves. They're made of neoprene, chemical resistant, and he's careful not to touch the outside of them as he slips them on.

The greenhouse door is locked with an electronic keypad beneath the knob. This high-tech addition was relatively cheap, and circumvents having to mess around with keys while wearing the gloves. It won't deter someone serious—after all, the greenhouse is made entirely out of glass and plastic—but it will keep the neighborhood kids out.

That kind of attention would be most unwelcome, after the years of planning.

He punches the code and opens the door. The thermometer on the wall reads 102 degrees Fahrenheit. Part of this is due to the gas heaters. Part is due to the towering compost heap in the back, which recently received a particularly large infusion of organic matter.

The Chemist loves being in the greenhouse. An untrained eye would only see the beauty of nature expressed by the ranks and files of growing, thriving plant life. A keener eye would be able to spot the cruelty beneath the veneer.

It's the cruelty that the Chemist adores.

He checks the hydroponics on a castor oil plant. Castors resemble hemp, but with six leaves rather than five. Next to it is a pallet of short green plants sporting delicate white flowers—lily of the valley. Behind them, oleander, the majestic flowers yawning open in the artificial light like pink fireworks. To their right, azaleas, with their startling bloodred buds, surrounded by netting much like his pith helmet, so the bees can't get to them.

The Chemist steps over a tank of nitrox, navigates around several stacks of fertilizer, past piles of piping and boxes of roofing nails, and approaches a ten-gallon saltwater aquarium. Roaming along the bottom, among the sand and bits of dead coral, are over a dozen brilliantly colored cone snails, none longer than two inches. In the tank behind them, next to the cockroach pen, are fingerling goldfish. He takes the small net off its suction-cup hook, scoops up several feeders, and drops them into the snail tank.

Normally he'd stay to watch the feast, but he has other things to do tonight.

Near the rear of the greenhouse, between the nightshade and the jimsonweed, is his workbench. Assorted beakers, petri dishes, test tubes, flasks, stoppers, swabs, eyedroppers, and a variety of tools are arranged carefully in the six foam-lined drawers. He drags a large plastic garbage can over to his stool, then bends down and lifts a case of premium vodka onto the bench. Removing a fresh bottle by the neck, he holds it over the can and shatters it with a hammer, glass and vodka spilling onto his gloved hands.

He picks through the mess, finds what he wants, and sets it on a place mat atop the bench, next to half a box of shotgun shells. A pair of garden clippers catches his eye, its blades stained with dirt and dried blood.

The Chemist smiles at the memory they invoke.

He picks up the shears and carries them to the large

industrial sink, between the refrigerator and the auto-clave, near the rear of the greenhouse. He turns on the faucet and scrubs the shears with antibacterial soap. He also scrubs the remaining vomit from the ball-gag and the handcuffs, and then drops all three items into a bucket with a twenty-percent bleach solution.

When everything is rub-a-dub-dub clean, he glances at the clock and decides to head over to police headquarters on Thirty-fifth and Michigan.

He doesn't want to be late.

CHAPTER 5

ASON ALGER RECEIVED his pension check at his home on the corner of Cortland Street and Hoyne Avenue, in the heart of a neighborhood known as Bucktown. He lived in an unassuming two-story residence with an ample backyard.

When we arrived on the scene, eight members of the Special Response Team—Chicago's version of SWAT—had already secured the perimeter and were scanning the building with optics. Their vehicle, a souped-up bus known as the Mobile Command Post, was parked on the street alongside several patrol cars.

The head of this SRT, a bull-faced sergeant appropriately named Stryker, was squinting at some fuzzy pink images on a laptop display. He wore the standard tactical gear: black jumpsuit, body armor, riot helmet, radio headset, and a utility belt stuffed with equipment, including a gas mask.

"I've got two heat signatures on the first floor, and one on the second," he said into his comlink. "No movement."

"Human beings?" I asked.

He didn't bother looking at me.

"Unconfirmed."

I watched an SRT member reposition the thermal optics, and another, a woman, sweep the building with a DOX sound cannon—a device that looked like a bullhorn but was actually an ultrasensitive unidirectional microphone. Two others were examining a printout that showed the floor plan of the building.

These guys were fast.

"Stryker," I said, tapping him on the shoulder. "Has your team been briefed?"

Again, the team leader didn't so much as glance at me.

"Sixty-three-year-old Caucasian male, considered armed and dangerous, probable location in the rear bedroom on the second floor, no other civilian activity, possible presence of biological agents. Two by two surgical entry, Taser capture takedown."

"He's a cop," I said. "His name is Jason Alger. I just cracked his file—his record on the force is golden. I also spoke to his former commander on the ride over. Alger was a straight shooter, family man, wife passed away six years ago, has a daughter and grandchildren in California. This isn't in character for him."

Stryker grunted, or perhaps it was a laugh. "Sometimes good apples get rotten."

"And sometimes they get thrown away while they're still good. Take it slow in there. Something isn't right."

"That's the only time we get called."

"Yeah. Well, good luck, Sergeant."

"Luck is for the unprepared."

I took a step back before the testosterone surging off

his body caused me to grow a mustache. Special Agent Rick Reilly sidled up behind me, so close I could feel his body heat.

Or maybe that was my imagination.

"These guys any good?" he asked under his breath.

"They're good."

"They've got a lot of fancy equipment. Is the subject inside the house?"

"We're not sure. Thermals have a few readings. Could be a person. Could be a radiator, or a fireplace."

"In June?"

"Or a water heater or a stove."

"I like his utility belt. He looks like Batman."

Normally I didn't mind jokes, but I was on edge.

"You're a biology guy, right?"

"I'm a doctor, actually. But saying *Special Agent Dr. Rick Reilly* is too much of a mouthful."

"Will those gas masks they have protect against BT?"

"They're standard NBC masks—nuclear, biological, chemical. NATO threaded filters. Should be fine. You look worried."

"I am worried. Show me a leader worth her salt who doesn't worry."

Rick pointed his chin at Stryker.

"GI Joe doesn't seem worried."

"And that worries me. Confidence is essential, cockiness is lethal."

This was my show. I wondered if there was anything more I should be doing. Go in with them? I didn't have that kind of training. And if I got into a *whose balls are bigger* spat with Sergeant Stryker it might be distracting, and I wanted him focused.

They know what they're doing, I assured myself.

"Why aren't you married?"

I narrowed my eyes at Rick, knocked off guard by the non sequitur.

"What does that have to do with this case?"

"Not a thing," he said. "But it might have everything to do with grabbing a bite to eat later."

"I have a fiancé," I said.

"Forget to wear the ring this morning?"

His eyes had a playful glint to them, which annoyed me. This wasn't the time or place for flirting. And cute guys had no right coming on to me only a few hours after the man I loved proposed marriage.

The man who was waiting patiently for me back at the house.

I excused myself and walked into the street, hitting the speed dial button on my cell phone.

"Hi, Latham."

"Hi, Jack. Any chance you'll be home soon? I made your favorite. Wiener schnitzel and spaetzle."

German food was comfort food to me. I mentioned it offhandedly on one of our early dates, and the next time I went to his place Latham cooked it for me. Men who could cook trumped men with sexy bedroom eyes.

Not that Latham didn't have sexy bedroom eyes.

I involuntarily glanced at Rick, noticed he was watching me, and gave him my back.

"You're a sweetheart, Latham. I'll try my best, but I'm in the middle of something big."

"I understand. I'll wait for you."

The man was a saint.

"No. Go ahead and eat without me."

"Are you sure?"

"I insist. I don't know when we'll finish up here. It could go late."

"I'll keep it warm for you."

"The food?"

"Everything."

Some paramedics pulled up. Standard procedure for a smash and grab, but it made me even more uneasy.

"How's that mariachi?" I asked. "Did he ever find the rest of his mustache?"

"No. I think Mr. Friskers ran off with it."

I smiled for the first time in hours.

"Look, Latham, I know I owe you an answer . . ."

"Focus on work, Jack. Keep your mind on the matter at hand. Everything else can wait until later."

That proved it. Latham was an alien pod person. No man could be this perfect.

"I love you," I said, and meant it.

"Love you too. Stay safe."

Stryker rallied his troops, and my leadership role was relegated to the sidelines to impotently watch his "two by two surgical entry." I stood alongside Herb, who'd been on the phone for over an hour organizing the task force teams, and snagged a headset from the SRT member monitoring the infrared. Beta Team marched around back, Stryker gave the radio command, and they rushed the front door. His partner did a knock-and-announce, Stryker hit the door with a handheld Thunderbolt battering ram, and they both stormed inside, weapons drawn.

"Team Alpha in," the radio squawked. *"Hallway clear."*

A similar banging came from the rear of the house.

"Team Beta in. Kitchen clear."

The headsets were so sensitive, I could make out four different breathing rates, four different footfalls. They had gone in under the assumption that anyone inside would have looked out the window and noticed the police carnival camped on the street, so this arrest was about speed rather than stealth.

"First bedroom clear."

Shuffling sounds. Some clicks.

"Hallway clear."

Then came a gunshot.

And screaming.

"Beta Team leader down! Repeat, Beta Team leader down! We have gunfire!"

A horrible gurgling came through my earpiece, like someone choking in a shallow pool of water.

"Alpha Team has been hit! Possible IED! Alpha—"

There was a popping noise, another gunshot, and static.

"Team Alpha, do you read," I said into the comlink. "Team Alpha, do you read."

Moaning, but no coherent response.

"Team Beta, do you read. Beta, are you there, god-dammit."

More gurgling, weaker this time.

Herb closed his cell phone and said, "Jesus."

I looked at the laptop monitor and could spot the heat signatures of all four SRT members. None were moving.

"Stryker, are you there."

The moaning became a keening cry, like a sick dog. It made the fillings in my teeth vibrate.

"Gamma Team going in!"

Two more SRT members, a man and the woman working the cartoid mike, rushed the house.

"Hold it!" I yelled.

·They didn't listen, quickly disappearing through the front door.

"Gamma Team, stand down," I said into the radio. "Repeat, stand down. I'm OIC. I want your asses back here now."

White noise. A groan.

"They're dead. They're all dead."

I gripped the headgear so tight, my fingers shook. "Get the hell out of there!"

"Jesus, what happened to his eyes—"

"This place is rigged. It's all rigged. Oh my—"

A snapping sound, then coughing.

"Gamma Team, do you read? Gamma Team, come in, over."

More coughing, and then the horrifying screech of someone screaming while throwing up. My skin got prickly all over.

"Gamma Team, come in."

The silence was suffocating. Then, after almost thirty seconds: *"Please . . . someone help me . . ."*

The final two SRT members made a try for the door. Herb tackled one. I used both hands to grab the other by the wrist.

"No," I told him.

"That's my team!"

"We'll get them out."

His name tag said *James, Joshua*. A kid, early twenties, barely old enough to shave. His eyes were wide, panicked, and he looked like he desperately wanted to believe me.

"How?" he asked.

I turned to the super, who appeared shaken, but not nearly as shaken as everyone on the line.

"I need a HazMat team, and the bomb squad, and that robot they have, the remote control one with the cameras."

"Bomb squad is at the Twenty-first District, the other side of town," she said.

"Tell them to drive fast."

Rick took my arm. "Make sure the HazMat uses self-contained breathers. I think something got through the NATO filters."

"I thought the NATO filters were safe."

"For BT, yes." Rick glanced at the radio unit, painful gurgling coming through the speaker. "That doesn't sound like BT."

"Do you have . . . what are those protective suits called?"

"Space suits. Back at Quantico. Not with me."

". . . *help me . . . please God help . . .*"

I racked my brain. Who would have a space suit? Fire stations? Nearby laboratories? I just saw a suit like that a little while ago. Where the hell was it?

Then I remembered what neighborhood I was in, and who lived nearby.

"Goddammit," I said, yanking out my cell phone, wondering if I'd ever bothered to erase his number.

It was still there. I hesitated two full seconds, then pressed the dial button.

"Harry's House of Love Juice, one hundred percent natural with zero carbohydrates, stop by for a free sample."

"McGlade," I said, swallowing my pride. "It's Jack. I need your help."

CHAPTER 6

MᶜGLADE BEAT THE BOMB SQUAD and the HazMat team to the scene, which was both a good thing and a bad thing. Good because we desperately needed his help, bad because being around McGlade was slightly less enjoyable than pulling out your own toenails with pliers.

"Hiya, Jackie," he said through the driver's-side window, pulling his Corvette alongside the curb. "You want me to park this big boy here, or shall I use your rear entrance?"

I briefly wondered what happened to his trademark 1968 Mustang, then realized he couldn't drive stick shift with his newly acquired prosthesis. McGlade had been a player in a homicide investigation of mine not too long ago, and he hadn't come out of the debacle entirely intact.

"Got the space suit?"

"I got it. You're lucky too—I just had it cleaned. There were stains, Jack. Lots of stains."

I put the thought from my mind. An eternity ago, Harry McGlade and I were partners. Since his dismissal, he'd been earning his living as a full-time private eye and part-time television producer. Along with boasting the

IQ of a tire iron, McGlade also had the unwelcome distinction of being one of the biggest perverts I know, and I'd met quite an assortment of them working Vice. Whatever he was using this space suit for had nothing to do with science.

"Where is it?" I asked.

"In back."

He popped the trunk, and I stared at a big pile of Day-Glo orange. I grabbed a sleeve and pulled the suit out of the car. The material felt like a combination of rubber and nylon.

"I should be the one going in," Rick said, coming up behind me.

"Those are my people in there, Agent Reilly. I'm going."

Herb ran over, looking even shittier than he had earlier.

"They're not responding anymore," he said. "Radio is silent."

"Can you hear anything? Moaning? Breathing?" Rick asked.

Herb shook his head. I kicked off my shoes and pulled down my skirt. Rick and Herb averted their eyes. McGlade whistled.

"This is a police matter, McGlade," I said, struggling into the suit. "You can leave."

"Ease up, Lieutenant. We still haven't worked out what you're giving me because I'm letting you use my suit."

I fought the material. The inside clung to my bare legs like plastic wrap. "It can wait."

"I want a liquor license."

Unbelievable. Herb must have thought so as well. He grabbed McGlade's shoulder.

"You need to leave. Now."

McGlade waved his artificial hand. It wasn't a primitive pirate claw, but it didn't look entirely realistic either. The flesh color was too light, and shiny like rubber.

"Don't shoot me, Sergeant," he said. "I'm unarmed."

Herb gave McGlade a push backward.

McGlade smiled and shook his head, raising both hands in apparent supplication. Then he placed his fake one on Herb's shoulder. There was a faint mechanical sound, like gears turning, and Herb yelped and fell to his knees.

"Modern technology," Harry said. "Six hundred pounds of pressure per square inch."

I got in his face. "Dammit, McGlade! People are dying! Stop screwing around!"

Harry shrugged. The mechanical hand whirred open. Herb had lost all color.

"Sorry, Jackie. I didn't know we were in such a rush."

I managed to snug the suit on over my shoulders. McGlade leaned close to me and whispered, "So . . . if I let you use the space suit, can you talk the mayor into letting me have a liquor license for the bar I'm open—IIIIEEEEEE!"

McGlade fell over, clutching himself between his legs. Herb unclenched the fist he'd used to induce McGlade's aria, then got up off of his knees, his other hand rubbing his shoulder.

"I hate that guy," he said.

Rick helped me strap on the SCBA tank. The gloves were thin, but not thin enough to get my finger inside of a trigger guard. Herb noted this and promised he'd be right back. The headpiece went on over the radio headset, a large hood with a Plexiglas faceplate.

It was hot in the suit. Steam-bath hot. And it smelled bad, like chili dogs. Sweat beads popped out onto my forehead, and my silk blouse clung to me at my armpits.

"Let me know when you feel the air."

Rick turned the dials on my self-contained breathing apparatus, and a wave of cool air bathed my face and circulated throughout the suit. The chest and legs began to puff out, like a balloon.

"I'll be with you on the radio," Rick said through the comlink. "Keep the chatter going, describe everything you see, maybe I can help."

Herb jogged back, cradling a Remington 870MCS shotgun with a pistol grip. He stepped over McGlade and passed it to me. My gloved finger easily fit into the oversized trigger guard.

"Bomb squad is still ten minutes away," Herb said. "Robby took a bad hit last week and is out of commission."

Robby was their remote-controlled robot.

"Give my respects to his family," I said, starting for the house.

"We could still wait for them. They've got better protective gear."

"No time."

"Dammit, Jack." Herb came up after me. "You're not even wearing a vest."

"Armor didn't seem to help the SRT."

I jogged toward the house. Herb and Rick flanked me.

"Her suit is leaking," Herb said. "I can feel the air."

"Positive pressure. It's supposed to do that. With air blowing out, nothing can get in."

Herb appeared ready to burst into tears.

"I've got a bad feeling about this, Jack."

"Me too."

I paused for just a moment, and stared at my partner through the Plexiglas face shield, wondering why this moment seemed so final.

"Okay." I took a big gulp of canned air. "Let's do this."

CHAPTER 7

THE CHEMIST WATCHES the cop in her space suit approach the front door. The suit offers more protection than the previous batch of cops had, but it still isn't enough.

She has seconds left to live. Minutes, if she's extremely lucky.

The Chemist has spent a very long time getting things ready. There are enough traps to kill at least a dozen cops. Even careful ones in protective biohazard suits.

He hadn't expected that the next death would be Jack Daniels, however. She's a celebrity. Now this will be national news for sure. He should have set the TiVo after all.

He wonders which one will get her. The modified M44? The rattraps? The pull-loop switch? The metal ball? So many terrible things await her.

And which toxin will it be? BT is perfect for food contamination, and the slower onset of symptoms has the desired effect of overburdening the hospitals and spreading panic and paranoia. But situations like this one called for something more immediate. More dramatic. *Convallaria majalis. Ricin. Rhododendron ponticum. Ornithogalum umbellatum. Thevetia peruviana. Strychnos toxifera.* Each of these induces instantaneous, messy death.

Of course, nothing is quite as cinematic as good old homemade napalm. Or potassium cyanide gas. He's covered those bases too.

The Chemist spent several months researching this particular phase of the Plan. Booby trap diagrams are easily found on the Internet, but he's taken them to the next level. They've become works of art. Fatal works of art. The slightest scrape of skin, the tiniest tear of fabric, the smallest misstep, and you're dead.

So exciting. So amusing. And he has the perfect view of everything.

He wishes he had a bag of popcorn.

A television news truck pulls up. It's about damn time.

The money will be nice. But what will really keep him company in his old age are the memories of moments like this.

CHAPTER 8

T HE SPACE SUIT WAS claustrophobic, hot, and cumbersome. I found it extremely hard to focus. The jog up to the front door had a surreal quality, as if I were indeed stepping foot onto another planet.

"Keep your eyes moving." Rick, through the comlink. *"Not only side to side, but up and down. Pay attention to where you're placing your feet, and what's overhead. You're looking for IEDs."*

Improvised explosive devices. Traps that released chemical or biological weapons. The things that decimated the SRT.

I stopped before entering the doorway and poked my hooded head inside, twisting my shoulders to get peripheral views. I could see the living room to my immediate left; the sofa and entertainment center looked completely normal. Beyond it, a hallway. To my right, several doors. No signs of Alger, or any of the fallen cops.

"Where's the first heat signature?" I said into my headset.

"To your right." Herb's voice. *"Second door."*

"Watch the thermals. If you see any signs of movement, let me know."

"Roger that. Take it slow in there, Jack."

I lifted up my right foot and crossed the threshold. The floor was dark wood, scratched, in need of refinishing. I noted some splinters and a screw; leftovers from the battering ram. I shifted my weight to my foot slowly, cautiously, as if I were on thin ice. It held.

"Attention, Special Response Team, this is Lieutenant Daniels, Homicide." I'd almost said *Violent Crimes*, but recently the suits had changed division names. "I'm coming into the house to find you. If you see someone in a big orange suit, hold your fire."

My words echoed in my earpiece, but had another added echo after bouncing off of my faceplate. I moved with care, as if every step counted, but the boots attached to the suit were too big for my feet and it was like walking around in clown shoes. Four steps into the hallway, my toe snagged on the base of a coatrack and I almost fell on top of my shotgun.

I was going to kill myself before I even got to the booby traps.

"What do you see, Jack?"

"It's a house. A normal, average house."

"It's not normal. Don't think that way. The IEDs will be hidden, or camouflaged. They might look like a child's toy, or a framed photograph, or a pair of slippers. Assume that everything is deadly."

I took a deep breath, let it out slow. Passed through the hallway without further incident, and stopped at the second door.

"How far into the room is the thermal reading?"

Herb said, *"It's about two yards in front of you. Not moving."*

Some sweat had beaded up on my forehead, and I didn't have a way to wipe it off.

"I'm going in."

My right hand kept the Remington at waist level. My left turned the knob and eased the door open.

I let out a nervous laugh when I saw the familiar rectangular object.

"It's a space heater."

"How many cords?" Rick asked.

That was a curious question. I lowered my line of vision to floor level and saw two.

"Thermal levels increasing." Herb sounded as edgy as I felt.

"Two plugs, leading to the same outlet."

"One is probably a motion detector, which activates a switch to increase the temperature. Certain poisons, like arsenic, become gaseous when heated."

"Good thing I'm wearing a mask. I can see some fumes coming off of—"

Because I had no peripheral vision, I didn't see the baseball until it was practically in my face. I jerked to the right, and it bounced off my faceplate. My finger reflexively squeezed the trigger, and I sprayed buckshot along the far wall, the boom of the shotgun rattling my teeth.

"Jack! Jack, are you okay?"

"I'm okay. Something hit me in the face. It's some kind of spiked thing."

It spun crazily in front of me, a baseball on a string.

Sticking out of it on all sides, like prickles on a cactus, were nails.

"Did it penetrate your suit?"

"I don't think so." I eyed the deep scratch in my faceplate, saw some sort of liquid dripping down the outside. I shuddered, wondering what those nails were coated in.

"You have to make sure, Jack."

"How?"

"Find a piece of paper. Hold it in front of your mask. If there's a hole, the positive pressure will blow the paper."

I looked around the room, found a paperback copy of *The Tomb* by F. Paul Wilson, and waved a page a few inches before the scratch.

"It's okay. No air coming out."

"Check above you, look for more projectiles."

I had to bend backward to see the ceiling. "There's a wire on top of the door. When I opened it, this thing was rigged to fall. Doesn't look like there's anything else up there."

"Remember to keep looking above you."

"Message received."

I racked another shell into the chamber.

". . . help . . ."

The word gave me gooseflesh.

"Did you guys hear that?"

"One of the SRT members." Herb's voice was pained. *"He sounds alive."*

"Where are you?" I tried to listen for noises in the house. "The first or second floor?"

Coughing, then, *". . . help me . . ."*

"We can't tell where he is."

I turned around and hurried down the hallway faster than I should have. Ahead, I saw stairs, and sitting on the bottom step, slumped over, one of my men.

I swiveled around, 360 degrees, looking for wires and traps and anything unusual. Finding nothing, I knelt next to the fallen cop and tilted up his head to see his face.

His gas mask was filled with bloody vomit, coating the inside of his goggles and oozing out the NBC filter.

I shut my eyes, then forced myself to place a hand on his chest, seeking evidence of breathing that I knew wouldn't be there.

"I found Buhmann," I said, sneaking a look at the name tag on his vest. "He's gone."

"Did you find what killed him? It might still be active."

Paranoia cut through my anger, and I stood up and took a step back.

Except for his gas mask, Buhmann appeared normal. No injuries, no blood, no—

"It's on the stairs." I squinted and moved in closer. The camouflage was insidious. Eight three-inch nails, protruding up through the carpeting, painted to exactly match the color of the shag. The only reason I spotted them was a drop of blood on the middle nail.

I wondered what kind of person thought up something like that. I could picture him, sitting quietly at a workbench, calmly putting together such a horrible thing.

Cold-blooded wasn't the word for it. This guy was a monster.

". . . please help . . ."

"I'm going up."

"There are several thermal readings nearby. Be careful."

I didn't need to be told to be careful. If the SWAT cop's combat boots weren't thick enough to stop a nail, my oversized rubber clown shoes wouldn't offer me any better protection. Still, I took the stairs as quickly as I could, anxious to find the poor soul crying for help.

The stairs ended at a hallway, and three more bodies.

"Three more down, at the top of the stairs."

"What do you see?"

"The nearest, vomit in the gas mask. The other two . . ."

It looked like their masks were filled with blood and bits of tissue. I remembered the wet coughing I'd heard earlier over the comlink. What kind of poison makes you cough up your own lungs?

". . . dead. They're all dead."

"Who are they?"

I didn't recognize the voice on the radio, and assumed it to be one of the remaining SRT members I'd made stay outside.

"Name tags are Winston, Banks, and Kordova."

"Look for what killed them."

I took a cautious step forward. The hallway was lined with floor-to-ceiling shelves on either side, filled with an extensive collection of NASCAR plates, framed pictures, and assorted knickknacks. A few of the plates had shattered and fallen to the floor.

"Two of the bodies, I see wounds on their calves. Might be buckshot."

"A hand-loaded shotgun shell packed with a fast-acting poison. Do you see any evidence of trip wires or pressure plates, or a gun or pipe sticking out of the walls?"

"No. Wait . . . there are some rattraps."

I was reaching for one, when Rick yelled, *"Don't move!"*

I froze in a crouching position.

"The traps fired the buckshot. It's easy to rig a trap to fire a shotgun cartridge. There's got to be tripwires in the hallway, stretching between the walls."

"I don't see anything."

"They might not be stretched tight. Might be hanging loose. Monofilament fishing line is very thin, and it's clear. How's the lighting?"

"Not very good." I saw a light switch on the wall. "There's a switch, I'll just—"

"Don't flip the switch!"

"Jesus Christ! I'm going to die of a heart attack before any of these traps kill me!"

"The switch may be rigged. Take a Maglite from one of the SRTs' utility belts."

I altered my course to reach down for one of the flashlights. I tugged it out of its little holster and felt like a ghoul, robbing the dead.

"Got the light?"

"Yeah."

"What color is the ceiling?"

"White."

"Hold the Maglite down low and point it at a forty-five-degree angle upward. You won't see the lines, but you might be able to see the shadows of the lines on the ceiling."

Smart. I was becoming very grateful Rick had come along.

I twisted on the Mag and kept it at waist level, sweeping it back and forth.

The ceiling became a spiderweb of crisscrossing gray shadows.

"There's a bunch. Maybe six to ten."

"He's probably not that way—he wouldn't have made it. What's behind you?"

I turned.

"A door. Closed."

Herb said, *"There's a thermal reading, three yards east of you. It's probably behind that door."*

The Remington was becoming heavy in my one-handed grip, and I was sweating so badly I felt like I'd just stepped out of the shower. I swept the Maglite around my immediate area, gently set the shotgun down against the hallway wall, and very slowly turned the doorknob.

I only got the door open an inch before feeling a small resistance.

"I think there's something—"

Then came the explosion.

CHAPTER 9

I FELL ONTO MY ASS, sitting atop one of the dead cops, and the gas came billowing into the hall.

"Jack! Jack are you there!"

"The door was rigged. Gas is everywhere."

Thick, gray gas, surrounding me completely.

"Is your suit breached?"

"I don't know."

The explosion hadn't been that powerful. I hadn't been knocked backward—I fell over from the surprise. Had it been enough to pierce my suit?

"Don't panic. You have to stay calm."

Easy for him to say. My ears were ringing, and my eyes stung like crazy.

Jesus, why were my eyes stinging?

The sweat, I realized. Dripping from my forehead. It must have gotten into my eyes.

At least, that's what I hoped it was.

"Get out of there."

That seemed like a good idea. I rolled onto all fours, but the gas had gotten so thick I couldn't see anything.

"Can't see. Too much gas."

My throat became very dry, and I couldn't swallow. Symptoms of panic, or something worse?

I reached out blindly before me, trying to find the stairs.

"Stay calm. Take it slow."

My breath came in ragged gasps. Death. I was surrounded on all sides by death. I began to crawl, unable to fight the terror. I had to get out of there. I had to get out of there now. If there was even the tiniest hole in my suit—

The shotgun blast was so close to my head I saw stars. At the same instant I felt a tug along my back, as if my suit had caught on a nail.

I'd tripped one of the rattraps.

As my hearing returned, I could hear three different people screaming in my headset, and I reached around to feel my shoulders, to feel if I'd been hit.

I couldn't tell. My back felt wet, but was that blood or sweat? This suit was bulky. The pellets might have passed right through.

But if I had holes in my suit the gas would get in.

I crawled faster, full-blown terror taking root in me like I'd never experienced before. I tripped another wire, and a gunshot peppered the shelving unit to my right, but I didn't stop, I picked up speed, climbing over a body, pushing away dead limbs, biting the inside of my cheek, eyes blurry with tears, had-to-get-out-had-to-get-out-had-to-get-out—

I reached the end of the hall and pulled myself through a doorway, entering a small room. The gas was dissipating, and I could finally see again. My stomach felt like a giant knot, and I teetered on the verge of throwing up. I was also holding my breath, freaked out that gas had gotten inside my suit.

Calm down, Jack, I said to myself. *Calm it down. You're still alive.*

I opened my mouth, trying to taste the air without breathing it.

Not surprisingly, it tasted like bile.

Squeezing my eyes shut, shaking from the lack of oxygen, I took a shallow breath even though my body craved more air.

No reaction.

I took a bigger breath, and began to laugh and cry at the same time.

"Jack! Are you there! Jack, please answer!"

"I'm still here," I said, my voice sounding very far away.

I looked around me, saw I was in a bedroom. There was a bed, a closet, a dresser, and a full-length mirror.

I stood up on wobbly legs and walked over to the mirror, getting a profile view.

There were a dozen tiny holes in my suit where the buckshot had ripped through.

"My suit has holes in it."

"Stay calm. As long as there's positive air pressure, nothing can get in."

"You son of a bitch—"

"McGlade, you little—"

"Give me the headset, lardass—"

"I'm gonna kick your—"

An oomph sound, coming from Herb.

"*Jack! It's Harry! You need to get your ass out of there! That tank is almost empty!*"

Once again, panic wrapped around me like a blanket.

"*Your fat sidekick punched me in the nards before I could tell you. I figure there was maybe four, five minutes of O2 left in that tank. How long have you been in there?*"

About four or five minutes, I figured. I looked back down the booby-trapped hallway, gas still lingering in the air, and made my decision.

"I'm going out the back window. Get the paramedics to put a ladder—"

I stopped in mid-step. Both bedroom windows were surrounded by black pipes that didn't look like they came standard with the house.

"I'm seeing some sort of pipes, sticking out of the window frames."

"*Describe them.*" Rick again.

I didn't want to get too close, but I forced myself to lean forward.

"Black. They have M44 written on the side."

"*Cyanide bombs. Used for killing animal predators. Don't go near them.*"

"You don't have to tell me twice."

Unfortunately, that meant I had to go back through the hallway to get out of there.

I began to hyperventilate, which made me even more light-headed than I already was. I got on all fours, reasoning that I'd already tripped the traps at that level and there wouldn't be any more. The gas had thinned out to the consistency of steam. Crawling over my fallen brethren was even worse this time, now that I could see their bloody faces up close.

"Look, Jackie, if you don't get out of there alive, I want to be sure that someone helps me out with this liquor license thing."

Harry sounded so close, I almost turned around, expecting to see him standing over my shoulder.

"McGlade, get off the—"

I was halfway to the stairs when I paused, wondering why the voice on the headset had gotten so clear.

It took me a moment to realize the radio reception hadn't gotten better—I could hear it better because there was no background noise.

The low, droning hiss of the SCBA had stopped.

I was out of air.

CHAPTER 10

I DIDN'T THINK. I moved.

I made it through the gas and to the stairs in less than three seconds, and then I slid down the first few on my belly like I was sledding.

The suit proved to be slipperier than I thought, and I picked up speed.

I stuck my hands out in front of me, trying to stop my momentum, but my gloves couldn't get a purchase on the carpet. My chest felt like I was getting repeatedly kicked, and my head bounced around on my neck in whiplash jerks.

BUMP BUMP BUMP BUMP. The ground floor rushed at me, blurry and off center.

And then I remembered the nails on the bottom step.

They were less than a body length away. No time to turn. No time to stop. I arched my back, reaching out my hands, palms up, trying to grab the shoulders of the dead cop slumped at the bottom of the staircase. I hit him, hard, my elbows bending from the impact, holding my chest a few inches above the deadly nails.

I did a push-up off of Buhmann, got my feet under me, and eased myself over the trap. Fresh air was only a dozen yards away, out the front door. I got ready to sprint for it.

"... *help me ...*"

I didn't move.

Stryker was still alive. It had to be him, because the only SRT members I hadn't seen yet were him and the woman.

I took a last, longing look at the door, then headed toward the rear of the house, to the kitchen, the only room I hadn't yet seen.

"*Jack, are you still there?*"

"I'm here, Rick. I think he's in the kitchen."

I concentrated on slowing my breathing. I don't know what poisons were clinging to me, or if anything had gotten in through the holes. Plus, the air inside the space suit was quickly becoming stale, since no new air was being pumped in. The less I breathed, the better.

Two steps into the kitchen, I found the female cop. I had no idea what killed her, but whatever it was made her eyes pop out of their sockets.

"Stryker, dammit, where are you?"

Static, then, "... *base* ..."

"Who's got a floor plan? Where's the basement?"

It was more talking than I wanted to do, and it emptied my lungs. I took a shallow breath.

"*I have the floor plan, Jack.*" Rick. "*There's a door in the back of the kitchen.*"

I spun my shoulders, taking in the room, and saw the refrigerator was open. I also noticed, sitting on a plate in the fridge, something horrible.

"The bomb squad is here, they're coming in."

Passing the refrigerator, I saw the basement steps, Stryker clinging to the top. His gas mask was also caked in vomit, but his chest was rising and falling.

I grabbed his belt and pulled.

It was like hauling a bag of bricks, but the tile floor helped, and I was able to yank the groaning SRT leader across the kitchen, toward the back door.

Three feet away, my vision began to cloud. My legs had become two sacks of jelly that could barely support my weight.

Two feet away. I felt hot and cold at the same time. A wave of dizziness swooped down on me, and I fell to my knees. Everything started to get dark.

A foot away. Beyond that doorway, fresh air. No more deadly traps. No more poison gas. Twelve inches away was Herb. Latham. Life.

I reached the jamb, straining from the effort of pulling Stryker, and then felt the floorboard shift beneath my hip.

I froze. My eyes followed the floorboard to an electrical outlet, under the sink. Attached to a cord, atop the loose floorboard, was a metal sphere the size of a golf ball. Surrounding it, like a jail cell, were metal bars. Next to the contraption was a fire extinguisher, its nozzle pointing at my face.

Even in my oxygen-deprived brain, I knew what I was looking at. If the floorboard moved, the metal ball would roll, touching the metal bars and completing a circuit, spraying me with whatever deadly substance was in that fire extinguisher.

I shifted my hip imperceptibly, and watched the ball roll forward, heading toward the bars.

I moved my hip back, and it returned to the center of its cell.

Things were really starting to get dark now. I didn't know if I'd been poisoned, or if I'd breathed too much of my own carbon dioxide. I tried to focus, tried to concentrate. The board beneath me was only a few inches wide. If I eased myself off of it slowly, keeping an eye on the ball, it would return to its original position and—

"*. . . please help me,*" Stryker groaned.

Then his foot kicked out, connecting with the trap.

CHAPTER 11

INSTANT INFERNO.

The flame that shot out of the extinguisher soaked Stryker, and covered the lower half of my body. I leaned over, trying to beat the fire off of him, but it stuck to my gloves like glue.

His screams cut into me, and then cut into me again through my headset. I wiped my hands on the floor, trailing fire, and then I looked around—for what, I'm not sure—maybe something to smother the flames, maybe something to end his agony, and then a powerful force yanked me backward.

I twisted around, trying to fight it, fearing what horrible trap had me now, wondering if I'd be gassed or burned or poisoned or punctured, and I lashed out with both hands, and one fist bounced off something fleshy and I stared up at Herb, pulling me out of the house.

"The suit," I tried to warn him. It was covered in God knew what kind of deadly substances. "Don't touch me."

But Herb didn't listen. He dragged me over to two firefighters waiting with a hose. They opened it up on us, knocking Herb over, pummeling me with water that looked, oddly enough, like a car wash through my visor.

Then Rick was there, yanking off my face mask, stripping off that horrible space suit, and paramedics were wrapping me in blankets. I glanced at Herb, my hero, and said, "Thanks, partner." He shook his head, his hound dog jowls jiggling, picked up a blanket, and walked away.

"Jack, look at me."

Rick had his arms around me, his face very close to mine. This time I was sure I felt his breath. It smelled like mint.

He looked at one of my eyes, then the other.

"Do you feel okay?"

"Headache . . . legs hot."

"First-degree burns from the homemade napalm. Like a sunburn. I could rub some cream on them, if you'd like."

"I'll manage."

I disentangled myself from his arms and took a last look at the house.

"Thanks." I took another deep breath, grateful for the clean air. "I probably wouldn't have made it out of there without your help."

"What, you think all Feds are brainless, regulation-spouting automatons who hinder local police departments' investigations?"

"Pretty much."

Rick smiled, and pretended to tip his hat.

"Happy to prove you wrong."

"Hey!"

We turned to look at McGlade, who was prodding the still-smoking space suit with his toe.

"Somebody owes me a space suit."

I ignored Harry, looking beyond him to try to find Herb. Two paramedics wheeled a gurney over. I declined. They insisted. I compromised, and they escorted me as I walked. The scene in front had become a madhouse of cops, media, and gawkers. I scanned the faces of the crowd. No Herb.

Joshua James, the SRT member that I prevented from running into the house, walked over to my car, tight-lipped and morose.

"They're all dead." He said it as a statement, not a question.

I nodded. "I'm sorry."

James hitched his thumbs into his belt and stuck out his chest.

"Sorry doesn't mean shit. Next time, let me do my fucking job."

His stare challenged me to say something back. I didn't. Then he turned his gaze to Rick.

"You got something to say, Fed?"

"In fact, I do. You need to focus your anger on the man that did this, not the woman that tried to save your team."

"She fucked up. I should have gone in there."

Rick jerked a thumb over his shoulder, pointing at two bomb squad cops, draped in so much body armor and protective gear, they each looked like the Michelin Man. Stretched between them was a body bag.

"See that? If you went in there, they'd be carrying you out in one of those."

The cop went to shove Rick, but Rick sidestepped the move and caught Joshua's wrist in a joint lock, forcing the larger man to his knees.

"They knew the risks," Rick said. "Don't disgrace their memories like this."

He released him, and Joshua glared at Rick, then at me, then at Rick again, and stormed off.

I grabbed my clothes and my purse from my car, and was then led to the rear of the ambulance. Again they tried to force me to lie down. Again I fought with them, insisting that I didn't want to go to the hospital.

"Let them help you, Jack."

Rick. He'd somehow eclipsed Herb as my omnipresent voice of reason.

"I just want to get home to my fiancé."

I coughed, feeling something wet in my lungs, and all thoughts of Latham were replaced by thoughts of the terrifying toxins I'd been exposed to. Rick caught my look of panic.

"Just because you seem to have avoided all of the fast-acting agents doesn't mean a slower one hasn't breached your suit. Like BT. Or something worse."

I coughed again, and let them strap me down. An EMT pushed Rick out of the back, shut the door, and they carted me off to the hospital.

CHAPTER 12

I WOKE UP AT FIVE in the morning in an ER bed, feeling like someone had beaten me up and used me as a pincushion. Antibiotics, antitoxins, and numerous vaccines had been administered. I was a little woozy, but it didn't seem like anything toxic had taken hold.

That was good enough for me. I had work to do, and it wouldn't get done with me lying down.

I called a cab, and he took me back to my car, still at Alger's house. During the ride I thought about Latham. I'd phoned him repeatedly from the hospital—at my house, at his apartment, on his cell. He hadn't picked up. What did that mean? Phone problems? Was he asleep? Watching TV too loud and didn't hear the ring? Or was he angry at me?

Yesterday, I'd called Latham my fiancé—twice—even though I hadn't officially said yes to his proposal. It felt . . . right.

I'd been married before. It hadn't worked. And even though my ovaries still had a few parting shots left in them, forty-six was too old to start thinking about babies, and families. If I got pregnant now, I'd be in diapers myself by the time the kid was old enough to buy me a beer.

So why did I feel all gooey inside when I pictured Latham and myself leaning over a crib, watching our child sleep?

The cab spit me out at my car. I paid the hack, and used my cell to try Latham again. No answer. So I turned my attention to the Alger house. Seeing it again made my stomach do flip-flops.

A few police vehicles and the SRT bus were still there. A bombie saw me and approached.

"Lieutenant Daniels?" Her name tag read *Wells*. She wore enough body armor to protect her from a point-blank bazooka hit. "There's something in the house you need to see."

My reaction was physical. The thought of going back into that chamber of death scared me more than anything had ever scared me in my life.

Wells seemed to sense this. "We've cleared the remaining traps. There were only two left."

"There may be others."

"We went in with X-ray, ultrasound, and a K9 unit. The house has been disarmed. You can use my mask . . ." Her voice trailed off, implying the *if you're afraid*.

"No need. Let's go."

I had to will my legs to move, as they'd suddenly become stiff. It was like approaching a firecracker that should have gone off but hadn't.

Bravery isn't the absence of fear. It's the ability to still function when fear overtakes you. Some people are naturally brave. Others, like me, learn to fake it. I still had no idea if faked bravery and real bravery were the same thing. Cops didn't talk about their fears. Instead they drank, got divorced, committed suicide, or all three. It beat dwelling on being killed in the line of duty.

So into the house we marched, stiff upper lips in place. Wells took me past the living room, past the staircase, and back into the kitchen, where a black, charred stain marked the linoleum where Stryker had burned alive.

The refrigerator was open.

Curiosity overtook my jitters and I peered inside.

Standard fridge contents. Milk. Cheese. Lunch meat. Beer. Condiments in the door. But one item was out of place.

On the top rack, laid out on a CorningWare plate, were three severed fingers.

I knew immediately whose they were.

Officer Scott Hajek, my lab guy, was short, plump, and needed both hands to carry his crime scene kit, housed in an oversized Umco tackle box. He came into the kitchen and set the heavy case by my feet.

"Anything good to eat in there?" Hajek asked.

"Only finger food," I replied.

Hajek squinted into the fridge through Coke-bottle glasses, then frowned.

"That's bad."

"It was that, or a *hand on rye* joke."

"Where's Herb? He has that gallows humor schtick down to a science."

I had no idea where Herb was. After he'd disappeared last night, I hadn't heard from him.

Hajek opened up his case, the hinged drawers expanding to three times the size of the base. After digging around for a few seconds, he came up with a vial of black fingerprint powder—to contrast the white appliance—and a horsehair brush.

He found several latents on the door handle, and several more on the front surface of the fridge. He used Pro-Lift stickers to remove and mount the prints.

"Got a glove mark."

He handed over the Pro-Lift card, and I noted the black oval smudge, no ridges. Someone had opened the refrigerator wearing gloves. I compared two other decent partials to a laptop display showing Alger's prints, and found that they matched. The homeowner used his own fridge; no surprise there.

Hajek then printed the severed fingers. He used modeling clay to avoid getting ink all over, and as I'd suspected the fingers belonged to former Chicago police officer Jason Alger.

It had been my suspicion that the cop had been killed, his fingers severed, and then his prints manually placed on the letter to the superintendent. The Chemist had known Alger's prints would be on file, and had wanted to lead us to this death trap.

"Can you lift any latents from the dead tissue?" I asked, hoping that perhaps the Chemist had handled Alger's fingers without using gloves.

"I could fume with iodine or cyanoacrylate, but let's try good old low-tech to start off."

Hajek dug around in his box and found a glass microscope slide. He handed it to me.

"Press this between your palms. My hands are always cold."

I did as instructed, and after a few seconds he took it back, wiped it with a nonabrasive cloth, and pressed the slide to the back of one of the fingers.

"Glass is great for picking up oils. The fingers are cold, so we warm the slide, and the oils cling to the glass."

He removed the slide and peered at it through a jeweler's loupe.

We repeated the process four times, and then he said, "Got one."

He dusted the slide, mounted the print with the Pro-Lift sticker, and frowned.

"Gloves."

The Chemist was careful. I didn't hold out hope for finding any prints elsewhere in the house, but sent Scott off to do the thankless work just the same.

"Dust any of the traps that the bombies have deemed safe. Hand railings. Toilet handles. Doorknobs. Light switches. You know the drill. Plus find Henderson—he's been taking swabs from the IEDs, which you'll need to identify some of the poisons."

Scott made a face. "I'll be here the rest of my life."

"Don't be silly. You'll be done in three years, tops."

I let him get to work, then pulled the pen from behind my ear and took out the notepad I'd been carrying in my waistband. So far the To Do list read:

      trace M44 purchases
      Alger—arrest record
      talk to neighbors
      question mailman who delivered letter
      security tapes at BT scenes
      witness search at BT scenes
      survivor interviews/background checks
      research IEDs

I scratched off *talk to neighbors*. Three teams had done extensive door-to-doors, and no one in the area had noticed anything unusual at Jason Alger's house. In fact, some of the neighbors didn't recognize Alger at all. I lamented how things had changed since I joined the force. Twenty years ago, people knew everyone on their block. These days, folks kept to themselves.

Maybe they were concerned some maniac might chop off their fingers and turn their house into a chamber of horrors.

I circled *Alger—arrest record*. There was a chance Alger had simply been a target of opportunity. But a plan this meticulous made me think that someone had a major beef against the former cop. I added *IA* after his name and decided it was time to get home to shower, change, and see what was going on with Latham.

The trip to Bensenville took almost an hour. Once I exited the expressway I fell in behind an ambulance, its sirens going full tilt. I hugged its bumper. Ambulances, fire trucks, and patrol cops had remote control devices called MIRTs—mobile infrared transmitters—used to change red lights into green ones. Being part of Detective Division, I didn't warrant the five-hundred-dollar gizmo, but following an ambulance worked just as well.

Luckily, the meat wagon appeared to be taking the same route I was. Hitting all of these greens, I might even get to the house in record time.

I considered what I'd tell Latham when I saw him. What was I afraid of? Trust? Commitment? Family? My living situation changing? Losing my independence? Love?

I didn't know. I was obviously afraid of something, but couldn't figure out what it was.

And then, abruptly, I decided that I didn't care what I was afraid of. I could fight the fear. I didn't feel brave, but I was damn good at faking it.

I would marry Latham.

I noticed I was still following the ambulance, which was a little creepy, considering I was almost home.

When it headed down my street, I felt downright paranoid.

And when it pulled into my driveway, I went from paranoid to panicked.

I threw the car into park and rushed onto the lawn. Two paramedics were approaching my front door.

"I'm a cop. This is my house. What's going on?"

"Had a call from this house a few minutes ago. Man complaining of abdominal pain, vomiting, and some paralysis."

Botulism. Those were symptoms of botulism toxin.

"It might be . . . it might be botulism. Do you have antitoxin?"

"Not in our kits."

I fumbled for my keys, trying to open the dead bolt, wondering how the Chemist could have found me so quickly. People close to me are always getting hurt. If Latham died because—

"Ma'am, can I try?"

One of the medics took my key and guided it into the lock. I flung the door open and rushed into the house.

"Latham! Latham!"

No one in the living room. In the kitchen, the table still set for a romantic celebration dinner that never happened, the bedroom empty, the bathroom—

"Latham! Oh my God . . ."

The man I loved was on his back, his shirt crusted with vomit, a portable phone still in his hand. It didn't look like his chest was moving. His face—his face was blue.

"Move out of the way, ma'am."

I couldn't wrap my mind around what I was seeing. The paramedics shoved me aside and knelt next to him. The next few seconds were a blur of words and actions.

". . . cyanotic."

". . . pulse is weak."

". . . airway clear."

". . . BVM."

They placed the mask over Latham's mouth and nose and pressed the bag, filling his lungs with air.

". . . BP is sixty over forty."

". . . get the cart."

One of the medics again pushed me aside and hurried past.

"Will he be okay?" I asked.

I asked this question several times as they strapped him to the gurney and wheeled him out to the ambulance.

Their only answer was, "We're doing the best we can, ma'am."

In the ER, Latham was put on a ventilator and given antitoxin at my insistence. I filled out his paperwork, naming myself as the primary contact.

In between worrying and hating myself, it occurred to me that the Chemist probably hadn't attacked Latham at my house. The food, the German dinner he'd prepared last night to celebrate, he'd bought at Kuhn's, a deli on Irving Park Road. The Chemist claimed to have contaminated a deli on Irving Park. I hadn't made the connection.

Latham wasn't sick because of my job. He was sick because of my stupidity.

I stared down at my left hand, at my naked ring finger, and cried until I had no tears left.

CHAPTER 13

THE CHEMIST WAKES UP ANGRY. Last night had been a bitter disappointment. Months of planning, and only six cops dead.

After morning coffee, he considers returning to the greenhouse, working on more liquor bottles. Instead he flips on the morning news.

Twenty seconds of taped action on CBS. On ABC, he only catches the tail end of the coanchor banter, their grave voices bemoaning the loss of police life. Channel 5 doesn't have anything at all.

He flips on CNN, and the story doesn't even warrant a scrolling graphic at the bottom of the screen.

Back to CBS, and they've wrapped his story, moving on to some earthquake halfway across the world. Channel 7 has a bit about the botulism outbreak, but the footage is recycled from an earlier broadcast.

Disappointing. Actually, more than disappointing. Infuriating.

How had Jack Daniels managed to get out of there alive? He'd almost died several times himself, setting up all of those traps. That bitch must be unbelievably lucky.

He lets the anger build. Living with anger is something he's become expert at.

What happens to rage deferred?

It explodes. It explodes in spectacular fashion.

He allows himself a small smile.

Last night went poorly, but the Plan hasn't changed at all. The second phase will soon be in effect, and he needs a patsy for it to work. Lieutenant Jack will be perfect for that. And she'll be all alone when it happens.

Not that 911 would help much anyway.

The Chemist switches off the TV. There will be more news in a few days. National news. World news. Books written, movies of the week, covers on *Time* and *Newsweek* . . .

But why not get the media ball rolling a little sooner?

"Do I dare?" he says, alone in his living room.

He has everything he needs. He even has a spot picked out, a backup in case one of the other locations went bust.

A deviation from the Plan doesn't seem smart. Everything has been thought through to the tiniest detail. Improvising at this point might lead to a mistake.

Still . . .

"Let's do it," he says.

There will be news. This very morning.

The trick to a good disguise isn't to hide your own features, but to make a certain feature stand out; one that witnesses will remember. He chooses a black mustache and a temporary tattoo of a black playing card spade that he applies to his right cheek. A ratty jean jacket, a bandanna, and some Doc Martens boots complete the transformation. Instant biker.

He types a note on his computer, prints it out, then fills the jet injector bag with a tincture of monkshood and lily of the valley. He hides the tube up his sleeve, arms the spring.

It's a beautiful day. Warm. Sunny. The Chemist walks past the semitrailer in his driveway, adjusts the tarpaulin that the wind had blown off the portable chemical toilets stacked against the garage, and considers which car, if any, to take.

He decides on neither—such a fine day is perfect for public transportation. Plus, no risk of a car being seen. Sammy's Family Restaurant is a few miles away. He takes the bus. Sammy's is open twenty-four hours, and at this time of morning it caters to the prework crowd and the people getting off late shifts.

It's part of a chain. He wonders if it's publicly traded. He wonders how much money will be lost when the stock takes a dive tomorrow.

Get ready for a bear market, he thinks, then enters the restaurant.

Just his luck, the place is so full there's a ten-minute wait for tables.

The Chemist studies the crowd. Lots of twenty-somethings. A few loners. Old people. Yuppies. And some off-duty cops, waiting to be served.

Perfect. This is going to be exciting. Really exciting.

He buys a newspaper from one of the coin machines in the restaurant lobby, leans against the wall, and waits.

A few minutes later, he's given a table for one. He makes small talk with the fat waitress, and eventually orders the all-you-can-eat breakfast buffet that Sammy's is famous for.

He approaches the salad bar like a sinner approaches an altar, reverent and nervous. The owners of Sammy's have installed a clear plastic sneeze shield at eye level, so germs don't contaminate the food.

How thoughtful of them, the Chemist muses. So concerned for their customers' health.

The Muzak can barely be heard above the loud conversations, so he knows no one will hear the hiss of his gun. He picks up a plate from the stack, still warm from the dishwasher, and gets in line behind two blond girls with jeans that just barely cover their butt cracks.

The big bowl of diced fruit, resting on a bed of crushed ice, gets his attention first.

Psssssssssst. Psssssssssssst.

Then he moves to the pan of scrambled eggs. Then the bacon. The dry cereal. The obligatory red gelatin. Sausages. French toast. Waffles. And a large tray of Danish and bagels.

The Chemist leaves the buffet spread with a large plate of food that he has no intention of eating. He surreptitiously detaches the jet injector and sticks it into his pocket. Then he returns to his table, opens the paper to a random page, and pretends to read.

But he's really watching the salad bar.

The cops are the first ones there, and he has to bite his lower lip to stop from grinning. They pile their plates with enough poison to kill a large town.

A yuppie couple next. Then some black guys. A father

with a young son who demands Jell-O—he should have gone to school today, Dad. A single guy going for toast seconds. One of the blond girls, returning for more eggs. An old man who is filling two plates, one for his crone of a wife waiting back at their table. The Chemist loses count after a dozen people have come and gone.

The first person begins to convulse less than five minutes later.

It's one of the cops. First he's patting his forehead with a napkin. Then he's clutching his stomach. Then he's on the floor, shaking like he's plugged into an electrical outlet.

The Chemist can stare openly, because everyone else is as well. One of the other cops places a call on his radio, doubles over, then spews a lovely green vomit all over his fallen partner.

People are on their feet now, their shocked expressions priceless. The Chemist stands as well, feigning horror.

The little boy is next. His face plops right into his plate of gelatin, and Dad begins screaming for help.

Soon many people are screaming.

One of the yuppies, moaning nonsensically, runs full-tilt into another table, sending food and patrons flying.

The old man has something spilling from his mouth that appears to be drool, and he's shaking with palsy so badly that his false teeth pop out.

More vomiting. More moaning. A mad rush for the door, where a girl who didn't even eat at the salad bar is trampled. The last cop, apparently hallucinating, fires his gun into the crowd, then begins aiming out the window at people on the sidewalk.

It is absolutely glorious. Truly a scene from hell. Seeing the immediate fruits of his labors is so much more rewarding than watching the victims on hospital ventilators on the news.

He yearns to be closer to the action, to become a part of it.

No one is looking at him, so he doesn't even try to conceal the jet injector anymore. He reattaches the hose, arms the unit, and then pushes his way into the throng of people.

Psssssssst. He gets a man in the neck.

Psssssssst. A woman's arm.

Psssssssst. A stray hand that got too close.

These first three he injects are so anxious to flee the restaurant that they don't even turn to look at him. The Chemist knows the jet injector doesn't hurt much. It's more of a mild discomfort, like having a small rubber band snapped against your skin. In the panic of the moment, none of them feel a thing.

He locates his waitress, the only person in the restaurant who got a good look at him, and gives her two trigger pulls under the chin.

She opens her mouth to scream, then falls over, convulsing.

The restaurant is almost empty now, except for the dead and dying. He hurries back to his table, drops the note, then picks up his plate and takes it along, dumping the contents on the floor. Ambulances, police cars, and fire trucks are starting to arrive. He crosses the street, tosses his plate into a Dumpster, and stands there for ten minutes, watching the commotion.

The news crews arrive next.

This will get more than a ten-second sound bite, he says to himself. Then he catches the bus for home, anxious to turn on the TV.

CHAPTER 14

I SPENT ALL DAY in the hospital, by Latham's side. I held his hand, cried, and listened to the doctors tell me there was nothing else they could do but hope the toxin's progression was stopped in time.

Latham didn't regain consciousness.

Since I wasn't a relative I wasn't allowed to stay overnight, even though I flashed my badge and made threats. They kicked me out when visiting hours ended.

Not having any other options, I went home.

Sleep wasn't going to happen. When all went well in Jack's world, getting to sleep was difficult. With everything currently going on, sleep would be impossible.

Instead, I worked out my frustration the way my mother always did. I cleaned the house.

I began by just tidying up, but that progressed to knee pads and rubber gloves and Lysol and Pine-Sol and ammonia. Everywhere I looked I saw germs, poisons, toxins. I individually bagged all the food Latham had bought at the deli and set it outside on the porch, and then threw away every other piece of food in the refrigerator and scrubbed it out with bleach.

Then I scoured the sink, disinfected the garbage can, mopped the floors, hosed down the bathroom, washed the bedsheets and pillowcases, and then the pillows themselves and the comforter. And, dressed in my Kevlar vest, safety goggles, and two oven mitts, I gave Mr. Friskers a bath.

He didn't like it.

After applying hydrogen peroxide to the gashes on my arm and cheek, I broke out the vacuum and wondered if I had time to do a room or two before I needed to get ready for work. My mother's bedroom was the smallest, so I figured I could at least get that one done.

I plugged the vacuum cleaner in, pushed Mom's twin bed over to the far wall, and bent down to pick up a shoe box she had under the bed.

Mr. Friskers, apparently still angry about the bath, launched a surprise attack, bounding into the room and leaping onto my back. I twirled around, feeling one of his claws dig into my shoulder, and the shoe box opened up and spewed paper everywhere like a snowblower.

The cat howled. So did I. Luckily, within reach was something he hated even more than the squirt gun—the vacuum.

I pressed the on pedal with my toe, and the sound alone was enough to make him disengage and haul ass out of the room.

All of those people who crow about how pets enrich our lives are full of shit.

I kicked off the vacuum, looked at the mess of paper around the room, and sighed as I began to pick stuff up.

It was mail, mostly. Some letters from one of my mother's old boyfriends. I inadvertently saw the phrase *nibble your luscious wet* and had to turn away before I saw any more.

One envelope, however, stood out because it was still sealed. Written on the front was the word *Jacqueline* in my mother's florid script.

I stared at it for a moment. On one hand, it was sealed and hidden in a box under my mother's bed. On another hand, it had my name on it.

On any other day, I would have put it back unopened. But I was exhausted, emotionally frazzled, and I didn't need anything else hanging over my head at the moment.

I opened the envelope and read the letter:

My Darling Daughter,

If you're reading this, it is because you've been going through my things after I've died. I hope my passing hasn't caused you too much distress.

I take that back. I hope you're completely devastated. I loved you more than life itself, and know you felt the same way about me. You're the one good thing I did with my life.

There's something you should know, something I've never had the courage to tell you when I was alive. You see, I can't forgive the man, and I knew if you learned the truth I'd have to deal with my buried feelings all over again. It was wrong, and you have every right to be mad at me, but now that I'm dead, I don't have to hear you condemn me for my decision.

I've lied to you, Jacqueline. When you were small, you were told your father died of a heart attack. In truth, he didn't die. He left us. One day, after supper, he calmly told me that he hated being a husband, hated being a father, and didn't want to have anything to do with us ever again. Then he walked out of our lives forever.

I told you he died because, essentially, he was dead to us. It was easier to tell a child that her father wasn't coming back because he was no longer with us, rather than he no longer wanted to be a father. I meant to tell you the truth, when you got older, but I feared you'd track him down and confront him.

It took a very long time for me to move on, after he left. You were a wonderful girl to raise, but you know how difficult we had it. I cannot ever forgive him for what he did to us, and never want to see him again.

I urge you to just let this go, but I know you won't. It isn't in your nature. You'll track him down, and ask him why he did what he did.

When that moment comes, dearest Jacqueline, give the bastard a swift kick in the family jewels from me.

                                                          Love, Mom

It took me a few seconds to process what I'd just read. Then it took me a few more seconds to get on the phone with Mom.

"Good morning, Jacqueline. How's my kitty cat? Is he eating?"

"Mr. Friskers is fine. I—"

"And how's Latham? I really like that man. If I were a few years younger—"

I didn't think this was the time to hit her with that news, so I held it back.

"Mom, I was cleaning up in your room, and I found the letter."

"Oh, don't be upset. So I exchanged a few dirty letters with a few men. I find the written word much more erotic than pornographic movies. Though I did date this one gentleman who took me to a peep show once—"

"Not that letter, Mom. The other one, with my name written on it."

My mother paused. "Oh. *That* letter. Did you read it? Of course you did, or you wouldn't be calling. Unless you're asking my permission to read the letter, to which I'll politely answer no."

"Dad is alive?"

Mom sighed, as if I was such a disappointment she couldn't bear it. "I honestly don't know. He might be. I really don't care, one way or the other. Did you read the part when I wrote that you were the one good thing I did in my life? Did that make you cry? I cried when I wrote it. But, truth told, I'd been hitting the schnapps."

I rubbed my eyes. "Mom, don't you think this is something we should have discussed before you died?"

"Well, I'm not dead, and we're discussing it right now."

"Who is it?" A male voice said in the background.

"My daughter, Charlie. Go back to sleep."

"Mom, are you in bed with someone?"

"Don't be shocked, Jacqueline. We were just sleeping." I heard her peck him on the cheek. "The sex won't happen until later, in the shower."

"Look, Mom, I'm upset right now."

"Well, don't be upset with me. I'm not the one who left us."

I set my jaw. "He's my father, and I should have known he was still alive."

"Why? So he could hurt you again? You don't know what it's like to have the man you married, the father of your child, look at you and tell you he wants no part of you. Believing he was dead was a much easier way to deal with the loss."

It was like wrestling with an octopus.

"That should have been my decision to make, Mom."

"Well, now it is. But if you find him, I don't want to hear about it. I don't want to know if he's dead or alive. I don't want to discuss it. Ever."

"Fine."

"Also, since you're obviously being very meticulous in your cleaning of my personal space, I suggest you stay out of my bedside cabinet, lest you find more things that upset you. Good-bye, Jacqueline."

She hung up. I marched into her bedroom, tugged open the drawer next to her bed, saw a variety of battery-controlled devices in different sizes and shapes, then closed the drawer and tried to get the images out of my head. Especially of the really long red one.

Mom knew I'd open the drawer. She did that on purpose to rattle me. I became even more annoyed.

Mr. Friskers appeared in the doorway and hissed in my direction.

"Not now," I warned him.

He seemed to consider it, then trotted away. I glanced at the clock, saw I was running late, and hopped in the shower. I didn't have time to condition, did a quick towel dry, dressed in a gray Tahari Mandarin collar jacket that I bought in a set with a beige cami and black slacks. God bless the Home Shopping Network. I eyed a pair of Emilio Pucci heels, which had so many different colors in their crazy design they looked like they were made of Care Bear skins, but ultimately went with some Taryn Rose "Stevie" flats, figuring I'd be running around all day.

The long drive to work gave me time to apply my makeup in the car and for my hair to air dry, providing it wasn't humid enough to give me the frizzies.

An hour later I was pulling into my District parking lot. The day turned out to be rain-forest humid, and the only thing I could do with my brown curls was tie them in a ponytail.

I took the stairs up to my office, hoping Herb had gotten there before me and was waiting with a big cup of coffee, because I needed caffeine.

There was a person in my office, but it wasn't Herb. And she didn't have coffee.

"That's my desk," I said, pointed to where she was sitting.

The girl smiled. "I know. It's your office."

She was in her early twenties. Blond hair with pink highlights, in a short bob. Enough makeup to shame a gypsy fortune-teller. Multiple earrings. And a multicolored blouse that clung so tight, it looked painted on.

"I'm Roxanne." She stood. Roughly my height, but slightly thinner in the waist and hips, and a cup size bigger. "Roxanne Waclawski. Call me Roxy."

She offered a hand, a zillion sterling silver wire bracelets jingling at me.

I kept my hand at my side.

"Why are you in my office." I added, "Roxy."

She smiled big. "We're partners!"

"I have a partner."

"Captain Bains told me that I'm your new partner. Your old one died or retired or something."

I spun on my Stevies and walked across the hall to Herb's office. He was packing stuff into boxes.

"Herb? What's going on?"

My partner looked at me with an expression halfway between pain and remorse.

"My transfer came through. I'm going to Burglary/Robbery/Theft. No more Homicide."

I felt like I'd been hit, like all the important people in my life were deserting me.

"Why?" I heard myself say.

"The stress. I can't take it. Too many years of people

trying to kill me. Or you. I think it's worse seeing you in danger."

"If it's about yesterday—"

Herb set down the box, hard. The noise made me flinch.

"Yesterday was just an example. It's been like this for a long time. I can't take it anymore, Jack. I've seen too many dead bodies. Talked to too many crying relatives. I'm done."

He pulled out his desk drawer and dumped all of the contents into the box. Most of the contents were empty food wrappers.

"Weren't you going to tell me?" I asked.

"Bernice told me not to. She said you'd talk me out of it."

"Of course I'd talk you out of it. You're a Homicide cop. A damn good one. It's in your blood. You can't walk away from this."

"I got less than ten years left in the Job. I'm spending them in Robbery. No crazed maniacs. No psycho killers. No lunatics poisoning the whole goddamn city. The next decade will be like a paid vacation."

I walked around his desk and put my hand on his arm. Herb was practically family. I'd had partners before, but never one that I felt such a bond with.

"You saved my life yesterday, pulling me out of that house. If you go to Robbery, who's going to save my ass next time?"

I said it half-joking, but his reply was so serious it stung.

"You'll have to find someone else to save you next time, Jack."

He gave me his back, pulling stuff off of shelves.

"I put all the task force stuff on your desk, which team is doing what. I'm sure Bains will assign you a new partner, if he hasn't already."

"He has. The paint on her isn't even dry yet."

Herb turned and managed a weak grin. "A younger partner, huh? I'd never put up with that shit."

Maybe I was the one who reached for him. Maybe he was the one who reached for me. But the very next moment, two tough macho cops were hugging like relatives at a funeral.

"You're going to make a great Robbery cop," I said to his chubby neck.

"You can come with me. Think it over. No shooting. No dead kids. No serial creepos. And if the bad guy gets away, he won't wipe out a preschool. The worst he'll do is steal a BMW."

"Sounds tempting. I'll think about it." But we both knew I was lying.

Herb broke the embrace, cleared his throat, and returned to the shelf. He came back with a cellophane package of Twinkies.

"Look at this." He squinted at the package. "Date says 1998. They look good as new."

"The best things in life never change," I told him.

"Actually, Jack, sometimes they do."

He tossed the package into his box. I didn't think I

had any tears left in me, but I felt them coming. I considered telling him about Latham, or about my father. Anything to make him stay.

Instead I said, "Call me when you get settled in."

Then I turned around and walked out the door.

CHAPTER 15

MEANWHILE, BACK IN MY OFFICE, Roxy had once again appropriated my desk. She even had her feet up, her Skechers in the spot normally reserved for my morning coffee.

"That's my desk." I tucked away all of my pain in a private, secret place, where it wouldn't get out until I allowed it, and forced a pleasant smile. "The next time I see you sitting at it, I'm going to roll you up into a ball and shove you back inside Cyndi Lauper."

Roxy quickly removed her feet and stood up.

"Who's Cyndi Lauper?" she asked.

"A girl who just wanted to have fun."

"She sounds cool. Hey, while you were gone, Captain Bains called. There's some big meeting happening downstairs that we're supposed to go to. Conference Room A."

"Are you really a cop, and not someone who just snuck in here?"

Roxy smacked her gum and grinned.

"I like you," she said. "You've got attitude."

I took the task force folder from my in-box. Roxy picked up her backpack—of course she had a backpack; how else could she carry her skateboard?—and followed me down the hall.

"I thought we were going to the conference room."

"I need coffee."

"Here." She tugged at my arm to stop me, then reached into her pack and produced a twenty-two-ounce can of energy drink.

"I don't want that. I want coffee."

"This is sugar-free. And it has twice the recommended daily allowance of taurine."

"What's taurine?"

"I dunno. It kind of tastes like pee. But it has a real kick."

The station coffee also tasted like pee, so I accepted the energy drink. The flavor wasn't pee so much as carbonated bile, with a hint of salt. But my body instantly reacted to the caffeine, and I perked up a little on the way downstairs.

"Your outfit is so cool," Roxy told me.

"Thanks."

"I'm *so* going to wear stuff like that, when I get older."

Captain Bains, Superintendent O'Loughlin, Special Agent from the Hazardous Materials Response Team Dr. Rick Reilly, the ubiquitous PR guy Davy Ellis, and several other people I didn't know were seated around the boardroom table, in a heated discussion. Roxy grabbed the last empty seat. I was about to strangle her with her hemp necklace, but Rick stood up and offered me his chair, leaving the room to find another.

"Jack," the super said, "this is Dr. Abigail Van Hausen from the Center for Disease Control, Major

Phillip Murdoch from the United States Army Medical Research Institute for Infectious Diseases, Dr. Sylvia Ng from the World Health Organization, and Dr. Wayne Astor, also from USAMRIID."

I shook hands all around. Roxy did the same.

"I'm Roxy, Jack's partner. Anyone need an energy drink? It's got taurine."

Everyone declined. Roxy removed a can and popped the top, taking a loud slurp.

"Has this become a DOD show?" I asked, eyeing the army guys.

The major answered, in a tone that was obviously military. "The Department of Defense is here to ascertain if the situation in Chicago is a threat to national security. Also, one of the victims at the diner yesterday was a dignitary from Japan, and we've been asked to assist in the investigation."

I'd heard about the diner massacre while at the hospital with Latham.

Bains appeared unhappier than usual. "Six dead, four more in critical condition. We've confirmed it's a Chemist attack—note found at the scene."

He passed over a piece of paper in a large plastic bag and went into details about the time and place. The font was bigger this time, but matched the previous letter.

> *Two million dollars or I tell CNN what's going on.*
>
> *The Chemist*

"We need to go public with this," I said.

"Not necessarily." This from Davy, of course. "If we went public—"

I interrupted. "It would cost the city billions of dollars. Which we all know is more important than the lives of a few innocent people."

"That's only part of it. The Chemist is bluffing. He doesn't want the media to know, because then it would be harder for him to spread his poisons."

"Explain how that's a bad thing."

"You need evidence to catch him. How will you find that evidence if he disappears?"

"Who is the asshole?" Roxy whispered in my ear. I ignored her.

"What will happen to the city's approval rating when the public finds out there's a lunatic poisoning their food, and we knew but didn't tell them?"

Mr. PR opened his mouth, but nothing came out.

"I'm calling a press conference," said the super. "We're going public."

Davy pursed his lips like a fish. "The mayor won't like this."

"Our job is to serve and protect, and keeping this from the public is doing neither. Dr. Ng, Dr. Van Hausen, I understand that you had colleagues at Cook County Morgue when they brought in the members of the Special Response Team from Alger's house. Have you found anything?"

Dr. Ng, a thin, attractive Asian woman, nodded at

Dr. Van Hausen, cleared her throat, and read off of a paper in front of her.

"The deaths all appear to be the result of poisoning. We've managed to isolate seven different toxins so far. Some of the deceased show symptoms and signatures of several toxins."

Rick came back into the room, dragging a chair. Roxy whispered in my ear, "Who is the stud?"

I ignored her, and suppressed a smug expression when the stud pulled his chair close to mine and sat down.

"*Nerium oleander*," Ng continued, "which is a cardiac stimulant and has an effect similar to digitalis. *Ornithogalum umbellatum, Tanghinia venenifera, Strychnos toxifera, Ricinus communis.* So far, we haven't discovered any evidence of disease. And it should be noted that all of the toxins we've found have been derived from plants . . ."

"Have you had similar findings, Special Agent Reilly?"

Rick turned his attention to the super.

"Actually, no. I found traces of hydrogen cyanide, arsenic trihydride, and parathion. These are all inorganic compounds, and can be purchased everywhere or made with a child's chemistry set. The Chemist apparently has knowledge of diseases, organic poisons, and chemical weapons."

"Parathion is a relative of sarin nerve gas." From Dr. Astor, the army guy.

"Yes. It's sold under various brands as a pesticide."

"Is everything the Chemist is using available domestically?" Major Murdoch asked.

"The big four haven't come up yet," Rick answered.

Roxy, who had been worrying a hangnail, perked up. "Big four?"

Rick turned to her. "VX gas, anthrax, smallpox, and plague. These would indicate a hostile foreign source."

"Or a domestic one." I faux-smiled at the major. "Doesn't the U.S. have smallpox in a freezer somewhere?"

Major Murdoch gave me a look that left no doubt I hated my country, then said, "Has there been any evidence that these compounds have been weaponized, or made more lethal?"

Rick snorted. "How can you make cyanide more lethal?"

"Please answer the question."

Rick's leg rubbed against mine under the table. I didn't know if it was intentional or not. My heart rate bumped up a bit, but I blamed that on Roxy's energy drink.

"No, Major. All evidence points to a single extortionist, not a sleeper al-Qaeda cell waiting to pop out of a cake and squirt you with Variant U."

"What is Variant U, Mr. Reilly?"

"It's Special Agent Reilly. Or Dr. Reilly. Variant U is a weaponized form of Marburg. And no, I haven't found any evidence of that either."

O'Loughlin focused on me.

"What have your teams uncovered, Lieutenant?"

I looked at the file before me, which I hadn't opened yet. Now seemed like a good time.

Herb, ever the professional, had written a condensed version of what he'd discovered so far.

"We've deployed eleven teams to each of the known sources of the BT outbreaks. They've already collected several hundred prints, hundreds of food products, have interviewed dozens of potential witnesses, and have the names and contact information for over one hundred more. Background checks are in the process of being done on all known botulism victims, and the store owners and employees at each outbreak nexus."

Major Murdoch leafed through the folder in front of him, and I noticed it actually had *Top Secret* stamped in red on the front. "How about the background of that cop Alger?"

"He's come up clean. Two Internal Affairs inquiries. Both shootings, both times he was cleared. We're looking at his arrest record for anyone who might have a grudge, which is just about everyone he'd arrested in thirty years on the force. The severed fingers in the refrigerator have been confirmed as belonging to Alger, and we suspect he's been killed."

"Maybe he cut off his own fingers to fool us," Roxy said.

No one said anything, but the stares she received made her shrink down in her chair.

"We've located the deli on Irving Park that the Chemist mentioned in his letter." I thought of Latham, and my voice caught. I coughed into my hand to cover it. "We've got a Crime Scene Unit there, gathering evidence, questioning the staff. It's going to take some time to sort through everything."

"We don't have time," the super said. "This nut wants

an answer in tomorrow's paper. To make the early edition, I need to get the personal ad in today by noon."

"Are we paying him?" I asked.

"I have received authorization to meet the Chemist's demands. It should go without saying that mum is the word on this." The super zeroed in on me. "We can say the city is under attack, we can name the businesses that have been hit, we can tie in Alger, but no word about the extortion."

I mulled this over. That was probably why the city hadn't outed the Chemist yesterday—they had been considering paying him off. If that got out, every loony with a Saturday Night Special would be moving to Chicago, trying to extort a few bucks.

"Who's in charge of setting the trap to catch him if we decide to pay?" I asked.

"We are, Lieutenant. You can start figuring out how right after the press conference. Plan on it at ten a.m."

The super adjourned the meeting, and both Roxy and Rick stuck to my shoulders, accompanying me to my office.

"You're cute for a Fed," Roxy said to him.

"I believe that looks are superficial, and it's what's inside that counts."

Roxy batted fake eyelashes. "Are you saying you'd like to get inside of me?"

"Sorry. I don't date women younger than the scotch I drink."

Score points for Special Agent Rick.

"You should date Jack. She's like in her fifties."

And points lost for the new partner.

"Have you ever done a press conference before, Roxy?" I asked, making my voice conversational.

"Who? Me? No. I was on TV once, at the MTV spring break bash in Fort Lauderdale. I never saw it, though. My friends told me about it. I was pretty trashed."

"I think you should sit this one out."

"Why? Are you afraid I'll steal your thunder?"

"No. I'm afraid you'll say something stupid that will get me fired."

Roxy tugged my elbow and stared me in the eye, petulant.

"I'm a detective third grade. I didn't get this promotion by giving blow jobs. I busted my ass. You, of all people, should know how hard it is for a woman to be taken seriously in this sausage fest."

I considered all the things I could say, about professionalism, and attitude, and image. Instead I said, "Chances are this lunatic watches the news. If we put an attractive woman up there, he could become fixated on you."

"Really?" Roxy grinned. "Cool."

"No. It's not cool. It's the opposite of cool."

"You think because I'm young I can't handle myself?"

"No. I think because you're young you can't handle yourself as well as you think you can."

Her grin disappeared.

"You know, you're an inspiration to a lot of women in the department, Jack. It's a shame that in person you're such a bitch."

I looked to Rick for support, but he'd taken an inordinate amount of interest in the bulletin board on the wall. Then I met Roxy's glare. I wondered if I disliked her so much because she reminded me of me at that age.

No. I would have gotten along with me just fine. This girl was a Gen-X car accident waiting to happen. But we all have to learn sometime.

I took a deep breath. "Fine. You can do the press conference with me."

"Are you serious?"

"I'm serious. But I'll do most of the talking. And we need to go over everything beforehand. Rule one, think before you speak. Don't repeat yourself or say *um* or *uh* a lot. Rule two, if you can't answer a question, say *no comment*. Rule three, always appear in control. Reporters can sense fear, and they pounce on it."

"I can do all that. How do I look?"

I gave her a once-over. "Do you have anything else to wear? That outfit is . . . cute, but it doesn't look very professional."

"Let me check my locker," she said, and hurried off down the hall.

Rick nudged me. "Is this a good idea?"

"We've all got to learn sometime."

"After this conference, how about lunch? I want to go over some points about the case."

"Lunch? I'm going to need a few drinks."

"We can do that. I need to check in with Washington and Quantico. I'll probably miss the conference. Can I meet you someplace?"

What is it about physical beauty? If Rick were average looking, I would immediately take him up on lunch. But because he was handsome, I didn't think I should spend any time with him outside of the office. It seemed like betraying Latham, even though we might be able to make some headway on the case.

It's only lunch, I convinced myself.

So I named the place and the time.

What was the worst that could happen?

CHAPTER 16

THE CHEMIST WATCHES the press conference with a frown on his face. He hadn't expected them to go public. Though this doesn't alter the Plan in the least; the city has followed his trail of bread crumbs quicker than he's expected.

They aren't showing his letters. They admitted that they did receive letters, but say they're keeping them under wraps to rule out bogus confessions. They also neglected to mention anything about his demands. Which means they're planning on paying him.

This is disappointing. He expected the city to stall for at least a few days, or to take a hard-line stance and refuse to deal with terrorists. That would have given him a chance to indulge in a few more surprises before the big bang.

Still, maybe he can fit one or two more in before crunch time.

He sets his TiVo to record, and then wanders over to his closet to pick a disguise. He decides on business formal. A Jack Victor suit, wool, three-button, vented, dark blue with dark gray pinstripes. A white shirt. A power tie. He slicks his hair back with mousse, applies a liberal dose of Lagerfeld, and then puts on the distraction—an eye patch.

A check in the mirror shows him to be roguish, mysterious. And all the witnesses will remember is a well-dressed man with an eye patch.

Along with the jet injector, he brings along a tiny contact lens case, containing a few drops of extract of Tanghin. The Chemist doesn't know if he'll get close enough to use either, but he's got the entire day free to try. Should be fun.

He considers taking the bus because parking will be terrible downtown, but with all the stops the bus makes, it will take twice as long. So he risks it and takes a car, one that can't be traced to him anyway.

The television told him the press conference was live at the 26th District police station, and that's where he heads. Traffic isn't too bad for lunchtime, and he manages to snag a parking meter spot from someone pulling out, only three blocks from the precinct house. Even luckier, the meter still has an hour left on it.

Fate apparently wants him to kill a cop today.

He decides to leave the jet injector in the car. Getting this close to the police, he doesn't want to be caught with it on him. That leaves only the Tanghin, but that should be more than enough.

He walks briskly, hoping to get there before everyone has left. There are still news vans parked in front, so that's a good sign. A hot dog vendor is set up on the corner. He approaches the forlorn figure and orders one with the works.

"Thanks, buddy. Business has been terrible."

The Chemist takes a bite of the red hot, smothering his grin with pickle relish. He considers poisoning this man's stand. It's the perfect location for it, right outside the police station. Cops probably eat here all the time.

Maybe later, when he comes back.

There's a bench on the sidewalk with a good view of the front of the station. He sits down and eats leaning forward, so nothing drips on his suit. Ten minutes pass, and he orders another dog, to the eternal gratitude of the vendor.

"Bless you, guy. I got two kids. Wish this city wasn't so chickenshit."

"You're not worried?" asks the Chemist.

"Hell, no. My food is fresh. No one will get sick off my dogs, that's for sure."

"Didn't you hear the latest?" The Chemist feels ripples of excitement, talking about this topic. "One man is doing all of this. They call him the Chemist."

"And if I ever met this Chemist, I'd bust him in the ass."

"What if he snuck up on you, poisoned your food while you were talking with another customer?"

"You got a sick mind, you know that?"

"I've been told."

The Chemist returns to his bench. After twenty minutes, he begins to wonder if he had gotten there too late and missed the mark, but like magic she walks out of the building. Alone. It's almost a hundred yards away, but he recognizes the hair, and the gray jacket she wore on TV.

He takes some extra napkins from the hot dog vendor. Then he trails the cop from the opposite side of the street, staying parallel to her.

She walks two blocks, turns onto Michigan Avenue, and enters a well-known grill pub, a chain place where kitschy things are stuck to the walls and the bartenders dress in sports jerseys. If it's like the others of its ilk, the interior will be crowded, smoky, with low lighting. Which is perfect.

Traffic is against him, so he has to wait for the light to change before he can cross the street. When he walks into the restaurant, it's exactly as he expected. The cheerful hostess tells him it will be a half-hour wait for a table. He declines, heading for the bar.

The bar is packed too, but he sees the cop standing between several men, trying to get the bartender's attention.

He moves in closer, getting to within a few feet. Up close, she seems smaller, less substantial, than she appeared on television.

"Dirty martini, up," she orders.

My, my, my. Our city's finest, drinking while on the clock. Still, who can blame her? It's been a tough morning.

A stool opens up, and she goes to it, and then does something that proves to the Chemist that fate is truly on his side: She takes off her gray jacket, places it over the stool, and asks the bartender where the ladies' room is.

He points over his shoulder, and she heads in that direction. A moment later, the bartender sets down her drink by her stool.

The Chemist doesn't hesitate. He opens the lens case, palms it in his right hand, and approaches the bar. With his left hand he reaches over, snagging some cocktail napkins from the bartender's side of the bar, and with his right he dumps the toxin into the drink.

Now it's a *really* dirty martini, he muses.

He shoves the napkins into his pocket, backs away from the bar, and finds a vantage point from several yards away. No one gives him a second glance.

A few minutes later she returns from the bathroom and sits atop her jacket. Grabbing the martini in one quick motion she brings it up to her lips—

—and drinks the whole thing.

He ticks off the seconds in his head.

One . . .

Two . . .

Three . . .

Four . . .

Five . . .

She touches her head.

Six . . .

Seven . . .

She wobbles slightly on the bar stool.

Eight . . .

Nine . . .

She rubs her eyes, then stands up.

Ten . . .

Eleven . . .

He cranes his neck up for a better look.

Twelve . . .

Thirteen . . .

She's bent over now, a line of drool escaping her mouth. It's followed by a flood of vomit.

Too late. Vomiting won't help.

At fourteen seconds, she falls over.

People give her a wide berth. Several say the word *drunk.*

It takes almost thirty seconds for an employee to approach and kneel next to her.

"Call an ambulance!" he yells. "She's not breathing!"

Of course she's not breathing. She's dead.

As the curious gather, he slips out the door, calm and casual. He has no doubt that several people are now frantically dialing 911. But according to statistics, a 911 response will take a minimum of ten minutes. Chances are it will take much longer. He knows this from experience. There is zero chance she'll be revived.

The Chemist uses the napkins to wipe out the contact lens case, then deposits them into a garbage can. It's a gloriously lovely day, and he takes off his blazer and uses one hand to carry it over his shoulder, Frank Sinatra style. Someone is bound to recognize the cop shortly. And when they do, it's going to be a media frenzy. He wants to be home in time to see it, but TiVo is taking care of that for him, and it has been so long since he's actually enjoyed a walk downtown.

In fact, it's been a while since he's actually enjoyed anything. A long while. Six years, three months, and thirteen days.

Revenge is a dish best served cold.

He considers heading to the lakefront, or walking through Grant Park. Then he remembers walking through the park with Tracey, and a foul mood overtakes him.

Who could have ever known that wonderful memories would someday prove painful?

He heads back to the car and climbs in, considering his next move. The satisfaction of watching the cop die is gone, replaced by a cold, dead feeling.

He wonders if this is why people become killers. That emptiness deep down that nothing—not drinking, not drugs, not therapy, not sex—can fill. Perhaps some people are born like that. Soulless. That's how he feels most of the time.

Before, he was a normal guy. Decent friends. Decent job. A hardworking, tax-paying, red-blooded American who voted for the current mayor because he promised to be tougher on crime.

It seems like it was someone else's life. But it wasn't. It was his.

And now, there's only cold.

He thinks about the hot dog stand, and that warms him a bit.

The Chemist snakes the jet injector tube up his sleeve and arms the spring. He's wrestling to put on his blazer in the cramped front seat when he hears a car horn, right next to him.

Startled, he looks up.

A man in a rusty, older model Chevy stares at him, the rage on his face an indicator he's been waiting there for a while.

The Chemist shrugs at him and shakes his head, indicating he isn't moving.

The man honks again.

"I'm staying," he says.

The man leans on the horn now, screaming, "Move your car!"

The Chemist ignores him, pockets the jet injector, and exits the vehicle. Some people just don't take a hint. He's actually doing this city a favor, reducing the population of idiots like—

"Hey, asshole! I've been waiting five fucking minutes for that space!"

The man has an unkempt beard and crazy eyes. In the passenger seat is an equally unkempt woman, obviously seething.

The Chemist shrugs. "This is my spot. Find another one."

"We're fucking late for court and we need that fucking space!"

No surprise there. The Chemist wondered what white-trash crime these two had committed. Set fire to their trailer to get the hundred dollars in insurance money? Or maybe sex with some sort of animal? His wife was so ugly, she'd qualify. He smiles at the thought.

And then the bearded guy is out of his car, walking right at him.

"You think this is funny, asshole?"

The Chemist is shocked. He's heard about this happening, people being killed over parking spaces, but he can't believe it's happening to him.

He manages to say, "I'm not laughing at—"

And then the guy shoves him, hard. The Chemist almost loses his footing.

"Think you're better than me, in that fancy suit and that faggy tie."

The man goes to shove him again, and on reflex the Chemist brings up the jet injector. When the guy grabs his shirt, he pushes the orifice into his chubby neck and squeezes the trigger.

The lunatic raises up a fist to hit him, then his eyes bug out and he clutches his throat.

He falls, dead before he hits the street.

"Arnie!"

The Chemist looks at the woman, who is now out of the car and rushing at him.

"What have you done to Arnie! You killed him!"

Like a picture snapping into focus, the Chemist is instantly aware of his surroundings. People are watching him. On the sidewalks. From their cars. This has become a scene.

"That son of a bitch shot my husband!" she howls. "Someone help me!"

The only person close enough to ID him later is Arnie's wife. He's on her in four steps, jamming the injector into her throat, killing her in mid-scream.

Then he hurries back to his car. People are pointing now, and shouting. A few of them are running over.

Hands shaking, the Chemist fishes the car keys out of his front pocket. He starts the car and realizes, to his horror, that Arnie's car is blocking him in.

There's no time to do anything else. He slams the car into gear, steps on the accelerator, and crashes into the car parked ahead of him. Then he puts it into reverse and hits the gas again, causing another collision.

He now has an extra few feet of room around his vehicle, and he squeezes onto the street between Arnie's Chevy and the car he'd just rear-ended. There isn't quite enough space, and there's a grind of metal on metal as he scrapes both sides of the Honda as he pulls away, hyperventilating, a crowd of people staring at him.

This is bad. Very bad. But he can fix it, if he moves fast. All they'll remember is the suit and the eye patch—thank God he kept it on.

They'll remember the car too. There's a good chance someone even took down the license plate number.

But that's okay. The car isn't his. He can tie up this loose end, if he hurries.

The Plan doesn't have to change. But now he feels an urgency he hasn't felt before, and that excites him.

He expected this to be emotionally satisfying. But in his sweetest dreams, he had never expected this to actually be fun.

CHAPTER 17

I SAT OUTSIDE THE CAFÉ, at one of their patio tables along the sidewalk. Rick hadn't been at the press conference, and it was twenty minutes past the time we said we'd meet.

We'd exchanged numbers, but I didn't call him. Instead I called Latham's hospital room, again, and was informed that there had been no change in his condition.

Another five minutes passed. An ambulance streaked by, sirens blaring. I dialed Dispatch, hung up, dialed them again, and asked the desk sergeant to give me a record and location of Wilbur Martin Streng, DOB October 16, 1935.

Traffic and people and time passed. A bee took an interest in the bud vase of cut carnations on my table, and I stiffened.

Don't bother it, and it won't bother you, I told myself. But I moved my hands away just the same. I was the lucky one person out of two hundred and fifty who was allergic to stings. When I was a teenager, a particularly nasty wasp had stung my hand, which quickly led to anaphylactic shock. My throat had swelled up to the point that I couldn't breathe, and only an emergency room injection of epinephrine had saved my life. It wasn't an experience I cared to repeat.

Luckily, the bee had interests other than me, and it buzzed off to molest some flowers at an adjacent table.

I sipped my iced tea. I closed my eyes. The sun felt good. I decided to order a club sandwich, not caring if Rick showed up or not.

"Sorry I'm late . . ."

Rick was slightly out of breath. I had the impression that he'd been running, and was more flattered by his hurrying to meet me than I was irritated at his lateness.

Rick sat down, then picked up the water glass at his place setting. He drained half of it in one gulp.

"Did you catch any of the press conference?" I asked.

"No. Conference call with Washington. How'd it go?"

"Fine. Roxy actually did okay. Remained calm and poised, answered everything correctly. And she looked better in my jacket than I did."

Rick leaned in, his eyes twinkling. "No. She didn't."

I was being honest, not fishing, but it felt nice to hear just the same.

My sandwich came, and I apologized for having ordered without waiting for him.

"Can we split this club, and then I'll order another one?"

"Sure. That's fine. But . . ."

"But what?"

I was hungry, but looking down at the food made

my stomach twitch. What if this restaurant had been on the Chemist's list? What if I took a bite and would be dead in thirty seconds?

Rick apparently sensed my hesitation.

"Life is about risk, Jack. You can run away, or you can face it head-on."

He leaned in closer, his knee touching mine under the table. Then he picked up half of the sandwich and took a big bite, some mayo dribbling down his chin.

I felt my heart rate increase. Maybe I was overtired. Or hormonal. Whatever problem I was having, I promised myself no more one-on-one time with Rick.

Another ambulance streaked by, followed by two news vans. I didn't like the implications of that at all.

I pulled my radio out of my purse and tuned in to the police band. A few seconds later Rick threw down some money and we jogged up the street.

I worked out three times a week, weights and aerobics, and twice a month I attended a four-hour tae kwon do class, so I was able to keep pace with Rick the three blocks to the station house without collapsing or throwing up. But I did feel sick when I saw the ambulances at the corner of my precinct building.

A dozen uniforms were cordoning off a section of street, directing traffic, and questioning onlookers. Several paramedics were milling around two bodies. They didn't seem to be in a hurry. I managed to locate Herb in the crowd. Even though he was no longer my partner, he still managed to beat me to the crime scene.

"What happened?"

"I just got here. Some kind of traffic dispute."

"The radio mentioned the Chemist."

"Could be. Two dead, no marks on their bodies."

"Don't touch him!" Rick yelled at one of the medics who was crouching down next to a victim. "Risk of contamination!"

If the witnesses weren't spooked before, that started a mass exodus to the police lines. Herb went north and I went south, explaining to the crowd that they were perfectly safe, and if anyone saw anything we'd like to talk to them. I managed to snag a retreating party of businesspeople, and Herb caught a kid on Rollerblades. While we did that, Rick produced a gas mask and some rubber gloves, and examined one of the bodies.

The trio gave me a rundown of what they saw, beginning with the honking and ending with the perp stabbing each victim in the neck with something. He wore a suit, had an eye patch, and drove a white Honda Accord with scratches on both sides. None of them got the license plate.

Herb's witness gave a similar version of the story, but said the victims were shot in the neck with some kind of gun, rather than stabbed.

As we conferred, a uniform named Justin Buchbinder came to us with a jackpot: a witness with a camera phone.

"My name is Doris, Doris Washburn. I took three pictures." She was young, chic, in business attire. "The quality isn't the greatest, but I got one of the killer, and one of his car."

She showed me how to view them on her cell phone.

The perp's head was turned, and the license plate on the car too pixilated to be read, but the forensics guys had digital filters that might help improve the images. The third picture unfortunately only captured the man who later died, pointing his finger and yelling.

"We'll need to keep your phone."

"I need my phone for work. Can't I just send you the images?"

"Will they lose quality?"

"No. I can send them to your e-mail address."

I called Hajek at the crime lab, and Doris sent the photos to him using her phone.

"Get anything?" I asked him while the data transferred.

"A headache. Neck strain. A sore back."

"No prints?"

"The Chemist used gloves for everything. I even found a glove print on the toilet handle."

I thought about that. The only people that paranoid about leaving prints are those with prints on file. This guy was in our system, somewhere. People who have been arrested had their fingerprints taken. So did government employees like cops, Feds, and military. Plus, fingerprinting was becoming more common in the private sector, for both security reasons and to ID workers.

"How about the devices? Any way to trace them?"

"The M44s had serial numbers, but they'd been removed. Acid etching didn't bring them up. Wildlife Services uses them to kill coyotes, but these seem to be older models. Could have picked them up anywhere."

"How about the other traps?"

"Made from common household items. I got a copy of the CDC report—even the poisons are from pretty common plants. Many are available growing wild, or at garden shops. All of them can be ordered over the Internet. No way to trace them. I'm getting the e-mail now, hold on."

This was becoming silly. How is it possible to kill so many people and leave zero evidence?

"Well, the bad news is, the pictures are awful."

"Can you fix them?"

"Let's see." I heard him typing, and then humming softly. "I'll transfer them to my image enhancer. Clean up the noise . . . resize the image . . . reduce JPEG compression . . . and it's even worse than before. Let me work on it. Will you be at this number?"

I told him yes, and hung up.

"Where's the new partner?" Herb asked.

"Lunch."

"Shouldn't you call her?"

"Probably. I want my jacket back."

I called Dispatch to get Roxy's number. Surprisingly, a man answered when I dialed her number.

"I'm looking for Roxanne Waclawski."

"Are you a friend or relative of hers?"

"I'm her partner, Lieutenant Daniels from the CPD. Can you put her on?"

"I'm afraid not, Lieutenant. I'm an EMT. We got a call of a woman passing out at a Willoughby's on Michigan and Huron. Your partner is dead."

I squeezed my eyes closed so hard, I saw stars under the lids.

"How did she die?"

"It appears to be heart failure. But in someone this young . . ."

"Okay, you need to be careful. She was probably poisoned, and some of it may still be on her. I need you to talk to the manager. Try not to let anyone leave until I get there."

"Was this—"

"Don't say anything more. I don't want to cause a panic. I'll be there in a few minutes."

I hung up and looked at Herb.

"She's dead. It's a few blocks away. I need you at the crime scene."

Herb hesitated for a moment, and then said, "No."

"Goddammit, Herb—"

"Goddammit, Jack, I'm not Homicide anymore." He looked as angry as I'd ever seen him. "This isn't my case, and you're not my partner."

"Fine," I said, the words forming in my mouth before common sense could override them. "Be a coward."

I didn't mean it. But before I could take it back, Herb was storming off, through the crowd, over the yellow police tape, and back to the station. I'd apologize later. Herb would forgive me. Especially if the apology included carbohydrates.

I turned to look for Rick, but he was still in full gear, hovering over the corpses. Figuring I'd need help at the restaurant, I grabbed the uniform, Buchbinder.

"How would you like a temporary promotion to Homicide/Gangs/Sex?"

"My sergeant will bust my balls if I leave my post."

"What's your post?"

"Parking enforcement."

"I'll smooth it over. You got a car?"

"A bike."

"Even better. Let's go."

That cheered me up a fraction. I liked bikes. My ex-husband, the man who gave me my last name, had a 1982 Harley-Davidson Sportster, and we'd go riding whenever we could. Which, as far as I can remember, was twice.

I worked a lot back then.

Unfortunately, when Buchbinder said *bike*, he meant *scooter*. The tiny little electric moped barely had room for two, and had a top speed of slow. A five-minute walk took us ten minutes on the bike, because Officer Buchbinder stopped for all traffic signals, pedestrians, strong breezes, and optical illusions. He also pulled behind a horse and buggy giving six geriatrics a tour of the Magnificent Mile—a tour so excruciatingly sluggish that I doubted all of them would live long enough to see its conclusion.

"Go faster," I said.

"If I follow too closely, there could be an accident."

As it turned out, there was an accident. Buchbinder couldn't brake in time, and coasted right through the largest pile of horse shit I'd ever seen.

"Apparently they can do that while trotting," I said.

"Did you see that? It came out of nowhere."

Actually, I did see it, along with where it came out of. But I chose not to mention it.

"Some got in the spokes," Buchbinder whined. "I just cleaned the spokes."

"Pay attention to the road."

"My God, my bike is trashed. What was that horse eating?"

"Let's get off this topic."

"What's that on the fender . . . peanuts?"

"Pass the damn horse or I'm firing you."

He made a hand signal and thankfully got around the horse and cart. But getting past it and getting past it were two different things.

"I gotta clean this quick, before it hardens. Don't want to have to chisel it off."

"Let's talk about something else," I said. I didn't say, "Like your non-future in the Homicide division."

Buchbinder, however, was fixated.

"I can smell it. Can you smell it?"

Jesus. It just wouldn't end.

"I got some on my pants."

"Buchbinder, shut the hell up about the horse already."

"Okay. But I never saw Mr. Ed do that, no sir. That manure pile was the size of a small child. Lucky we weren't both killed."

I didn't feel lucky. Not even a little bit.

"Do you smell peanuts?"

We got to Willoughby's shortly thereafter. I instructed

the Horseshit Whisperer to take witness statements after he cleaned his pants. Then I spoke with the bartender.

"She came in alone. Sat down, ordered a dirty martini, up. Took off her jacket and asked where the bathroom was. I made the drink and set it down by her stool."

I looked at the empty glass, an olive at the bottom.

"Did you see anyone near her drink?"

"Some guy came to the bar, took some napkins."

"Did he touch her drink at all?"

"I only saw him out of the corner of my eye."

"Can you describe him?"

"White guy. Suit. Had an eye patch."

Dammit, Roxy. After that long talk about making yourself a target and being extra careful, how could you leave an unattended drink on the bar? I stared at my gray jacket on the bar stool, and could picture her on camera wearing it, looking so confident and professional.

I left it on the stool. I'd never wear it again.

I switched focus to the martini glass, trying to figure out how to transport it. The Crime Scene Unit would have the materials. They needed to be here anyway, to dust for prints.

I used the cell phone to call in the CSU, and some members of my team, including an Identikit artist. Maybe with all of these witnesses, we could give the Chemist a face.

My phone rang. Rick. I picked it up.

"Where are you?" he asked.

I filled him in.

"Shit. She was a good kid. You can't blame yourself."

"Sure I can."

"She was a professional. She knew the risks."

"She was a child."

"Put the guilt on the back burner for a little while. I think I figured out his delivery system. What he's using to tamper with food."

That got my attention. "What?"

"He's also been using it directly on people. It's called a jet injector."

"What is that?"

"I can do better than just tell you. I'll show you. When will you be free again?"

I looked around, at the several dozen people in the restaurant.

"A few hours at least."

"We had to cut lunch short. Up for dinner?"

I thought of Latham, unconscious and on a ventilator.

"I've got something to do after work."

"How about a quick bite? I'll bring some food to your office. I can show you there."

I hadn't eaten anything, and by dinner I'd be ravenous. And if I ate at work, it would give me more time with Latham.

"Fine. Meet you there at five."

No big deal, I assured myself. It wasn't like we were going to have sex in my office.

Right?

CHAPTER 18

I GOT BACK TO the office a little after four. A copy of the personal ad set to run in tomorrow's newspaper was on my desk.

Chemist—the answer is yes.

My stomach was growling loud enough to make passing dogs growl back. I visited the office vending machine, plunked in two quarters for a candy bar, and then stopped when I remembered that candy bars were on the list of tampered food items.

What was left to eat? Food in cans, and things I hunted and cooked myself. And I wasn't even sure about the cans—the CDC found evidence that a can of chicken soup might have been dosed with BT.

What the hell can contaminate canned food?

I had half a roll of breath mints that had been in my purse for a year, and I wiped off the lint and ate those, along with water from the tap.

The CSU had lifted a bajillion fingerprints from Willoughby's. The crime lab, in conjunction with the CDC/WHO/HMRT, had confirmed that Roxy's martini had been dosed with *Tanghinia venenifera*, known as the ordeal bean of Madagascar. It also grew wild in Hawaii. As few as ten drops of extract were fatal.

Poor Roxy.

I flipped through a few reports from witnesses at the restaurant, and three of them had put together a composite picture of a generic-looking guy. It was so featureless, it looked like a Ken doll with an eye patch. A hot dog vendor a block away had corroborated the sketch, adding that the Chemist spoke with a Midwestern accent, stood about five feet nine inches, and was between twenty-five and forty-five years old. But even though he had extended contact with him, all he really had focused on was the damn eye patch. Basically any thin white guy could be our perp.

I guessed the eye patch to be a disguise, because it hadn't been mentioned in any of the scads of reports. We ran it through the registry just the same. Over two thousand guys in our database could fit the description. I put a team on it.

The mints did nothing to curb my hunger, so I wandered over to Herb's office, to apologize for being an ass and to see if he still had those antique Twinkies.

His office had been cleared out, and there was no Herb to be found. No food either. He'd even taken the wrappers.

I passed the vending machine again, and paid special attention to the packaging. Chips—could be tampered with. Candy bars—could be tampered with. Mints—it would be hard to inject toxin into mints.

I bought a roll, then spent five minutes turning

them around in my hands, looking for evidence of tampering.

Life is about taking risks, Rick had said. I opened the package and popped one in my mouth.

I didn't die.

As I sucked on the candy, I went through the reports that Herb had compiled, and made some calls to get updates on the questioning of the victims, witness searches, security tapes, and Alger's arrest record. None of it pointed in any specific direction. I took out my To Do list and stared at it.

> ~~trace M44 purchases~~
> ~~Alger arrest record~~
> ~~talk to neighbors~~
> question mailman who delivered letter
> ~~security tapes at BT scenes~~
> ~~witness search at BT scenes~~
> ~~survivor interviews/background checks~~
> ~~research IEDs~~

I added to the list: gardener, fingerprints probably on file, disguise/eye patch, white Honda Accord, local, two million dollars.

I stared at the new list. Why two mil? It was a lot of money, but not that much. He could have demanded more than that. Did it have some kind of significance?

I also noted that *question mailman* was still on the list. I leafed through Herb's folder and found the statement from Carey Schimmel, USPS. It was the shortest statement in the history of statements, amounting to: *I delivered the letter.* Carey also admitted that since the anthrax scare, he wore gloves, which explained his lack of fingerprints on the extortion envelope. I crossed that off the list.

I was about to give Hajek a call to see how he was coming with the camera phone pics, when Rick came in, carrying a bag of heaven.

"Do you like Chinese?" he asked, eyes sparkling.

"Are you kidding? I could eat Mao Tse-tung raw right now."

The smells were intoxicating. Sweet and sour. Rice. Soy. Beef. Veggies. My mouth filled with saliva.

But wariness prevented me from tearing open the bag with my bare teeth.

"Are we sure it's . . ."

"So far, the Chemist has only struck in the city, right? I got this in Cicero."

We dug in. I ate an egg roll in two bites, wondering how that might look to a guy, but not caring. Then I dug into some beef chop suey, some kung pao chicken, and a potsticker that had to be the single greatest thing I've ever put in my mouth.

Rick had also brought a six-pack of Tsingtao. My job would be in jeopardy if just one reporter with a long lens caught me through the office window, drinking beer. I took the risk anyway. I wouldn't call myself a beer aficionado—I liked Sam Adams and I liked a local brew called Goose Island even more—but that Tsingtao went down quicker than any beer I'd had in ages. Rick popped open another for me, and then one for himself.

"To catching the bad guy," I said, raising my bottle.

"And to making new friends."

We drank to that.

When my stomach had distended to the point where my innie became an outie, I threw in the chopsticks.

"So what is this lunatic using to tamper with the food?" I asked, kicking off my shoes and pulling my feet up under me in my chair.

"I'm not a hundred percent sure, but it would explain the lack of needle holes or surface toxins, and I confirmed it with the deaths of the couple on the street, and several of the victims of the Sammy's massacre yesterday. It's called a jet injector."

"Which is what?"

He dug into his satchel and took out a small blue object shaped like a phaser from *Star Trek*, only child-sized. It had a white plastic tube jutting out of the handle, which extended about eighteen inches into a silver cylinder.

"It's a needle-less injection gun, used for mass immunizations. Invented years ago, to counter the cross-contamination caused by needles, along with the fear factor and high cost of sterilization. Diabetics also use them. This model can administer a dose of liquid up to three cc's. Its orifice is many times smaller than a needle—less than the width of a human hair, actually—so the hole it makes is very hard to spot. And unlike a needle, it evenly disperses liquid once it penetrates the skin. It's the perfect system to introduce medicine subcutaneously."

I looked at the thing with a mixture of dread and fascination.

"How does it work without a needle?"

"Air pressure. This one uses a spring. Other models use compressed gas, like CO2. You arm the device"—Rick turned a key on the cylinder—"then squeeze the trigger."

I flinched at the hissing sound, and saw a spray of vapor appear around the nozzle of the gun.

"The pressure causes a jet stream, which forces the liquid through the skin and into the muscle. Smaller hole, less central concentration of fluid, less pain. Some of these models are tough too. You could inject insulin into a basketball."

"What about plastic wrapping, or butcher paper, or aluminum cans?"

"Conceivable, yes. It would probably even work on thicker plastic, or cardboard. And look how small it is."

Rick turned his palm and closed his fingers. The gun was completely hidden by his hand.

"I think this is what the Chemist used on his last two victims, on the street outside. They died so quickly there wasn't even bruising, and the puncture wound could only be seen under a microscope. But I biopsied neck tissue where witnesses say he held his weapon, and found uneven concentrations of ricin, a toxin found in castor beans. I think he injected it directly into their throats."

Rick was smiling, and while I was happy to know what we were up against, I wasn't able to share his enthusiasm. Truth told, the Chinese food was doing somersaults in my stomach. The thought of someone using a device invented for good to do so much evil gave me a giant case of the creeps.

"Can we trace these things?" I asked.

Rick's smile faltered.

"No. There are about two dozen companies that make them, and only six of them make a model small enough that it can be concealed, but that still gives us thousands of possibles. The guy might have picked it up at a garage sale, or on the Internet, or stolen one."

He set the jet injector on my desk, where it coiled like a snake among the half-empty food cartons. Rick, so full of energy a moment ago, looked like he'd deflated.

"This still helps narrow it down," I said. "We're looking for a white male, local, with a greenhouse and a jet injector."

Rick raised an eyebrow at me. "He's local?"

"He has to be. Roxy was just assigned to the case, and he got to her right after she appeared on television. I'm guessing he was watching at home, then put together a quick disguise and went out after her."

"Why the greenhouse?" Rick asked.

"He uses toxins, which are organic. I'm guessing he makes these himself, which means he has a garden some-where. Some of the plants are tropical, so unless he keeps his house at ninety-five degrees, he probably has a green-house."

"Smart. That could mean hydroponics, special lamps, fertilizers. Chicago is a big town, but it shouldn't have that many specialty gardening stores."

My turn to frown. "You're forgetting the Internet. All that stuff can be purchased online."

We were quiet for almost a full minute. It didn't surprise me that Rick looked adorable while deep in thought.

"You're paying him?" he finally asked.

"That's the idea."

"You'll try to make the arrest when he picks up the money?"

"Of course. But I'm sure he's anticipating that."

Rick rubbed the stubble on his chin. I liked stubble. I liked the feel of it, against my cheek. Between my thighs.

Dammit, Jack, quit it. So, he's pretty. So what. Get over it.

"Two million isn't a lot," he said.

"I was thinking the same thing."

"Might be using that small number because it's easier to handle, easier to carry. Even using hundred-dollar bills, it makes a pretty big pile. About the height of your desk. One person couldn't carry it all."

"Which means, what? A drop-off point? He'll ask for the money in a big metal box and then swoop down in a helicopter carrying a big magnet?"

Rick grinned. "That's what I was thinking."

"We know all the tricks. Transmitters. Tracking devices. Exploding ink packs. Consecutive serial numbers. Coating the money with spy dust."

"What's spy dust?" Rick asked.

"An invisible powder that shows up under UV light."

"You use that stuff?"

"No. I saw it on a TV show."

We shared a laugh.

"I guess we won't know what to do until we hear from him," Rick said.

"Which should be tomorrow, once he reads the paper."

I looked at my watch. Visiting hours at the hospital were until eight p.m. I needed to get going.

"Jack, you have something on your cheek."

Rick did the mirror reflection thing, wiping his own cheek off. I wiped in the same spot.

"Did I get it?"

"No. Here."

He reached for me, caressed my cheek, and our eyes locked and I couldn't believe I fell for that stupid trick, but I didn't pull away, even when he moved in and placed his lips against mine.

I didn't kiss him back.

Well, not at first.

His lips were warm, soft, and when the tip of his tongue entered my mouth, something snapped in me and a little sigh escaped my throat and I put my hands behind his head and pressed his body against mine.

He grabbed me by my waist and picked me up out of the chair like I weighed nothing, and then his hands were on my ass and mine were on his ass and—*damn*, did he have a great ass.

As our mouths fought for better purchase, his hand came around my hips and undid my front button, or perhaps just tugged it off, and then his fingers touched the top of my panties and he was a few inches away from seeing how excited I really was. Then common sense overrode hormones and the World's Worst Fiancée pushed him away.

"I . . . can't," I said between deep breaths.

"Sure you can. I bet you're really good at it."

I wanted him, but a small voice inside me said I was just using sex to cope with all of my problems. Then another small voice tried to convince me that there was nothing wrong with that, sex was a perfectly acceptable way to cope, and that voice was louder than the first. And then a third voice, louder than both of the others, reminded me about a boyfriend on a ventilator whom I was afraid to marry because I feared making mistakes.

And then it all made sense.

"I'm afraid to get married because I'm afraid I'll screw it up," I said, surprised at the self-realization. "So I'm subconsciously trying to sabotage that."

Rick reached for me again, but I kept him at arm's length.

"I . . . I fear failure," I said to Rick. But it wasn't really to Rick. It was more to myself. "So I'd rather cop out of a situation than take a chance. I mean, look at me, I'd rather sabotage a good thing instead of giving it a try."

I stared at Rick, who somehow had his shirt open—had I done that?—revealing as nice a chest as I'd ever seen outside of a movie.

"I'm going to see my fiancé," I told him.

"Are you sure?"

"Yeah. I'm really sure."

Rick smiled. "He's a very lucky man."

I checked my pants button, and saw that he'd also gotten the zipper down. I zipped them back up, suddenly embarrassed.

"If it doesn't work out . . ." Rick said, letting his voice trail off.

But I knew it would work out. I'd make sure it would work out. I loved Latham, and I'd do everything within my power to make our marriage succeed.

"We're not going to happen," I told Rick, pointing at him and me. "I'm sorry."

Rick sighed, then buttoned up his shirt and left my office, closing the door behind him.

I adjusted my blouse and realized he had unhooked my bra as well. How the hell had he done that so fast?

The phone rang, and I knew deep in my heart that it was Latham, and he was conscious again, perhaps even well enough for me to screw his brains out.

But it wasn't Latham. It was Hajek at the crime lab.

"I'm a genius, Lieutenant. A certifiable genius."

"What happened?"

"I got the license number. And even better, I traced it."

"Meaning what?"

"Meaning we've got the bastard's address."

CHAPTER 19

WHAT'S THE ADDRESS?" I asked.

"Don't you want to know how I did it?"

Hajek spoke with the same enthusiasm as a child showing off the construction paper snowflake he made in school.

"Give me the quick version."

"JPEG compression didn't work, and neither did resizing or noise reduction, so I used a program that could change the blur width by—"

"You're a genius," I said, interrupting. "What's the address?"

"But changing the focus points wasn't enough. I had to rearrange the pixels using—"

"The address, Scott."

He sighed. "Vehicle belongs to a Tracey Hotham. Her apartment is on Thirty-first and Laramie in Cicero."

"Did you run priors?"

"Of course. No records. I checked DMV, and her license had expired. So I tried Social Security, and found out Tracey died six years ago."

"How?"

"I didn't dig that deep. But you can ask her parents. According to 411, they're still living at the Cicero address."

Two scenarios came to me simultaneously. Maybe they no longer had the car, or maybe a member of Tracey's family was the Chemist.

I yawned. Not from boredom—my lack of sleep was catching up with me. "Nice work, Scott."

"Thanks. Maybe we could discuss it over dinner."

"Sure. I'll call you tomorrow, during dinner."

I hung up, my fingers pressing the speed dial for Herb before my mind remembered he and I were no longer a team. I hit the disconnect button.

Abruptly, I felt very alone.

I could get in touch with Bains, have him assign me a new partner, but that wouldn't happen today. I wasn't even sure I wanted a new partner on this case. I didn't like wearing a bull's-eye, and didn't want to hang one on anyone else.

Calling Rick wasn't an option. I didn't want to see him again unless I was wearing a suit of armor. I could try Scooterboy Buchbinder, but going solo was preferable to hearing him wax prolific about the World's Largest Road Apple. Before leaving Willoughby's, he had taken me aside and confessed that right before the unfortunate collision, he'd sworn the manure pile looked exactly like the Lincoln head on Mt. Rushmore.

"I keep seeing it. President Lincoln's face, getting cleaved in half. And that haunting, squishing sound . . ."

The guy had issues. More than issues—he had a whole subscription.

So I had no choice. I'd be going stag to Cicero.

On my way to the car, I called the Cicero police, and

was bounced around until I connected with a sergeant named Cooper.

"You think the Chemist lives in our burg?"

"I have no idea. As of now, the Hothams are persons of interest. It's your jurisdiction, if you want someone there."

"We'll meet you at the apartment. You need a warrant?"

"I just want to ask some questions. Don't . . ." I thought about walking into Alger's house. "Have your people wait for me before they go in. This guy likes to set traps."

And then I hopped in my car and headed for Cicero.

The drive only took fifteen minutes. Cicero bordered Chicago on the west, blending into it seamlessly. Mostly Hispanic, a population of around eighty thousand, middle class, blue collar, more like a neighborhood of Chicago than a distinct town.

Their patrol cars were black with silver accents, and there was one of them at the address when I arrived. It was empty.

On the drive over, I'd gotten a little sleepy. But this put me into full alert mode, complete with adrenaline sweat and a tug of nausea. They'd gone in without me.

I dug out my .38 and stared at the apartment building. Three stories, brick, dirty beige. Black wrought iron railing along the walkway, rusty and broken. Security windows on the first floor. Front door open a crack.

I hung my star around my neck, drew in a big breath, and went through the door.

Hallway was well lit, the walls freshly painted. I took the stairs two at a time, up to the second floor and 2-C, where the Hothams resided. Their door was also open a few inches. I nudged it with my shoulder, peering into the apartment but keeping my face well away from the crack.

I heard static, then, "Car seventeen, this is base, please copy."

"Police," I announced. "I'm coming in."

I eased the door open, still not daring to breathe the air coming out of the apartment.

I saw the legs first. Male, black shoes, sidearm still in his rocker holster.

"Seventeen this is base, what's your twenty, over."

He lay on his back, bloodshot eyes wide, mouth hanging open and coated in froth and mucus. I didn't see any movement, but I knew I needed to check for a pulse to be sure.

The problem was, I didn't want to go into that apartment.

I parted my lips, still not breathing, but trying to taste the air, to see if it was safe. I didn't taste anything.

"Is anyone inside this apartment?" I said loudly.

No answer.

My options were to call for backup, or go inside and look for possible survivors. If this was the Chemist's apartment, it could be booby-trapped.

"Car seventeen, this is base, please respond. You there, Smitty?"

I let in a tiny bit of air. It seemed fine. No strange smell. No physical reaction, other than a strange sense of déjà vu that I'd been in this same situation before, which wasn't déjà vu at all.

But this time, I didn't have a space suit.

I went in, crouched next to the fallen cop, probing his carotid. Nothing. So I reached for the radio clipped to his chest.

"This is Lieutenant Daniels, Chicago PD. We have an officer down at 1730 East Thirty-first, apartment 2-C. Request immediate assistance."

The radio crackled a response, but I wasn't paying attention; my eyes focused on the two people sitting on the couch.

A man and a woman. Early sixties. She had brown hair, cut short, with gray highlights. He was mostly bald. Both wore glasses. Both stared straight at me.

Both were dead.

It took a moment to realize that. After the adrenaline startle, I stood erect and took a few steps toward them. Their eyes were dry, lifeless. Their faces devoid of color. They held hands, and I noticed the lividity blush to their fingers, where the blood had pooled.

What killed these people?

My paranoia kicked up to near panic, and I looked up, down, left and right, in every direction I could, for traps, for gas, for IEDs, for poison, for anything dangerous or out of place.

Cobwebs on the ceiling. A clean carpet. An easy chair. Two floor lamps, glowing. A window air conditioner. A large floor-model humidifier, silent. Photos on the walls, of the old people. It was their house.

"Is anyone in here?" I shouted.

No response.

I walked past the fallen officer, through the living room, nice and easy, aware of my center, my footing, my balance, eyes sweeping the floor for wires and fishing line.

Another cop was in the kitchen, facedown on the tile floor, a pool of vomit surrounding his head like a green halo. Gun clenched in his fist. No signs of any injury, just like his partner.

Had they surprised the Chemist, and he dosed them all and then ran out?

Or had they run into some of his improvised traps?

Or was the Chemist still inside, waiting with his jet injector?

The phone rang, and my finger flinched. I was a millimeter away from shooting the dead cop before I caught myself and eased back on the trigger.

It rang again. I stared at the phone, one of those older desktop models the phone company once called "Princess," on the kitchen counter between a coffee machine and a tabletop humidifier—apparently the Hothams preferred a humid household.

I moved in closer, searching for trip wires or switches attached to the phone. It seemed untampered with. On the third ring, I picked it up.

"Hello?"

"Who is this?" A male voice, whispering.

"Lieutenant Daniels, of the Chicago Police Department. Who am I speaking with?"

A pause. I could hear him breathing. Slow and even, like a metronome.

"You know who this is, Lieutenant. Did they assign you a new partner yet?"

Anger overrode anxiety. "Why are you doing this?"

"You're the cop. You figure it out."

I clenched the phone so tight, my knuckles turned white.

"You're killing innocent people."

"No one is fully innocent," he rasped. "Especially not the police."

"How about these people in this apartment? What did they do to you?"

"Unfortunate, but I needed the car. I believe the government would call them casualties of war, or collateral damage."

"We're not at war."

"I am."

I waited. An old police trick. Give a suspect silence, and he'll fill the silence with talk.

"Are you wondering if I'm a terrorist?" the Chemist finally said. "I'm not. I'm not out to cause terror. I'm out to cause pain. An eye for an eye. And I might as well make a little money along the way. Have you decided to pay me?"

"Yes. The ad will run tomorrow. If we pay you, you'll stop this?"

He chuckled.

"You're very attractive. Not like that younger woman, the blonde. She had a better body, but she didn't have that look that you have. The haunted look. You've seen things, I bet. Done things. Any sins to confess, Lieutenant?"

I knew I could get the phone records, trace this number, but he probably knew that as well. Why did he call? To ask about the money? To see if there were survivors?

"If you come in voluntarily, we can work out a deal. I know the assistant state's attorney. We could waive the death penalty."

"Lieutenant Daniels." He was speaking normally now, no longer whispering. "*I am* the death penalty."

I had talked to my share of psychos, but this one was really freaking me out.

"Why did you call here?"

"For two reasons. First, to get your phone number. You're the person I want to deal with from now on. What's your cell?"

I didn't like that much, but I gave it to him.

"What's the other reason?"

Another chuckle. "It's awfully dry in there, don't you think?"

I glanced at the tabletop humidifier, noticed that the green light was blinking.

"Perhaps you should leave, Lieutenant. A dry environment isn't very healthy."

I dropped the phone and backed away, stumbling over the corpse, almost losing my footing, forcing my throat closed in mid-gasp. Back in the living room, I heard the faint humming of the floor-model humidifier next to the sofa. It had been off before, but those things had sensors and timers and started automatically. Now it was running full tilt, billowing lethal steam throughout the room.

I clamped a hand over my mouth and sprinted, still not breathing, and ran out into the hallway into a band of Cicero cops storming up the stairs.

Four men trained their weapons on me. I exhaled, raising up my hands, saying, "I'm police."

And then my stomach twisted, and my vision got wiggly, and I grabbed on to the railing and thought *Oh my God no* just as the vomit escaped my lips.

CHAPTER 20

AN OVERLY HAIRY MEDIC named Holmes stuck an electronic thermometer in my ear as I sat in the rear of his ambulance, breathing into a plastic bag.

"Ninety-nine point one," he declared.

The plethora of unpronounceable poisons, toxins, and diseases I'd been exposed to in the last few days raced like a stampede through my mind.

"So I'm sick?" I asked, my voice small.

"BP is normal. Reflexes are normal. Headache or stomachache?"

"Both."

"Open wide."

I opened, self-conscious about my breath after throwing up.

"Throat looks fine." He shined a penlight in my eyes. "Pupil response normal."

"So what have I got?"

"Nothing, as far as I can tell."

The CPD Mobile Command Post drove up, and six SRT cops got out, all wearing full space suits.

"I threw up," I told the medic. "Should we go get a sample?"

"Why?"

"I don't know. To test."

Holmes gave me a patronizing look.

"You aren't the first cop to throw up at a crime scene. It's nothing to be ashamed of."

"That's not why I threw up. I've seen corpses before."

"Have you been under a lot of stress lately?"

"Maybe."

"That's probably what did it."

"But you said I have a fever."

"A slight fever. Could be due to stress, or overheating."

"And my headache?"

"Stress."

He packed up his kit.

"If I drop dead, you're going to feel really stupid," I said.

He winked at me. "I'll risk it."

A Cicero cop came over, *Cooper* on his name badge. The sergeant I'd spoken with on the phone. Short, dark, and brooding.

"What a giant clusterfuck. Those were good guys."

He didn't seem to know what else to say. I didn't have much either.

"You want my statement?" I eventually asked.

"Yeah."

We spent half an hour going over it, backward and forward and backward again. Cooper got on the horn with the phone company and a few minutes later found out that the Chemist had called from the Hothams' own cell phone, which he'd apparently taken with him after their murder. Cooper tried pinging the number—a system that the 911 Emergency Center uses to triangulate cell phone locations to within twenty-five meters—but the Chemist had probably destroyed the phone after calling the apartment.

With my statement in the can, I asked if I could poke around the apartment. When Cooper said no, the relief I felt was a physical thing.

"We'll keep you in the loop, get you the reports, but you going up there now isn't going to happen."

From the hard looks of the Cicero cops who walked past, I understood Cooper's reasoning. If I hadn't called earlier, two men would still be alive.

I drove home. Even though Cicero was closer to Bensenville, it still took an hour.

A call to the nurse's station told me Latham had awoken briefly, but was now sleeping again. I asked them to call me if there was any change. Then I fished my notebook out of my purse, and found the number of Wilbur Martin Streng that Dispatch had given to me earlier. He lived in Elmwood Park. No priors, other than some minor traffic violations.

My dad.

I stared at the number, wondering how I should feel. I didn't remember much about my father. All I had were impressions of him. The old leather slippers he always wore around the house. The dark-framed Clark Kent glasses. The smell of Old Spice and cigars.

One memory stood out, so clear that I had no idea if

it was a real memory or a fabrication. We were in Grant Park for some kind of summer festival, and I was on his shoulders, and there was an ice cream vendor on the street. Dad bought me an ice cream, and I dropped it. So we went back to the vendor, and he bought me another one. I accidentally dropped that one too. He didn't get mad. No lecture. No yelling. Not a single word. We just went back to the ice cream man, and Dad bought me a third.

This was the man who left me and Mom. The man who destroyed our family.

I wanted to drum up some hate, but couldn't seem to find it. All I had was curiosity. I wanted to hear, in his words, why he left. Why he never tried to get in touch. How he could completely absolve responsibility for the lives of two people he was supposed to have loved.

I put the number away. Now wasn't the time.

I came home to a package outside my door. Shoes I'd ordered from some TV shopping club. Normally that would perk me up. This time, it was a chore to even pick them up.

Upon opening my door, I was greeted by the pleasant surprise of a living room coated in kitty litter. This was impressive, considering the cat box was in the kitchen. Mr. Friskers had also asserted his dominance over the sofa, having shredded one of the armrests.

He missed my mother, I guessed.

I'd once gone so far as to battle Mr. Friskers into his cat carrier, in preparation to get him declawed, and if possible, detoothed. Mom, in her mother tone, reminded me that the cat had saved both of our lives, and removing his claws would be like taking away Wyatt Earp's Colt Peacemaker.

I told her, "Wyatt Earp didn't terrorize the West, maiming innocents and destroying property."

"Let the kitty out of the carrier, dear, and help yourself to my Valium."

The cat was the one who needed the Valium. But Mom won, and the weapons of mass destruction weren't removed. Mr. Friskers celebrated his victory by tearing apart a section of carpeting in my bedroom.

He never seemed to destroy any of Mom's things.

I went into the kitchen, litter crunching underfoot, and saw Mr. Friskers on the countertop, playing with something small and dark.

That poor mariachi's mustache.

"You're the Antichrist," I told him.

He ignored me.

I checked his food dish, saw that it was filled with kitty litter (how did he do that?), and rinsed it out. I dumped in some dry food, refreshed his water, and plodded into the bedroom.

As I undressed, I thought about Latham and got pretty choked up. Not only because he was sick, but because I should have said yes when he proposed. I looked at my left hand and felt an itch where the ring should be.

Where *was* the ring?

Latham had appropriated a few drawers in my dresser, and I opened up the top one. The ring box was resting on top of his jeans. I took it out and opened it up.

It was gorgeous. Bigger than I remembered. And I wanted it so badly.

I considered putting it on, so he could see it when I visited him. But I wanted him to put it on me. I wanted the mariachi players again, and the kneeling, and the sweet speech, but this time I'd say yes, and no one would lose any facial hair, and then we'd have a romantic dinner and wild sex and I'd soon be Jacqueline Conger. Jacqueline Conger-Daniels. Jacqueline Daniels-Conger.

Well, we'd figure out the name stuff later.

I closed the box and put it back in the drawer.

A hot shower burned away some of the stress, but not much. I threw on one of Latham's undershirts, rubbed some Oil of Olay into my wrinkles, and plopped into bed as exhausted as I'd ever been.

Sleep refused to come.

After twenty minutes of tossing and turning, I flipped on the Home Shopping Network. I had their 800 number on speed dial, my customer number committed to memory, and I bought a portable steamer, a hair-coloring system guaranteed to get out the gray in five easy minutes, and an assortment of fake eyelashes because I'd never owned fake eyelashes and because they looked like fun and because I was seriously overtired.

"Would you like to put this on your Visa, Ms. Daniels?"

"That sounds perfect."

Some people had cocaine. I had HSN. It was still up in the air as to which was the more expensive addiction.

The phone rang, and I wondered if it was Stacey

from HSN, telling me their computer burst into flames when they tried to authorize my credit card.

But it wasn't HSN. It was the hospital.

"Are you the next of kin for Latham Conger?"

I tried to swallow, but couldn't. I managed to say, "Yes."

"You'd better get here are soon as possible."

"What's going on?"

"His condition has deteriorated. He may not last the night."

I glanced at the drawer, the one with the engagement ring in it. Then I threw on some clothes and headed for the hospital.

CHAPTER 21

HIS GREEN SWEATPANTS have holes in the knees, and have been rubbed with grease and grime from his gas grill. He wears a blue hoodie, equally stained, and over that a black rain slicker. His shoes are an old pair of white Nikes that have been scribbled on with black permanent marker. Grease also coats his forehead and both cheeks. The glued-on goatee has bits of crackers in it.

Taped to the insides of his jacket are eight large-sized ziplock bags. They're full, and when he cinches his jacket closed, he can feel their contents wiggling.

He carries a stuffed backpack, also dirtied up. If he puts his ear to it, he hears a soft rustling sound.

He checks the mirror, rubs more grease onto his face and over the backs of his hands, and then pulls on a wool cap, covering his hair.

Then he walks to the corner and waits for the bus.

Even at three in the morning, it's unbearably hot. It's only June, but Chicago already has that oily humidity so common during summer nights; part garbage smell, part sewage smell, with just a hint of Lake Michigan. It's bright out—traffic, shops, streetlights—and the bus stop is especially well lit. To discourage criminal behavior, he assumes. He's not discouraged in the least.

The movement inside his jacket is creepy, repulsive. He forces himself not to fidget, to keep the coat on and relax. When the bus arrives, green and white and almost as dirty as he is, he puts his quarters in the money box and the driver makes a show of not looking at him.

The bus has a few occupants. A single black man. Some college kids talking loud. A woman who might be a hooker. He sits in an empty seat and places his backpack between his feet. He stares at it, and tries not to think about what he's got under his coat, tries not to think about what he's going to do.

His stop comes up. He gets off the bus. There are a few people on the sidewalk, but not nearly as many as before. He's sweating hard now, and can smell himself. It adds to his disguise.

The police station is ahead, and he hesitates. He'd been inside a few months ago, to get a layout of the place. This will work. He just needs to remain calm.

He walks through the front doors, up to the desk sergeant seated behind the bulletproof glass.

"I was robbed," he says, putting a little alcohol slur into the words. Then he gives a fake name. Brian Pinkerton.

The cop frowns at him. He can guess the sergeant's thoughts. No one likes the homeless. They're a blight on the city. Who cares if one got robbed? But a crime is a crime, and they have to take the reports.

He's told to sit down in the lobby and a police officer will be with him, but it may take a little while.

Which is perfect.

He takes a seat on a cracked vinyl bench the color of cigarette smoke, and places the bag between his feet like he did on the bus. But this time, he unzips the top.

There are half a dozen people in the lobby. An old woman, black and fat, obviously homeless, muttering to herself. A Hispanic lady who keeps dabbing at the tears in her eyes with a wadded-up tissue. Two white guys with various facial cuts and bruises. A man in a reverend's collar. An angry-looking old man, swinging his cane around like he's swatting flies.

The first cockroach climbs out of the backpack, hesitates for a millisecond, then climbs down the side and tears across the room.

Two more do the same thing.

Then thousands.

One of the white guys is the first to notice. He stands abruptly, pointing and saying, "Holy shit!"

His companion also stands.

"That is disgusting."

The angry old man also stands up, uttering a round of expletives, the favorite being, "Goddamn!"

Crying lady leaps to her feet and runs across the room, screaming. The reverend watches, mouth agape, and then also gets up and retreats to a corner of the room.

The Chemist remains still, even as the roaches crawl up his legs. He's been preparing for this for many months, breeding and feeding the bugs, sticking his hands into the roach pen to overcome his inherent squeamishness. He reaches inside his raincoat, pulling open one of the bags. Roaches erupt from the holes in his clothing like he's bleeding them out of his veins.

The homeless woman also remains still as the roaches swarm her. He watches as several crawl across her face, and tries to remain just as unaffected as they crawl across his.

Someone is yelling at the desk sergeant, and two plainclothes cops come into the lobby, take one look at the stampede of insects, and join the old man in the "Goddamn" chant.

In a radius of ten feet and growing, the white tile floor has become brown with shifting white specks. Some of the roaches beeline for corners, cracks, hiding places. Others run in straight lines, apparently assured of their safety in numbers.

A female uniformed officer comes in, takes a look, and exits the way she came.

The Chemist stands, hands in his coat, opening more bags. He was hoping to free at least half of the bugs before they kicked him out, but no one is rushing over to grab him. More cops enter the lobby, and they just stand there, looking revolted. No one acts. One of them tiptoes across the room, roaches crackling underfoot like dry leaves, but he heads for the exit rather than trying to secure order.

There is more talking now. The Chemist catches the words *filthy* and *homeless*. Freeing the contents of the final bag, he walks toward the exit, pausing at the bulletproof glass to stare at the desk sergeant, ass up on his desk and feet raised from the floor as if the room had suddenly flooded.

"You got a bug problem," he says.

Then he walks casually out the door and into the humid Chicago night.

CHAPTER 22

I SPENT THE NIGHT by Latham's bedside, holding his hand. He had developed pneumonia, his lungs awash with pus and fluid. He was mercifully unconscious for a horrific procedure called a lung tap. The doctors and nurses used big words like *empyema* and *nosocomial* and *rhonchi* and *pleural effusion*, but none would give me the straight facts on what his chances were.

He looked terrible. His entire face seemed to hang loosely, as if it no longer was attached to the bone. His color was sickly pale, his red hair slicked to his head, his hand clammy and hot.

I played the fate game for a little while, thinking about my telling him to eat without me, realizing that if I hadn't we would have eaten together and I'd be in the bed next to him. No one wins thinking those thoughts, but I punished myself with them just the same.

I slept a little, on and off, Latham's mechanical ventilator oddly soothing. But I always awoke with a startle shortly after sleep began, panicked that the man I loved had died without me being there for him.

At a little after seven in the morning, I again startled myself awake, and looked into Latham's eyes and saw that his droopy eyelids were halfway open.

"Are you awake, honey?"

I pushed a damp lock of hair off of his forehead and noticed his skin was cool. His fever had broken.

"Do you know where you are?"

His eyelids twitched, and I felt him weakly squeeze my hand.

"You're in a hospital. You have botulism poisoning. It's paralyzed many of your muscles, including your diaphragm, so you're on a ventilator."

Another light squeeze.

"It's not permanent. You'll get better, but it will take a few weeks. I was thinking . . . I was thinking about our honeymoon. I've never been to Hawaii. I was thinking maybe we could go there."

His eyes closed again. I didn't think he'd heard me.

And I had to go to work.

I went home, forced myself through some sit-ups and push-ups and a twenty-minute workout video, showered, searched my cupboards for food and found some instant oatmeal, nuked it, and forced myself to keep it down, even though my stomach didn't like the idea. Then I threw on a light blue Barrie Pace wing-collar jacket, a matching skirt, and what I called my tough-girl boots—black suede Giuseppe Zanotti knee highs with low heels, rubber soles, and silver and crystal skull details on the ankle buckles. Socks, no nylons. Then makeup.

The sleep had helped reduce the enormous black bags under my eyes to only slightly gigantic, and my concealer made easy work of them. My mom, a cop herself, was never a fashion plate, but she taught me one valuable girlie lesson: The more expensive the cosmetics, the less you have to fuss with them.

It was humid, and my hair frizzed up in a Mary Elizabeth Mastrantonio way. Straight-haired women all wanted curls, and I hated my curls and wished someone put out a shampoo that promised less volume instead of more. I checked my purse for mousse or gel or spray. All out. I was stuck with poofy.

An hour later, I tried to pull into the station parking lot, but every slot behind my building was filled, mostly with trucks bearing the names of exterminators. I had to park across the street, next to a hydrant.

"What's going on?" I asked a uniform named Collins when I came in.

"Roaches. Some homeless guy brought them in this morning. They were living in his clothes."

I stared as three men with backpack spray canisters and multicolored jumpsuits walked past.

"All this for a few roaches?"

"More than a few. Nasty things are everywhere."

I took the stairs to my office, eyes alert for roaches. I saw something on the wall that turned out to be a stain, and a wad of gum stuck to the railing, but no insect activity.

There were reports waiting for me on my desk. More victim interviews, witness interviews, a crime lab report from Willoughby's, and a fax from the Cicero PD—my statement, autopsy reports, and an inventory of the crime scene. My machine had run out of paper, but had eight more pages saved in memory, so I reloaded the tray and let them print. Then I sat down and settled in to read.

The task force was doing a good job gathering information, but since I was the only one going over everything, there might have been connections that I was missing. I corrected that by calling one of my teams and switching them from interviews to data review. Then I loaded up the fax with reports and read the one that had just printed. It was a background check of the Hothams, and they came up clean, but there was another mention of their daughter Tracey's death. Except this mention labeled it a homicide.

I called Cooper in Cicero, but he had no more information about the daughter—the crime hadn't happened on their turf. So I ran Tracey Hotham through the Cook County database, and found the death certificate. She'd died six years ago. GSW to the stomach. I didn't recall the case, but there had been thousands of murders in Chicago since then.

I located a case number, along with the assigned officer—J. Alger. It also had another case number—an arrest—attached. I looked that up, and found that Tracey Hotham's assailant, a man named Dirk Welch, had been charged with her murder. A Department of Corrections search informed me that Welch got life, but died in prison after serving two years. Back to the CC database. Welch's death certificate stated he'd died of a digitalis overdose.

I wanted to read Alger's case files, but that required a trip to Records on the first floor. So instead I Googled

"Tracey Hotham" and found the newspaper articles about the attack. Thirty-one-year-old postal worker Tracey Lynne Hotham had been beaten, raped, and shot in the stomach. She was taken to the hospital, and died en route. Welch had been living across the hall in the same apartment building. Jason Alger arrested Welch two days after the attack, he confessed, and it was an unusually speedy trial.

So what was the Chemist's connection? Did he have ties to Tracey or to Welch or to Alger? Or was this just an unhappy coincidence?

I'd have to visit Records and crack open the file for more info.

I leaned back in my chair, ran my hand through my hair . . . and felt something.

I thought maybe it was a twig, or maybe some plaster from the ceiling had fallen on my head. But the something twitched and crawled right out of my fingers.

I abruptly stood up and shook my hair side to side like a Vidal Sassoon commercial, without the sultry smile. I bent over to give my hair another shake, and glanced at my boots, along with the several dozen roaches climbing up them. Then I felt them inside the boots, between the suede and the naked skin of my calves.

I freaked out, complete with full-blown girlish screams and hopping up and down. This knocked over my garbage can, and the remains of the Chinese feast Rick had delivered last night. Except that I didn't see any garbage, because it was swarming with hundreds of scuttling cockroaches.

I ran out of that office like it was on fire. It took me five steps before I got any control back, and luckily no one saw me. I wound up sitting on a boardroom table, tugging off my boots, dumping about ten live roaches onto the floor. And a few dead ones, that I'd squished underfoot.

Yuck. Yuck yuck yuck yuck.

"At least they weren't bees," I said, my voice a wee bit higher than normal.

My white cotton socks, covered with roach guts, went into the garbage.

It took courage I didn't know I had to put those boots back on, and then I flagged down one of the jumpsuited exterminators—one who looked a lot like Bill Murray in *Ghostbusters*—and gave him directions to my office.

"Kill them," I said. "Kill them all."

"That's why we're here, ma'am."

He walked past, but I grabbed his elbow.

"Do, um, cockroaches carry any kind of disease?"

He scratched at his stubble. "They aren't the cleanest. Like to eat spoiled food, and excrement. Tough little buggers too. A roach can survive a few weeks with his head cut off. Eventually starves to death. Can live if you flush them down the toilet. Can even survive radiation equivalent to a thermonuclear explosion. But they don't carry any germs harmful to humans."

"Thanks."

"No problem. And hold still, you got one in your hair."

I clenched my teeth as he reached up to my scalp and pinched a roach between his bare fingers.

"Thanks again," I said, forcing on a smile.

"Ah, there's another one. Hold on."

I forced myself to stay still.

"Just a sec . . . little fella crawled around the other side."

Bill Murray walked behind me, rooting through my hair like he was giving me a hot oil treatment.

"Looks like you got a few in here. Maybe they're having a party."

And that was the straw that broke me. I ran squealing to the bathroom, leaned over the sink, and gave my scalp to the tepid spray. I got water up my nose, started to choke, but kept my head under, running my fingers through my hair over and over until I was sure every last bug was out.

Then I squeezed out the excess water, tried not to stare at the five bugs trying to crawl out of the slippery porcelain sink, and positioned myself awkwardly under the push-button hand dryer.

The air was hot and strong, but it took twelve button presses before I'd dried my head and jacket.

I checked the mirror. My expensive makeup hadn't washed off, and my hair had lost the poofiness and actually looked pretty good.

I wasn't going to go back into my office until I was sure it had been fumigated, sterilized, and hermetically sealed, so I took the stairs down to Records.

Chicago had twenty-six Police Districts, divided

into four Areas. Each District housed their duplicate reports at a single Records facility in their Area. My District had that honor for my Area. Alger had worked the two-four, making him part of my Area, which meant copies of his files would be kept in my building.

Every year, we griped about digitizing the files and putting them in a database. And every year, we were told that there was no money for it. So even in this enlightened technological age, the CPD was still killing trees.

Records was an expansive, open room with floor-to-ceiling shelves. The shelves held document boxes labeled according to case numbers, which were divided by District and in semi-chronological order.

The cop running Records was a portly woman named Martel Sardina who'd worked here for six years and didn't know where a damn thing was. It took a special talent to learn absolutely nothing about your job in that amount of time. I asked Sardina about it once, and her reply was jovial.

"I like it here. It's quiet. I can read magazines. Records is considered scut-work, a stepping-stone to other positions. If I did a good job, I'd be promoted out of here. So I don't do a damn thing."

It made a warped kind of sense.

Sardina offered a friendly smile and wave when I walked in. Instead of reading magazines today, it appeared that she was working on crayon drawings. I asked where the two-four files were, and she shrugged.

"Come on, Officer Sardina. Just point me in the right direction."

"I have no idea. Do we even have records from the two-four?"

"Yes. And I'm sure a thousand people have asked you where they are, over the years."

"If they found them, they never shared their location with me."

"If you had to guess, where would they be?"

"I couldn't even guess."

"Come on. I won't tell. I'll even put in a bad word to your superior."

"I can't help you, Lieutenant. And in all honesty, I don't wish that I could."

She smiled pleasantly.

"What if I told Captain Bains you're doing a great job, and that I wanted you transferred to Homicide?"

"Threats won't work," she said. "He just threatened to suspend me, because of my art."

She held up a poorly done stick figure crayon drawing of a man with a very large mouth yelling, "I'm a big stupid poop head!" The title at the top read *Captain Bains.*

"You got the eyes wrong. They're brown dots, not blue dots. And I don't think he has a pig snout."

"Artistic expression. Want to see the one where he's rolling around in the mud?"

"Maybe later."

"Ask Mr. Creepy Exterminator Guy if he wants to see it. He's around here somewhere, spraying for bugs." She squinted at her drawing. "Think the captain would look good as a cockroach?"

"Just make sure you get the eyes right."

While she hunted for a brown crayon, I walked down the ranks and files of shelves, trying to remember where I should begin. I had the case numbers, but where were the two-four files?

I checked the nearest box as a reference point. But the boxes on either side didn't seem to be in order. Was that also part of Sardina's plan to appear incompetent? Putting the files back out of order? If so, I was impressed. She deserved to be in management.

I moved an aisle over, and here the numbering system seemed to work. I opened a box to confirm. This was, indeed, the two-five section. I skipped the next aisle, turned, and almost bumped into a guy in a bright red jumpsuit, digging through one of the boxes.

"Are they eating our files?" I asked.

The exterminator looked up and smiled. He had a port-wine birthmark covering most of his right cheek, just above a thick goatee. Aviator glasses that reflected like mirrors. And a dark smudge on his forehead, grease or dirt.

"Little fellas like it dark. Gotta check everywhere."

He set the box back on the shelf and picked up his chemical pack, slinging it over his shoulder. Then he held out the sprayer wand and squirted along the bottom of the shelf he'd been searching, coating the carpeting with white powder.

"Is that stuff dangerous?"

He winked. "Only to vermin."

Sardina was right. Creepy guy. We passed each other,

and I followed the numbers until I got to Alger's case files. My internal alarm sounded—they were in the same box that the exterminator had been looking through.

I took off after him, rounding the corner, not even thinking that my piece was upstairs in my purse, and then I skidded to a stop because he was waiting for me, his sprayer extended.

"Take a deep breath," he said.

And then he squeezed the trigger, blasting me right in the face.

CHAPTER 23

LIKE I'D DONE AT the Hothams' apartment, I closed my throat and sealed off my lungs, halting my breathing in mid-inhale. I also shut my eyes on reflex.

The chemical, or whatever it was, clumped onto my face and neck. It felt warm, slightly moist, almost like a beauty peel or a mud wrap.

I reached up to wipe the poison off, to get it off my face.

"Don't touch," the Chemist said. "That's tetraethyl pyrophosphate. Also known as TEPP. It can be absorbed through the skin, and the mucus membranes. If you rub it, you'll force it deeper into your pores."

I stopped. Time seemed to stop too. I had one of those *this can't be happening to me* thoughts, which did nothing to improve my situation.

"The first symptoms will be eye pain, headache, and cramps. That quickly progresses to chest pain, vomiting, loss of sphincter control, convulsions, paralysis, low blood pressure, and finally, death. Chances are, unless you can wash it off, you'll be dead within fifteen minutes. Sooner if you inhale."

I stuck my hands out, touched the fabric of his uniform, but he pulled away.

"Not on the first date, Jack. But maybe later. If you live through this. Bye, now. Best of luck."

I heard him walk off, and then all I could hear was the beating of my heart in my ears, and it was beating much too fast for me to make it through this alive.

I pushed aside the panic, which wasn't that hard to do because I had panicked so many times in the last few days, I didn't have much left in the tank.

Officer Sardina wouldn't be of help. She probably wouldn't even look up from her crayon art. And I dared not open my mouth to yell, because some poison might get in.

I needed to wash this off. That meant a sink. There was one on this floor, but I wasn't sure of the exact pathway. But on the second floor, I knew the bathroom was right down the hall from the stairs.

Could I make it to the second floor, with only half a chestful of oxygen, blind as a bat?

I had to try.

In my mind, I pictured where I stood in the Records room, tried to remember where the door was. Straight ahead, and to the left. I held my hands in front of me and began to walk in what I thought was a straight line.

I ran straight into a shelf, jamming my right pinky.

Readjust. Step to the left. Keep walking.

"Hey, don't point that thing at me, Creepy Man."

Sardina. Then she screamed. It was followed by choking. And gagging.

I had to focus. I walked fast, using the shelf as a guide. When it ended, I kept going forward until I reached the wall, and followed that left, seeking the doorway.

Vomiting sounds from Sardina. Then an eerie, pain-racked wail.

The wall stretched on. I bumped into a chair. Tripped over boxes. Walked fifteen steps. Twenty. Twenty-five.

Sardina began to scream. Wet, gurgling screams.

Where was that goddamn doorway? Did I miss it? Did I go the wrong way?

And then my hand met empty space and I fell through, onto my knees. The tile was cold, hard. I tried to think. The stairs were to the right. I began to crawl until I found the wall again, then followed it to the staircase.

How long had it been since I breathed? Thirty seconds? A minute? It seemed like a long time ago, and my diaphragm spasmed, wanting air, wondering why I wouldn't allow it. The pounding in my head became louder, and my eyes had begun to sting. The first symptoms.

Again I fell when the hallway opened up into the stairs. I landed on my chest, and that knocked some precious stale air out of my lungs, but I couldn't dwell on it. I was on all fours, climbing the steps, reaching for the handrail, coming up to where the stairs turned, taking them as fast as I could go to the second floor.

When I reached the hallway, I couldn't remember if I needed to go left or right.

Panic worsened. The spasm in my chest was now a full-blown cramp, almost doubling me over.

Left or right? Left or right?

My office had been here for ten years. *Dammit Jack, focus. This is an easy one.*

Left. It was left.

I kept my hand on the wall, found a doorknob, but that was an office, not the bathroom. My head was screaming now, and my legs were giving out, and my vision through my closed eyes—already black—seemed to get even darker.

Dizziness set in. I'd need to breathe within the next few seconds, poison or no poison. Rational thought had been overtaken by animal instinct, and I felt the scream well up in my throat, my whole body beginning to quake.

And then I was in the bathroom.

I ran, my hip crashing into the sink, my shaking hands turning on the water and splashing it onto my face, over my eyes, wiping at my nose and mouth, and then I was sucking in air, crying, still wiping and rubbing and splashing and I opened my eyes and saw they were bloodred, and I started screaming until everything went blurry and finally black.

CHAPTER 24

AN EXTERMINATOR HAD SEEN me crawling blindly through the hallway, and alerted some cops on my floor. Shortly after I passed out I was whisked away to the hospital. They revived me en route, and I semi-coherently informed them it was TEPP poisoning.

The ER nurses scrubbed my face and neck until I appeared to be sunburned. My eyes were irrigated, a process as painful as it sounds. I was given atropine. Pralidoxime. Activated charcoal.

Somehow Herb appeared at my side during the treatment. I gave him bits and pieces about what I remembered, but couldn't give much of a description beyond the port-wine stain on the Chemist's cheek, which I guessed to be fake. Even though Herb was no longer my partner, he dutifully took down the info.

I was in eight kinds of pain. The drugs made my heart jittery. My eyes itched, my skin was on fire. My nose and throat felt like I'd been sniffing broken glass.

"My face hurts," I told Herb. I was setting him up for the punch line, "Yeah, it's killing me too." But he didn't bite. He just stared at me, sadly, his walrus mustache drooping at the ends.

"I brought your purse. It's next to the bed. We've

also got a team on the way, to watch your room after you're admitted."

"Thanks." It was painful to talk. "How's Sardina?"

"She didn't make it."

I couldn't take the way he was staring at me, so I turned away, focusing on the green ER curtain that surrounded my cot. Humble pie time.

"I'm sorry I called you a coward, Herb. You're no coward."

His hand touched my arm, above the IV.

"This has to stop, Jack. You've almost died twice in three days."

It was actually three times, if you count the Hothams' apartment in Cicero, but I saw no reason to share that. Instead, I spilled out everything else.

"Latham proposed and then got poisoned with BT, I made out with the Fed, my father is still alive, and I can't catch the Chemist without you."

Herb let it all soak in, and then said, "You made out with a Fed?"

I forced myself to look at him. "Out of everything I told you, that's what you latch on to?"

"That HMRT guy?"

I nodded.

"I thought he was gay."

"Why do men always think that all really cute guys are gay?"

"It helps us sleep better at night. So how far did he get? Second base?"

"Second base? What, are we in junior high?"

"Third base? Did he violate your Constitutional rights?"

"You sound like McGlade. Can't we talk about my father, or the fact that I'm engaged?"

Herb lifted up my left hand, scrutinizing it.

"Where's the ring?"

"I didn't say yes yet. Before I had a chance, he got sick. He's critical. I almost lost him last night."

"I'm sorry, Jack. I like Latham. You're going to say yes?"

"Yes."

Herb smiled. "Congrats. If you need a maid of honor, I look great in pink. And your father isn't dead?"

"He lives in Elmwood Park. My mother admitted that he left us, and she told me he died to stop me from looking for him."

"Have you spoken to him?"

"No."

"But you're going to?"

"I don't know. I—"

I heard my phone beep. Herb handed me my purse, and I checked the number. The Hothams' stolen cell.

"It's the Chemist," I told Herb.

He picked up his notepad and put his head next to mine so we could both hear. I answered the call, made my voice strong.

"This is Daniels."

"I'm glad you're still alive, Jack. You've got a great set of lungs on you, if I may say so. How are you feeling?"

"We've agreed to pay you. What are your demands?"

"I asked you a question, Lieutenant. How are you feeling?"

I spoke through my teeth, anger masking all of my symptoms.

"I'm fine."

"Good. Because I want you personally to deliver my two million. Here's how it will work. I want a hundred thousand dollars in cash, three hundred and thirty-two thousand dollars in platinum eagles, and the remainder in uncut diamonds, at least three carats per stone. No tricks, no transmitters, no laser-engraved serial numbers on the stones, no moissanite, you get the idea. If you screw around with me, I'll be very angry. Put everything in a leather suitcase, and paint it bright yellow. Then stand outside the Daley Center, near the Picasso, at ten thirty a.m. tomorrow. Got all of that?"

I looked at Herb, who was furiously scribbling notes. He nodded at me.

"I got it."

"Good. Have your cell phone on you, and wear some running shoes. You're going to need them."

"I know about Tracey," I said, trying to catch him off guard. "And Dirk Welch. You killed him in prison. Were you cell mates?"

There was a pause.

"I'm planning something big. Very big. If everything goes well tomorrow, I'll tell you what my plan is, and you'll be able to stop it in time. If anything goes wrong, many will die. If you try to find me, many will die. If you pull any tricks or try to catch me, many will die. The elderly.

Women and children. I know you don't want that on your head. But it won't stop there. I'll come after you as well. You and everyone you know."

He hung up. I stared at Herb. He didn't say a word, but I could read his mind.

Burglars don't call you up and threaten you and half the city. Robbers don't spray poison in your face and put you in the hospital. Thieves don't attack the people you love.

Yeah, well, he was right. But I couldn't do anything about it.

A nurse opened the curtain and stuck her perky head in.

"We've got a room available, Ms. Daniels."

I might have protested, demanded to be released, but the nurse divided into two identical nurses and I wasn't sure which to talk to. Earlier, I'd been told to expect double vision. It wasn't as much fun as I'd hoped it would be.

"Herb, I hate to ask . . ."

He held up his notes. "I'll pass this along to the super. We'll work out the details. You get some rest."

"Thanks. Also, in Records, I was looking for the Alger case file for Tracey Hotham's murder investigation. The Chemist was in the box. I don't know if he took it or not. If he did, we need to see if the records are still on file at the two-four."

"I'll check."

"There was a guy named Welch involved, died in prison."

"Jack . . ."

"I know. We're not partners anymore. Pass it off on a subordinate."

Herb nodded, gave me an informal pat on the shoulder, and left.

I asked the nurse(s) for some water, and she gave me a cup and took my blood pressure. As she did, my whole body began to shake. First mildly, and then it became violent enough to make me spill water all over my bed.

"She's seizing!" the nurse yelled.

A doctor rushed over while the nurse forced something rubber between my teeth. Then I couldn't see anything else, because my eyelids were fluttering too fast.

"Administering diazepam push."

I felt a calm flow through me, and the convulsions stopped. The nurse fished out the mouth guard, and I squinted at her, trying to focus.

"It's okay," she said. "You're fine. TEPP can cause seizures. We gave you some Valium, which will work with the atropine and pralidoxime to relax your muscles."

"Thanks," I said. I was pretty freaked out, but the Valium went a long way to helping me over that.

The nurse draped a dry blanket over me, then promised to be back shortly. While I waited, my phone rang again. A blocked number.

"This is Daniels," I said. My voice sounded kind of thick.

"Hiya, Jackie. How's it hanging?"

Harry McGlade.

"Hi, Harry. How's the space suit?"

"A tax write-off. I cornered your superintendent, and

she threatened to have me arrested if I didn't vacate the scene. A real piece of work, that one. Feisty. If her cankles weren't the size of hams, she'd be my type of woman. Speaking of dates, are you going to PoliceFest on Sunday?"

"No."

"How about going with me? The mayor will be there, and you could get me an audience. He likes you, right?"

"I'm not going."

"Of course you're going. Every cop in the Midwest is going, and this year it's in Illinois."

"Every cop but me." I grinned. Valium was a pretty nice drug.

"You owe me one, Jack."

"Ask the super to take you. Maybe she'll do it if you promise to rub lotion on her cankles."

There was a long silence, which was unusual for Harry.

"Jack, I . . . I gave up my business. No more private investigating."

"Chicago will never get over the loss."

"It isn't funny. Could you stay a cop if you lost your gun hand? I suck lefty. Hell, I can't even wipe my damn ass lefty. I'm completely useless with a gun. And I had to sell my baby, my Mustang, because of the goddamn stick shift. My electric bill was sent back because they thought a retarded child had signed the check. I even had to pay for sex, because no woman wants to sleep with me."

"What does that have to do with your hand?"

"Dammit, Jack, my life is destroyed. Show some sympathy."

Maybe it was all the medication, or the residual effects of the TEPP, but I actually felt for him. "That's too bad, Harry."

"If the city doesn't let me open up this bar, I might as well shoot myself. And I'd need your help doing that too, because I'd miss my fricking head."

"You think? You have a pretty fat head."

I laughed at my drug-influenced assessment. He *did* have a fat head.

"Take me to PoliceFest. Introduce me to the mayor. Help me get the liquor license. And I promise, I'll never bother you again as long as I live."

"That's a tempting offer."

"We were partners once. I know I did wrong by you, but I've helped you out several times since then. Please. I need this."

Harry McGlade had caused me more annoyance than I cared to recall, but in a warped sort of way he was kind of a friend. A friend who needed a hand. Really.

"Fine, McGlade. But I can't promise the mayor will go for it."

"Thanks, Jackie. I'll drop by Sunday morning. You still at the place on Addison?"

"No. I'm a suburban girl now. I live in Bensenville."

I gave him my address.

"See you Sunday. Maybe afterward I can buy you a beer."

"Maybe."

"And after that, sex."

"Good-bye, Harry."

"I've got this attachment for my prosthesis—"

I hung up before he could finish. Then I took a deep breath and closed my eyes, thinking about PoliceFest with Harry . . .

PoliceFest with Harry? What the hell was I thinking?

Maybe I'd get lucky, and the Chemist would kill me tomorrow so I wouldn't have to go.

I fell asleep, strangely comforted by that thought.

CHAPTER 25

THE CHEMIST SHATTERS the last bottle of vodka over the garbage can, spraying glass and alcohol on his heavy work gloves, a shard bouncing off the facial netting on his helmet. He's in his greenhouse. It's dark, quiet. Night is the best time to work, because insect activity is minimal.

He reaches into the glass shards and fishes out the bottle neck, moving with speed and efficiency. He's getting near the end, a culmination of years of effort. This should be savored. But all of the recent excitement has put him behind schedule, and he has to catch up.

He places the bottle neck on his workbench and uses a hammer and pliers to break all of the glass away from the aluminum cap. When he's finished, the cap, with its tamper-proof ring along the bottom edge, is intact.

Next he selects an identical brand of vodka, and twists off its top. The tamper-proof ring separates along the perforated line where it is attached to the cap and remains on the bottle neck. He snips the ring off using nail clippers, pours out four ounces of vodka, and adds an equal amount of colorless, odorless ethylene chlorohydrin. It blends invisibly with the liquor.

Then he takes the intact cap—the one he removed from the broken bottle—and carefully screws it onto the full bottle. It now appears to be new, unopened. He places it in the cardboard box next to the eleven other poisoned bottles of alcohol, and gets started on the beer.

Beer is even easier to tamper with. A local brewing supply shop, the same place he got some of his hydroponics equipment, also sells bottle cappers. He carefully pries the tops off of a dozen popular import beer bottles, adds a few drops of conotoxin to each, and then uses the bench capper to reseal the caps until they're as tight as when they left the brewery.

After finishing a full case of beer, he stands and stretches. There are things that need to be double-checked. He makes sure the Little Otter has a full charge. He lays out the dry suit, places a bottle of talc next to it. Tests the gauge on the nitrox canister.

Then, outside, he changes out of his protective suit and checks the cement mixer, which has another three yards ready. It takes ten minutes to pour. He's an expert with the forklift, and gets it into place on the first try. Two more to go. He loads the mixer with three more bags. Adds a touch of aluminum. A dash of diesel. A healthy handful of roofing nails.

Inside, he practices for the last time with the TelePC. He's adjusted for delays. He's taken the route himself, so the timing should be perfect. This should all work out.

Finally, he uses spell-check on the letter, and prints out a copy.

This will be a nice surprise for Lieutenant Jacqueline Daniels. A beautiful end to a beautiful relationship.

After six years, three months, and thirteen days, Tracey will finally get her revenge.

And then he'll get his revenge.

CHAPTER 26

AGAINST DOCTOR'S RECOMMENDATION, I checked myself out of the hospital at seven a.m., wearing loaner clothes. A cab took me to my car, which was still in front of the fire hydrant. I drove back to the suburbs, rush hour traffic helping me chase away the groggies.

I felt pretty good, considering. A little weak. A little raw. But ready to work.

Once home, I fed the cat, forced down some oatmeal, hopped into a tepid shower—hot hurt my skin—changed into a pair of boot-cut Levi's, some Adidas running shoes, and an Anne Klein blouse and jacket—black over white—and called Latham. He was sleeping, but the nurse informed me he was stable. I took that as a good sign.

Next, I climbed in my car and headed back to Chicago. When I got on the expressway, I called Herb.

"Any word on the Hotham file?"

"Missing. That one and the Welch file. From the two-four as well."

"That's what I figured. There's something there the Chemist doesn't want us to find. What's the set-up for today?"

"You'll be carrying a GPS phone, a clone of your cell

number. It will track you wherever you go, and has a booster for indoors. They've got six cars, two bikes, four teams on foot, and chopper support. You won't get lost."

"Any luck finding Tracey's cell phone, or her car?"

"The Staties found a white Honda in a parking lot in O'Hare. No plates, but the VIN matches. Unlikely they'll find prints—the car was torched. No ping on the cell phone. They think he's removing the battery between uses. We'd have to catch him during a call."

"How about the money?"

"Cash, coins, and stones are all clean, as he demanded. We've got the yellow leather suitcase."

"What's in it? Radio transmitter? Another GPS?"

Herb didn't answer.

"Herb?"

"Nothing. There's nothing in it, Jack. If you run into the Chemist, you're ordered to stand down. No arrest. No shooting. The mayor doesn't want to mess with this guy."

I processed that, but it didn't get any better the more I thought about it.

"What if I have a chance to catch him?"

"You remember what the loony said if you try." Herb kicked up his voice to Mickey Mouse level and mimicked, *"Many will die, many will die."*

"Many will die anyway. He's not going to stop."

"I'm only the messenger," Herb said. "I don't like this any more than you do."

I'm not a person who spits, but I was angry enough to.

"Will you be there?" I asked.

Another pause. Then, "No."

"Herb—"

"We're not partners anymore, Jack. I'm not Homicide. I've got another case I'm working on."

"And what case is that?"

"Last week, someone stole a semi full of portable toilets."

"Well, that's a lot more important than tracking down the mass murderer who's terrorizing our city. What do you call that? Grand theft potty?"

"Good-bye, Jack. Be safe."

Herb hung up.

I had no right to be mad at Herb. The secret to reaching old age in our profession is knowing when to call it quits. If he felt he couldn't do it anymore, my goading him wouldn't help either of us.

But Herb was Violent Crimes to the bone. If you cut him, he bled Homicide. Robbery was a waste of his time and talents. He must have known that. He just needed someone to remind him.

I called him back. I was going to open a line of honest communication to get to the bottom of his fears and intentions instead of resorting to blaming and name-calling.

The first words out of my mouth were, "Don't be an idiot, Herb."

He hung up on me. I thought about calling his wife, remembered she was in on his silly plan to stay alive until retirement, and instead called Rick.

"I'm glad you called, Jack. I heard about what happened. I wanted to visit you in the hospital, but I figured . . ." He trailed off.

"No problem. Did you hear what the mayor said?"

"I was at the meeting last night."

"He wants to give the guy his money without trying to catch him."

"That's the plan."

"You're not going along with that, are you? The federal government doesn't make deals with terrorists, right?"

"Not as far as you know."

"Are you saying—"

"I'm saying that this guy has the means to kill more people. If we pay him off, there's a good chance he'll stop. I talked to some special agents on the Behavioral Science Team, and the profiling computer says—"

Great. I'd been down this route several times, and it never led anywhere worth visiting. Was I the only sane cop left in this hemisphere?

I interrupted his profile-speak. "What do you think? You personally?"

"I think he's got something big planned, and if we bring him in, he'll let people die."

"So we just let the guy go?"

"The case won't be over, Jack. We have a mountain of evidence we haven't even sifted through. We'll catch him eventually. And we won't be risking the lives of civilians."

It was tough to talk while biting my tongue, but I managed. "So we run away to fight another day."

"You sound pissed off."

"I am pissed off."

"Not to put a price on human life, but it's only two million dollars, Jack. That's nothing."

"You're wrong. It's two million too much. Tell me about the profile. Let me guess—starts fires, wets the bed, tortures animals, abused as a child . . ."

"Not even close. Single white male, between thirty-five and fifty-five, college education, white-collar job, lives in Chicago, possibly a leader in the community, does volunteer work, bi-polar—"

"You think? Maybe his problem is he ran out of Zoloft."

"—above average intelligence, minor criminal infractions in the past, single, some background in theater—"

"Sure, he did *Arsenic and Old Lace* in summer stock."

Rick sighed. "This is a decent profile, Jack."

"Where's the part about dressing up like Snow White and collecting Donnie Osmond lunch boxes?"

"Actually, the profile says he probably collects something, like comic books or baseball cards."

"Or poisonous plants. Look Rick, letting this guy go is a bad idea. Does the profile say he'll stop if he's paid?"

"Yes."

"Well, he won't. I've talked to him. This is all a big game, and he's enjoying it way too much. Once you give a bully your lunch money, you have to keep paying him forever."

"What are you planning on doing?"

I thought about the .38 in my purse.

"I'm going to be a bigger bully than he is."

"And what if more people die?"

That was the question, wasn't it? If I caught him, and people died, I'd never forgive myself. But if I let him go, and people died, I'd never forgive myself.

Burglary/Robbery/Theft was looking better and better.

I bid adieu to Rick and spent the remainder of the drive going over scenarios, trying to find one with a decent outcome.

None sprang to mind.

I parked in front of a hydrant on Randolph, kitty-corner to the Daley Center. It looked like a scene from *The Blues Brothers*. Twenty members of the SRT were there, in formation. At least forty cops. Some brass, including the super. Eight squad cars. Four motorcycles. Two scooters. Four horses. Two mountain bikes. The Mobile Command bus. And a Segway.

The Daley Center served as Chicago's main courthouse. It was an imposing six-hundred-foot-tall structure, all steel and glass, bounded on all four sides by streets. The area around the Picasso—an impressive metal sculpture in rusty brown that resembled a horse mating with a harp—had been cordoned off with yellow police tape, and onlookers as well as media had gathered around the perimeter to watch whatever was happening.

I popped the trunk, dug out my spare shoulder holster, and put it on under my jacket. I also strapped on an ankle harness that held a five-inch AMT Backup II. It weighed about eighteen ounces. I loaded five 9mm short rounds into the clip, jacked one into the throat, and added one more. My boot-cut jeans covered it easily, plus the wider bottoms made my hips seem slimmer. A win-win jeans experience.

I went back to the front seat and removed my Colt Detective Special from my purse, along with a speed loader, and a roll of antacid tablets. I chewed four antacids while strapping the .38 and the speed loader into the Velcro webbing of my holster.

Then I opened the glove compartment and took out a balisong, a Filipino butterfly knife. It had a four-inch stainless steel blade, which stayed hidden between two halves of the handle. With a few flicks of the wrist, the handles would separate, the blade would come out, and the handles would rejoin. I'd taken it off a suspect last year, and often played with it while driving. I'd gotten pretty good, and could open the blade in less than a second.

The knife went into my back pocket. Then I stuck some Ray-Bans on my forehead, locked the car, and jumped into the fray.

I pushed my way through the crowd, past the SWAT guys, sidestepping the horses and a manure mound that looked disturbingly like Richard Nixon, and sashayed up to Superintendent O'Loughlin. She wore what appeared to be a man's blazer, which pinched her waist and made her shoulders look like a linebacker's. The slacks were even less flattering. Someone needed to take away her Macy's charge card, because she was wasting it.

The omnipresent Davy Ellis, attired in gray Armani, offered me a big smile and a wink. Captain Bains didn't seem to be around.

"Lieutenant," the super boomed, "I've gotten word that you don't want to play by our rules."

Who ratted me out? Herb or Rick? Had to be Rick. Herb would never do that. Right?

"I don't think we should let the Chemist go," I said.

"I'm sure your personal opinions won't interfere with your ability to do your duty."

"My duty is to catch bad guys."

"Your duty is to serve and protect. Engaging this guy won't do either."

"Neither will letting him go."

O'Loughlin was hard to read. I knew that somewhere, deep down, she had to agree with me. But her face was granite.

"I'd like you to relinquish your weapon, Lieutenant."

I blinked. Then I blinked again.

"You're kidding."

"You're going to be watched every step of the way. Air support. Snipers. Even a police marine unit. We'll make sure nothing happens to you."

I thought about my AMT backup, safe in the ankle holster, and then handed her the Colt.

"Now the backup piece."

I made my face blank. "What backup piece?"

"You gave up the .38 too easily. That means you have a backup."

Smart lady. I should have thought of that.

"I need to have a gun on me, O'Loughlin."

"You'll address me as *Superintendent* or *ma'am*. Now give me the backup."

"What if I refuse?" I added, "Ma'am."

"Then I call over some men to take it from you, and at the end of the day I fire you."

"And then I go to the media and tell them all about you paying the Chemist off." I looked at Davy. "Think that would be good for PR?"

"That would be bad," Davy said.

O'Loughlin got in my face. "You do what you have to do, Lieutenant. I'll do what I have to do. And right now, I have to take your piece."

We played stare-down for what seemed like twenty minutes, but was probably only a few seconds, and then I gave her the AMT.

"If I get killed, it's on your head."

"I've got a lot of deaths on my head right now, Lieutenant. Do I have to frisk you for any more weapons?"

I lifted up my arms. "If that's what turns you on."

For a moment, it looked like she was going to do it, but then some SRT guys came over with a big yellow suitcase and interrupted our tête-à-tête. A tall one with a unibrow handed me something silver.

"This is a tracking phone programmed with your number. It sends a GPS signal to the Mobile Command Post, and we can pinpoint your location to within three feet. It will also transmit the number he's calling you from, and we can trace that number to either an address or to a cell phone within twenty yards."

"And if you find him, you'll do what? Deliver a pizza?"

"After we've deemed it safe, we'll get the guy," the super said. "He won't get away with this. He'll pay."

Another SRT cop, a black guy with biceps larger than my waist, opened up a map of Chicago.

"There's a chance he'll run you around town, to try to lose any tails. That's pretty much impossible with the GPS, but we have teams stationed around the city, all with receivers." He pointed out a dozen red dots on the map. "We also have people stationed at O'Hare and Midway in case you're required to get on a plane. Plus three teams dogging your every move. We won't lose you."

I wasn't worried about getting lost. I was worried about the guy dosing me with something lethal before any of the ten thousand cops around me could do anything to stop it.

But I said, "Thanks, Officer," just the same.

They wired me up with a radio headset/walkie-talkie combo, gave me an extra GPS tracker, and an extra phone.

"Do you want armor?" Biceps asked.

"No need. He's not a shooter. But I could use some of this."

I sidled up to Unibrow and put my hands on his utility belt.

"May I?" I asked, taking a can of pepper spray.

"Help yourself, Lieutenant. It's rated at five million Scoville heat units. Hit him anywhere on the clothing, or just get the stream close to him, he'll feel it."

"Thanks. A girl needs her protection, right, Super-intendent?"

The super didn't seem amused, but she didn't pre-vent me from tucking the pepper spray into my holster.

"So now we wait," Biceps said.

The wait wasn't long. Less than a minute later, my tracking phone rang. A blocked number. I nodded at the group, and said, "It's showtime."

Then I answered the call.

CHAPTER 27

"GOOD MORNING, JACK. HOW are you feeling?"

His voice provoked a reaction in my stomach normally reserved for warm oysters and cheap tequila.

"Nervous. I've got all this money, and no one to give it to."

"I don't see the suitcase. Hold it up."

I fought the urge to look around. He could be in one of the surrounding buildings, in a car, in the crowd, on the street, or even in the Daley Center itself. Ultimately, it didn't matter where he was. We were going to let him go anyway.

I hefted the yellow bag, surprised by its weight. Forty, maybe forty-five pounds, and bulky. I had Biceps hold my phone, then I pressed the suitcase up over my head, made sure it was balanced, and did a 360-degree turn.

Biceps had casually plugged in an earpiece, and Unibrow casually walked back to the Mobile Command bus.

"Good," the Chemist said when I got the phone back. "Here's how it is going to work. I'm going to call you, and tell you to go to an address. When you get to the address, you'll wait for me to call again with more instructions. You're to go alone, no escort. I don't want to see any cops with you, near you, or following you. If I do, I'm calling it off, and many people will die. Understand?"

"Yes."

"I saw that SWAT guy give you some things. A radio. An extra phone. And what was that black thing?"

"Pepper spray."

"Naughty girl, Jack. Don't you know that chemicals are dangerous? But I'm not referring to the spray. I'm referring to the small black box, looks like a PDA."

"That's a GPS tracker."

"Put all of those things on the ground."

I complied.

"The pepper spray too. I wouldn't want you hurting yourself."

I made a face, but added that to the pile.

"Very good. Now, I know that you're going to try to find me. That you'll try to trace the calls. I'm sure that large phone you're talking on right now has all sorts of tracking goodies on it. So we're going to switch phones. Walk over to the Picasso. Bring the suitcase with you, and make sure everyone keeps their distance."

This was getting better and better.

"Everyone needs to stay here," I informed the group. The super nodded at me, either a *good luck* nod or a *you'd better follow orders* nod. Then I yanked out the telescoping handle and pulled the suitcase behind me, grateful for the wheels.

"Look by the base of the sculpture. There's a coffee cup. Put down the phone you're talking on and pick up the cup."

I saw it immediately, stark white contrast to the brown metal of the Picasso. As I stared, it began to ring.

I didn't want to touch anything the Chemist had touched, but I took a chance, assuming he wouldn't kill me this early in the game. I set down the tracking phone and gently lifted the cardboard cup by the rim. Inside was a cell phone, an older, larger model.

I answered the call.

"I found it."

A pause. Then, "Walk east. I'll be watching. If I see anyone approach you, this is over, and people will die. Keep the line free for further instruction. If I try calling, and it's busy, people will die. Remember the rules."

And then silence.

I had no choice. I began to walk.

In a way, this was all pretty funny. The Chemist was working damn hard to make sure no one arrested him, when all he had to do was knock on the mayor's door and His Honor would gladly sign over a personal check. Unfortunately, I had a hard time seeing the humor when I had no backup, no radio, no GPS, and no guns. I assumed my fellow officers would still be able to follow me, but that didn't mean they would. The city of Chicago had made it abundantly clear that the payoff was more important than my personal safety.

I walked east to Dearborn, went right, then continued east on Washington. The day was hot, muggy, in the upper eighties. The sun hurt my face, still pink from the rough scrubbing the hospital had administered. I moved the sunglasses from my head to my eyes, and kept my pace casual even though my heart rate was set on sprint.

After a block, I had an unhealthy film of sweat covering my body, and a really good feeling I was being followed. A yellow cab, creeping along ten yards behind me, matching my pace. I stopped, pretended to adjust the suitcase handle, and looked at it over my Ray-Bans. The taxi also stopped. I couldn't see inside very well—the sun glared off the windshield—but the cab was hired and it looked like a single occupant in the backseat.

In truth, I didn't know if I'd recognize the Chemist even if I was staring right at him. The only thing I remembered from my brief encounter with him in Records was the port-wine stain on his face, and his beard. Both were fake. Just like the eye patch.

If I ran into someone with a single distinctive feature, that might be our man. But if he went without a disguise, he could be anyone. Maybe even someone I've already met.

I stopped futzing with the bag and continued east on Washington. I sensed that the cab resumed pursuit, and then actually saw it peripherally as it came up on my right.

"Handoff, from a jogger, soon," Unibrow said through the open backseat window.

Then the cab accelerated past and turned right on Wabash.

The cell phone rang. I connected after the first ring, wondering if the Chemist was going to go ballistic because he spotted the cab.

"Hello?"

A pause, then, "Go to the Art Institute and wait on the steps. You have four minutes."

That was about four blocks away, one east and three south. I couldn't make it in time by walking.

I began to jog.

Normally, a four-block jog wouldn't even get me winded. But heat, exhaustion, sickness, and a forty-five-pound anchor all conspired to have me wheezing like an asthmatic after the first hundred yards. I kept up the pace, my eyes scanning the crowd ahead, looking for the police jogger who was going to hand off something to me. I hoped it was a cold beer.

The jogger, wily little devil, came up from behind after I turned onto Wabash. He ran past me with ease, not so much as a bump, and I almost didn't think it was him until I thought to check my blazer pocket.

No beer. But he had left me a walkie-talkie and a wireless earpiece. I switched it on, leaving it at whatever frequency they'd set it at, and stuck the receiver/mike combo on my ear.

"This is Daniels," I panted. "He told me to go to the Art Institute."

"This is Reynolds, SRT." It was Unibrow. "We know. Miller took a guess, and the cell phone the Chemist gave you is Tracey Hotham's. We're listening in, and we can ping your location. We're also tracing his calls. It's not as easy, because they're being routed through a PC—one of those computer phone lines. It's not the same phone he called you from initially. That was one of those pay-by-the-minute cells. We're *not getting anything from it. But we should have his new lo-cation in a few minutes.*"

I didn't waste any breath answering. The Art Institute was a block away, on my left, and I only had about a minute to get to it. I was sweating freely now, my shoulder beginning to ache from tugging the suitcase. The side-walks were packed, and the citizens of Chicago paid me little attention as I ran. A few stepped aside. Most ignored me. None offered to give a struggling lady a hand. I passed the Prudential building, and saw the green lion sculptures in the distance, standing vigil on either side of the steps in front of the Art Institute, and then the phone rang.

"Daniels."

"Now go to Buckingham Fountain. Stay on foot. You have seven minutes."

"I need—"

I wanted to say *more time*, but the connection ended. The fountain was another three blocks north, and maybe three more blocks east. I couldn't do six blocks in seven minutes, not as tired as I already was.

"Did you get that?" I said into my radio.

"*Affirmative. We got a lock on the phone he's calling from, and it doesn't make sense.*"

"Why not?" I huffed.

"*It seems to be coming from Jason Alger's house.*"

The retired cop whose home had been turned into a death trap and whose fingers had been left in the fridge.

"*We're sending a team to check it out.*"

"Bad idea. Last time—"

"We'll be careful. But Alger is uptown. How did he get across town so fast?"

I made it to Jackson, and the light was against me, so I couldn't cross. It would delay me, but I was grateful for the rest.

"Could have had a remote video camera planted at the Daley Center," I said. "Or he was watching from a distance. Or maybe he's forwarding his calls through Alger's computer somehow."

"Or maybe he has an accomplice."

I didn't like that possibility. Not at all. A guy on the corner next to me gave me a sideways glance, then resumed his cell phone conversation. Suddenly everyone on the street was a potential spy. Or a potential poisoner.

The light changed, and I put it into second gear and charged across the street, almost pulling off my arm when the suitcase wheels caught on the curb. I switched to my left hand, couldn't find my rhythm, then switched back. I cut left on Van Buren into the cul-de-sac leading to Congress, and huffed and puffed up the bridge over the railroad tracks.

When I reached the apex, my legs, arm, and lungs were pudding. But I could see the Buckingham Fountain ahead, one of Chicago's most recognizable landmarks, the center jet shooting a hundred and fifty feet into the air. When I got there, I was seriously considering jumping in to cool off. Or to slake my thirst.

Strangely, I was in the same part of Grant Park where my father bought me those three ice creams, years ago. Where were all the damn vendors now that I really needed one?

My phone rang, even though I hadn't yet crossed Columbus.

"I'm almost there."

"New destination. Navy Pier. Take Columbus to Grand Avenue on foot. You have fifteen minutes."

Then he hung up. That little mother . . .

"Lieutenant, this is Reynolds. We have a team en route to Alger's house."

"Why? So you can shake his hand and congratulate him when he gets his money?"

That might have been harsh, considering the casualties they'd suffered, but I was exhausted and in a mood.

"We're going to watch and wait. The mayor doesn't want him picked up until we get the all clear. But you can be damn sure we won't let him out of our sights."

Reynolds sounded pissed, and I realized he didn't like playing by these rules any more than I did. Maybe during their surveillance the Chemist might accidentally have his head blown off. The thought made me smile.

I paused for a moment in front of the giant fountain, the Windy City blowing a mist of its water onto my face. I had no idea how clean the water was, but it felt wonderful.

Navy Pier was a mile away, maybe a little more. To make it in fifteen minutes, I needed to haul ass. But something was bothering me. The Chemist liked to talk. Even after he sprayed me with TEPP, he stuck around for a bit to chat. But his last several phone calls had been abrupt, clipped. Either he was worried about being caught on the phone, or . . .

"Reynolds, what's the number the Chemist is calling from?"

He read it to me.

"Have you tried calling it?"

"No. We don't want to tip him off that we know."

But I could call him back without letting on that I knew his number. I pressed *69. The phone rang ten times. No answer. I tried entering in the number Reynolds gave me. Another ten rings, no pickup.

Then I waited. If the Chemist thought he was being messed with, he'd call me back to scold me. But my phone didn't ring.

"He's not in the house," I said. "He's not watching me. He's at the drop point already."

"Are you sure?"

"Have your team do a thermal scan of the Alger house. I bet it's empty."

I knew I was right. But how could we use this to our advantage? I had fourteen minutes to make it to Navy Pier, and if I wasn't being monitored, I could use that for something else. What could this extra time buy us?

"Get me transportation. The nearest cop in the area. And if Rossi is available, have him come along."

"Rossi?"

"If not him, try Taurus or Wesson or Daewoo. Any of those guys."

"Okay. Got it."

I waited two minutes. My breathing and heart rate returned to normal. The Chemist didn't call, demanding why I was still at the fountain. Now I was positive he wasn't watching me. I briefly toyed with the idea of grabbing a cab, getting on a plane to the Bahamas, and seeing how long two million bucks would last.

I heard a motor coming from the right, and did a double-take at the police scooter heading toward me, the manure-fixated Officer Buchbinder at the helm.

"Hello again, Lieutenant. I was the closest cop in range. How's that for a coincidence?"

"Get me to Navy Pier," I said, securing the suitcase on the small rack at the rear of the bike with bungee cords. "And watch out for horses."

"Don't need to tell me. I scrubbed my bike for so long I had dung stuck in my fingernails."

He offered me his hand for inspection, which I judiciously ignored.

I mounted the scooter and asked, "Where's the gun?"

"The what?"

"Rossi. Daewoo. Those are gun manufacturers."

"I was on parking detail. No one told me to bring you a gun. Just to pick you up."

"Give me your gun."

"Why?"

I spoke between my teeth. "Because I need one."

"It's my gun. I bought it."

It's a good thing he didn't hand it over, because I would have shot him.

"Take Lake Shore Drive," I ordered Buchbinder. Then I hit my call button. "Reynolds, I'm going north on LSD. Have Rossi meet me on Monroe."

"Roger that. The SRT has checked the house for thermals. Negative."

Buchbinder refused to turn onto Lake Shore.

"What the hell are you waiting for?"

"There's a lot of traffic."

"Jesus, take the damn footpath."

"What if I hit somebody?"

"Buchbinder, get the damn bike moving or . . ." What the hell could I threaten a parking cop with? "Just get the damn bike moving."

He crossed the street and pulled onto the footpath.

"What's our next move, Lieutenant?"

I had to choose my words carefully. I knew O'Loughlin was listening in.

"I think he's using an auto-dialer on the computer. Like telemarketers use. That means he's not at Alger's house, it's just a recording. If you can get your team into the house safely, maybe we could find out where the drop point is before he gets there, so you can get men in place." I added, "To follow him."

"Roger that."

"Lots of people taking walks today," Buchbinder whined. "Dogs too."

"Go faster," I told him.

We zipped past some Rollerbladers, but Buchbinder was still driving like an old lady in a rainstorm. A blind old lady, with gout in her accelerator foot.

If I got a gun, and if I had some private time with the Chemist, I'm sure I could convince him to tell me what he was planning. That might not be what the super, the mayor, or the city wanted, but letting this psycho go not only went against everything I believed in as a cop, but more people were going to die. I was sure of it.

Buchbinder picked up a tiny bit of speed. On our left, Lake Shore Drive, eight lanes packed with cars. On our right, a strip of grass and trees, and beyond that, Lake Michigan, a giant black mirror dotted with tiny white boats.

I checked my watch. Eight minutes left.

Maybe this would all work out. Maybe—

"Dog poo!" Buchbinder screamed.

He jerked the handlebars left, then right, avoiding the little brown land mines dotting the walkway.

"We've been hit! Did you see the size of that pile?"

"Buchbinder, dammit, you need to—"

And then he turned too fast, the bike spun, and we hit a tree and both went flying through the air.

CHAPTER 28

I OPENED MY EYES and wondered what kind of crazy dream I was having. My neck hurt like I'd slept funny, only worse. I had a pounding headache, and someone had removed the roof of my house so I faced blue sky.

I tasted something metallic, delicately probed a fat lip, and looked at my fingers. They had a few blades of grass clinging to them, and blood.

I looked around, saw the lake, saw the cars, and remembered where I was. The motor scooter lay about fifteen feet away from me, crumpled like a frat boy's beer can. Someone, a tall white guy, was leaning over it, inspecting the damage. The Chemist? No. Too big.

"Police," I said. "Get away from there."

I had meant for it to be a yell, but it came out as a croak. Then I searched for Buchbinder, saw him sitting on the lawn a few yards from me. He was wide-eyed and holding out his hands in front of him, Lady Macbeth style.

"No no no no no," he moaned.

"Buchbinder! You okay?"

He held up his palms for me to see. They were covered in dog shit.

I sat up, the motion bringing a world of dizziness.

Someone helped me to my feet. Someone else asked if I was all right. I reached for my radio earpiece, discovered it was gone. So was the radio. Thankfully, I still had the cell phone. And I wasn't the only one. Several people had their cell phones out, calling 911.

"I'm a cop," I said. "Everyone put down your phones."

If the Chemist saw a big gathering of emergency vehicles, it might spook him. I must have looked like an authority figure, because everyone put their phones away. Now I needed to find my radio. I looked through the grass, between me and the wrecked scooter.

"It's on my face!" Buchbinder screamed, high-pitched and manic. He began to rub his face, but since his hands were already coated, he wasn't doing much in the way of cleaning.

I glanced at the bike again, and saw the curious tall white guy remove the final bungee cord and begin to drag the suitcase up the walkway.

I automatically reached for my holster, which did about as much good as Buchbinder's face-rubbing, and then took off after the guy. My legs felt good, strong, but my vision was wiggly and my neck hurt like I'd been playing tetherball with my head.

"Freeze! Police!"

My voice was in full effect, but Tall Boy had apparently misinterpreted my order as "Run away faster," because he picked up speed, heading in the direction Scooter and I just came from. I checked my watch. Six minutes left. If I turned around and ran the rest of the way, I might make it to Navy Pier in six minutes. But I didn't have a gun, and I would owe the city of Chicago two million bucks. If they took it out of my paychecks, I wouldn't be able to retire until I was 163.

I gained on Tall Boy, part of me wanting to shout, "Hard to drag that bastard, isn't it?" I managed to restrain myself, and instead reached out and caught the suitcase by a strap.

One of Newton's Laws got involved, something to do with objects in motion and pulling and pushing, and I jerked him off his feet and ate my own asphalt sandwich a millisecond later. When the tumbling stopped, Tall Boy was on his knees, opening up a folding knife and snarling at me.

It's never a good time for a knife fight, but this *really* wasn't a good time.

"I'm a cop," I said, trying to sound stern despite my fear and exhaustion.

"I'm Charlie Manson," he said.

Great. A loony.

I reached into my back pocket and took out the butterfly knife. I opened it slowly, with some flourish, letting the handles swing back and forth a few times to show this punk I knew what I was doing.

"I'm not going to kill you," I said, getting to my feet. "I'm only going to poke out your eyes."

I closed and opened the knife again, as fast as I could. His bravado cracked a bit.

"Just turn around, and run away. After I take your eyes, I'm going to take your ears."

I changed my grip on the knife, did another blindingly quick open and close, and sliced open my knuckles pretty good.

"Son of a—"

Tall Boy saw my mistake and attacked. He came in low, his weapon held in an underhanded grip, blade up, stabbing at my chin. I pulled back, wincing at the pain in my neck, but avoiding the cut. He followed up with another jab, to my chest, but momentum was already taking me backward and I twisted my shoulders and all he caught was the fabric above my left breast, making me thankful for the first time in my life that I was a B cup.

My knuckles were bleeding, but functional, and my grip on the butterfly knife was solid as I brought it down on his thrusting arm, jamming it a good two inches between his radius and ulna. His knife flew into the grass, but leverage was on his side and as he fell the balisong was jerked from my hand.

He howled, staring at the handle protruding from his forearm, his entire body shaking.

"Leave it in," I told him. "If you pull it out, you could bleed to death."

I checked my watch. Four minutes and some change left. I hurried to the suitcase, happy to find it intact, and began to jog back to Monroe. My bottom lip was now so swollen I could see it if I looked down my nose. It throbbed with every step. I tried to find my rhythm, tried to find the cadence, but my feet weren't moving as swiftly as I wanted them to.

I passed Buchbinder, who was wiping his hands on

the grass and moaning, "I need a moist towelette," and one of the onlookers pointed at me and screamed. I must have looked pretty bad to provoke such raw fright. But then I realized she wasn't pointing at me, she was pointing behind me.

I chanced a look, and Tall Boy was a few steps away from me. He hadn't taken my advice about leaving the knife in his arm. The knife was now in his hand, raised over his head like Mrs. Bates during the shower scene in *Psycho*, and his expression confirmed he wasn't in a happy place.

I stopped in four steps, pivoted my hips, and swung my right leg around, planting the mother of all spin kicks into his stomach. It knocked me backward, but I stayed on my feet. Tall Boy fared worse. He fell onto all fours, retching. I was on him in five steps, kicked him squarely in the jaw, and he sprawled out onto the lawn, where he'd probably stay until he bled to death.

"Buchbinder! Tourniquet!"

Buchbinder stared at me like my nose had grown five inches. I tried a different tactic.

"This guy has antibacterial wipes."

Buchbinder scrambled over to him, and I headed back up the footpath, toward Monroe, dragging the suitcase, two minutes to go, hearing Buchbinder cry behind me, "I crawled through vomit!"

And then a wheel on the suitcase broke.

I hefted the bag up to waist level and tugged the strap over my shoulder. *Heavy* wasn't a good adjective to describe it. *Impossible* was better. I couldn't run, but I broke into a kind of quick hobble. The only thing on me that didn't hurt was my ass, but there was still time for that.

When I reached the intersection, I looked all around for the cop who was supposed to meet me.

Naturally, there was no cop. I should have expected that. I thought of Herb, sitting behind his desk at Robbery, making a few phone calls to track down his missing toilets, and felt a jealousy so intense I almost started to weep.

A car honked. The cab, with Reynolds in the backseat. He opened the door and said, "Hop in."

Getting the suitcase off my shoulder was a relief on par with a death row reprieve. I shoved myself into the backseat after it, and Reynolds ordered the driver to Navy Pier.

I checked my watch. The fifteen minutes were up.

"Couldn't find Rossi, but I got a Mr. SIG-Sauer for you."

He handed me a P228, semiauto, blue finish. Cocked and locked.

"Thanks. Mr. SIG-Sauer will do just fine." I adjusted the Velcro straps on my holster and tucked the gun inside. "You need to send an ambulance to the walkway a few hundred yards back on LSD. And make sure they have some towels."

"Trouble?"

"A little. Lost my radio too."

Reynolds dug around in his pocket. "Here's an extra."

"Any luck with Alger's house?" I asked, plugging in the earpiece.

"It's been booby-trapped again. No casualties, but my team can't get to the computer."

"Probably too late now anyway. We'll try Plan B."

Reynolds narrowed his eyes at me. "You gonna drop this guy?"

"I'm going to have a talk with him."

"This asshole killed a lot of my buddies."

I thought of Officer Sardina in Records. "Mine too."

"Don't be a hero. He looks at you funny, waste him. No one will shed any tears."

"And if more people die?"

"They would anyway."

The unibrow notwithstanding, I liked this guy. The cabbie pulled onto Streeter, and I told him to park it. Navy Pier was less than a block away, and if the Chemist was watching, I wanted him to see me walk up.

"Good luck, Lieutenant."

Reynolds offered his hand. I raised mine, noted the bloody knuckles, and gave him a salute instead. Then I manhandled the bag out of the cab, pulled the torture strap up onto my shoulder, and walked toward the giant letters that welcomed me to Navy Pier.

CHAPTER 29

As the name implied, Navy Pier was a pier. It stretched east into Lake Michigan, three hundred feet wide and ten times as long, boasting a dozen restaurants, several theaters, fifty-plus shops, two museums, a fun house, a miniature golf course, a carousel, and a giant Ferris wheel.

I stood in front of the entrance building, known as the Family Pavilion, and watched people come and go. A minute ticked by. Then two. I was wondering if the Chemist had gotten cold feet, and then the phone rang.

"Is this a recording?" I said.

"Take Grand Avenue east, past the Beer Garden and the Grand Ballroom, to the end of the pier. Look for the tree with the red bow. You have three minutes. If you try anything, people will die."

"Are you a psychotic bed-wetter?"

The call ended. That was definitely a recording. The Chemist was probably already in place, making sure the scene was clear. I heaved the suitcase up and headed east.

I hadn't been to Navy Pier since it was renovated about ten years ago, and if I hadn't been there to deliver extortion money to a mass murderer I might have enjoyed the music, the foliage, the myriad of smells, the distinct carnival atmosphere. Instead, I focused on moving as fast as I could and ignoring the many signals from my body that I should stop moving so fast.

Halfway there, I had to stop to move the strap from one shoulder to the other. My blouse was soaked with sweat, and some blood. My jeans were grass stained, my watch bezel was cracked, and my lower lip had swelled up to football size.

The three-minute time limit passed. Then four minutes. I limped onward, finally making it to the end of the pier at the five-minute mark. Beyond the Grand Ballroom building there was some outdoor seating, a semicircle of flags, and a handful of evergreens. The one in the center, next to the railing that prevented people from falling into Lake Michigan, had a red ribbon tied around the trunk.

I approached it slowly, partly out of caution and partly because slow was the only speed I had left. At the base, covered by dirt, was a white business-size envelope.

I looked around, but no one seemed to be paying any attention to me. Figuring the Chemist wouldn't try to kill me until he got his payoff, I picked up the envelope by the corners and fished out a piece of paper.

> *Jack, be a good girl and throw the suitcase into the lake, directly ahead of you. Do it now. Then wait for my call.*

I started to laugh. The son of a bitch had actually gotten away with it. He'd been there watching at the Daley Center, then used his auto-dialer to send me running all over the place while he put on some SCUBA gear and waited in the lake for the money to come.

"Reynolds, the Chemist left me a note. He wants me to drop the money into the lake. Where's the police boat?"

"Burnham Park Harbor, about a mile away."

"Do they have diving equipment?"

"I think so. Hold on."

I waited a few seconds. Out on the lake, a tour boat glided peacefully by.

"They have equipment," Reynolds said, *"but it would take them a minimum of ten minutes to get it on."*

So much for that.

"Ask them where he could come up."

"There are a few harbors, and three beaches, plus he could be on the lake somewhere. There are dozens of boats out there."

So that was that. There was nothing else we could do.

I walked to the perimeter fence, which only came up to my waist, and set the suitcase over the top. Then I climbed over after it, walked a few feet to the end of the pier, and gazed down into the inky blackness. Ten yards deep, at least. Probably more. I couldn't see past the first few feet.

But he'd be able to see it, painted bright yellow.

"I hope it lands on your fucking head," I said, and dropped the bag into the water.

It hit with a big splash, and then sank immediately; of course it did, with twenty pounds of platinum to weigh it down. I stared for almost a full minute, then hopped back over the fence and sat down at one of the outside benches and watched the waves roll in.

CHAPTER 30

THE CHEMIST BREACHES the surface alongside a pier in Chicago Harbor, less than a mile away from where he picked up the suitcase. He drops the Little Otter—the underwater jet scooter that got him here so quickly—and lets his SCUBA tank, still half full of the nitrox air mix, sink to the bottom. He doubts they'll be found, but if they are, they can't be traced to him.

Next, he hangs the bag handle on a mooring cleat, pulls off his flippers, and then eases himself onto the pier. There are some people in a boat a few yards away, but they aren't looking in his direction.

It's hard, getting the suitcase out of the lake. The money inside is soaking wet, as is the leather, and he almost pops a blood vessel in his forehead hoisting it onto the pier. Once it's up, he walks casually over to the *Miss Maria K,* the twenty-three-foot boat that rents this slip, and removes the black vinyl bag he'd tucked under her cover tarpaulin. Another quick look around, and then he opens up the suitcase and stares at the cash, the platinum, and the felt bag full of uncut diamonds.

"For you, Tracey," he says aloud. But there's no joy in his words.

That's okay. The joy will come later.

It takes him thirty seconds to put everything into his new bag, and then he drops the yellow suitcase back into the water, where it slowly sinks. Getting out of the dry suit is like wrestling with an inner tube, but he manages, tucking it into the nylon bag atop his loot. Wearing only a bathing suit, he slings the bag over his bare shoulder and walks down the pier, to the sidewalk, and into the parking lot, where his car awaits.

After locking the nylon bag in the trunk, he starts the car, waits for the light, and pulls onto Monroe.

He makes a few random turns, watching his mirrors. When he's sure no one is following him, he reattaches the battery to his buy-and-go cell phone and calls the good lieutenant.

"Daniels."

"Hello, Jack."

"Is it you this time, or another recording?"

He smiles. She thinks she's so clever. If that's the case, why is he the one with two mil in his trunk?

"It's me. And it's also the last time you'll be hearing from me. You kept your end of the deal, and I'm keeping mine. Today, a prominent Chicagoan is getting married. I helped out with the refreshments. If you don't intercept them in time, the reception will be really dead."

He had planned on saying that, but it isn't as funny out loud than it had been in his mind.

"Whose wedding is it?" Jack asks.

"That's for you to figure out. Better hurry; you only have a few hours."

"And that's it, then? You're done terrorizing the city?"

"Rest assured that I'll never poison anyone again."

"I think you're lying."

He smiles. "Believe what you like. I did what I set out to do. Now I'm going to disappear. Think of me, next time you go out to eat."

"You're a monster."

"Good-bye, Lieutenant. I hope I showed you a good time. I had a blast."

He separates the battery from the phone, and tosses it in the backseat to dispose of later. He would like to feel a sense of accomplishment, of completion, but there is still much to do. The wedding reception is in a few hours, and he wants to be there to watch the show.

Supermarkets and restaurants are easy to sabotage. A reception is difficult. It requires a lot of work, and more than a little luck. But it can be done, if you know how.

Two weeks before the event, call the banquet hall, speak to the banquet service manager, and ask if he would like to switch liquor distributors. Some chitchat will get you the name of the distributor they're currently using, and even the day of the week they deliver.

Next, wait around the back entrance of the hall for the distributor to show up. Tail him during his route until you have a chance to kill him—many toxins can imitate heart attacks. Then take a look at his invoice clipboard until you find the weekly liquor order for the hall. Make a copy of it. Also make copies of his keys, and take a look in back at how the liquor orders are packaged. Then return everything where you found it. Someone will discover the driver and the truck eventually.

On delivery day, wait for the new driver at an early stop in his route. When he dollies in the boxes of alcohol, he leaves the truck unattended. Use your keys to get into the back of the truck, and substitute your order for the hall's order. It might not be exactly the same, but who cares? They might make some exchanges when they check the invoice, but enough of the tampered alcohol will get through.

The Chemist finished this last step early this morning. He also noticed that on the banquet hall marquee, there are two receptions scheduled for the day. Fortunately, he poisoned enough alcohol to kill everyone at both weddings. He also tampered with a dozen two-liter bottles of soda, using the jet injector and a tiny dot of superglue to plug the hole so the CO_2 wouldn't escape. Non-drinkers and the kiddies shouldn't miss out on the fun.

It's possible that the police will stop it in time. But that's okay. As much work as this has been to set up, it's just a diversion.

The real show hasn't even started yet.

CHAPTER 31

REYNOLDS PICKED ME UP in the cab after I walked back to Streeter.

"Maybe we should stop by the ER," he suggested.

"It's just a fat lip," I told him, except I said *fab lib*. I handed him back the SIG and his radio.

"What next, Lieutenant?"

"We need to stop a wedding reception. Know of any big shots getting married today?"

He didn't need to answer. SWAT guys didn't read the society column.

Which gave me an idea.

I called information, got the number for the *Tribune*, and had the front desk connect me to Twyla Biddle, a reporter who did a column about celebrities. I'd never spoken with Twyla directly, but I'd been in her column a few times, mostly in connection with a TV show I'd done some consulting for against my better judgment.

"Lieutenant! Thanks for calling. What have you got for me? Something juicy, I hope."

Twyla had a deep whiskey and cigarette voice, like Marge's sisters on *The Simpsons*.

"Maybe. I need to know what famous Chicagoans are getting married today."

"Why? What have you heard?"

"Just rumors and innuendo."

"I make a living on rumors and innuendo. Spill it."

"Give me a list, and if it pans out, you'll get the scoop."

Did reporters even use the word *scoop*? If they didn't, Twyla didn't call me on it.

"Well, the wedding of the week has to be Maurice Williams."

"Who is that?"

"Former Chicago Cub. All-Star catcher. Abs you could eat a six-course meal off of, and believe me, you'd want to lick the plate when you finished."

"Who else?"

"William Kent. Owns a lot of real estate, including the Krueger Building. His daughter is getting married tonight. And how could I forget Corndog Watkins? Chicago blues legend, marrying a woman forty-five years younger than he is. Reception is tonight at Buddy Guy's Legends."

I was writing all of this down in the margins of a *Time* magazine—no one in the cab had any paper.

"Anyone else?"

"Those are the majors."

"No one political?"

"Not that I'm aware of. Hold on, I'm at my computer. Let me search through the marriage announcements for tomorrow's issue." I faintly heard fingers hitting keys, at a much faster rate than mine ever could. "Let's see, he's a nobody, she's a nobody, she's a nobody, he's a nobody, he's a—wait. The Bains and Harlow wedding. Jeremy Bains is the son of a police captain."

I'd completely spaced that out. Captain Bains wasn't at the Daley Center today because his son was getting married. Two weeks ago someone at the District had taken up a fund to buy a gift, a chafing dish or something equally useful.

"That's all?"

"All that matter."

"Thanks, Twyla. If I get anything, I'll let you know."

"So how are things with you, Lieutenant? Still dating that hunky accountant?"

I wondered how she knew, but I suppose it was her job to know.

"We're engaged. He proposed a few days ago."

"Congratulations! And how is that famous PI friend of yours, the one missing his hand?"

"It's still missing."

"And how is—"

"I gotta run, Twyla. Thanks again."

"Take care, sweetheart."

I ended the call and wondered if I'd see my name in next week's column. And if I did, if I would save it. I'm not much for collecting things. I didn't even have any pictures of my first wedding. We hadn't bothered to hire a photographer. The wedding might have failed, but I still regretted having no pictures of me in my dress, and regretted it on a semi-regular basis.

"Congratulations on the engagement," Reynolds

told me. "Though I have to admit, I was hoping you were single."

"It's not me," I said. "It's my look. Men are suckers for big, sensuous lips."

It came out *sensubus libs.*

Reynolds raised an eyebrow—well, the right half of his unibrow.

"Actually, I think you're one of the bravest women I've ever met."

"Thanks. And thanks for watching my back."

We exchanged a meaningless *mutual admiration society* glance.

"Where to now?" he asked. "Back to your District?"

"The Daley Center. My car."

Reynolds told the cabbie, and I called Superintendent O'Loughlin, and ran through the list of wedding possibilities.

"Four teams," I told her. "We'll need to check food and drinks, search for traps, interview staff for anything out of the ordinary, and if needed, confiscate everything."

"That will piss some people off," she said.

"Not as much as their entire guest list keeling over. We'll make the two-six the base of operations. The conference room. I'll be there in half an hour."

"Meet you there."

"Good. I want my guns back." I hung up and nudged Reynolds. "Round up your team and as many cops as you can find." He got on the radio, and I called the Crime

Lab. Officer Hajek wasn't in, but a cop I knew named Dan Rogers was.

"I need four CSUs, fully loaded, at the two-six, thirty minutes."

"I've only got four guys here."

"You've also got a phone. Get more. The superintendent is authorizing the overtime."

"She is?"

"She will. Haul ass."

The cab dropped me off, and I drove back to my District. The exterminators had been replaced by a Haz-Mat team, cleaning up the poison in the Records room. Maybe it was oversensitivity on my part, but I could swear the entire building smelled like acrid chemicals, and I tried not to breathe much when I took the elevator to the second floor. The staircase and the bathroom I'd used to wash off the TEPP were being decontaminated, so I had to use the bathroom at the other end of the hallway.

I spent ten full minutes washing off blood and dirt. My mouth was puffy. My hair was a bird's nest. I'd sweated through my jacket, and ripped the shoulder. In short, I looked like I died yesterday but no one had bothered to inform me. Reynolds was the brave one, hitting on me when I was like this. Maybe he didn't like bravery so much as he liked scary.

I didn't feel much better than I looked. I found Advil in my purse, popped three, then combed the knots out of my hair and used half a tube of thirty-dollar lipstick to try to cover up the lip injury. I inadvertently called attention to it instead, like painting a football red.

I went a little heavy on the mascara to compete with it, some rouge to highlight my cheeks, and the next thing I knew, I looked like a hooker. A hooker with bad hair who just got her ass kicked.

Fine. No makeup. I scrubbed it all off.

Then I put just a touch back on.

After making myself appear somewhat human, I went to the water fountain and drank like a camel—not the easiest thing to do with a fat lip, but the cold water felt nice. I had a brief spell of double vision, worked through it, and then showed up in Conference Room A to talk with forty-plus cops, Feds, and others, including the folks from the CDC, USAMRIID, and WHO.

My speech wasn't particularly inspiring, witty, or even pithy. But I made up for all of that by being brief.

"I recently spoke with the Chemist. There are four high-profile wedding receptions taking place in Chicago today, and if we're to take him at his word, he's poisoned the refreshments at one of them. We need to shut all four of them down until we can figure out which one is the deadly one. I need four teams. Each will have a Crime Scene Unit with full gear, an SRT to check for booby traps and IEDs, and as many officers as we can spare to interview the staff. If possible, let's get in touch with the wedding parties, ask them if anything unusual has happened in the last few days or weeks."

Rogers raised his hand. "How can we test for toxins or poisons in the field? We need to take samples to the lab, run them through the GCMS. There will be hundreds of samples."

"Our guy is touchy about leaving fingerprints. Look for things that have been wiped down, or for glove marks. People at the distillery, distributors, busboys, bartenders, servers, managers—they all leave their latents on bottles of booze. Any bottle that's clean should be given top priority."

I spied Rick sneaking into the room and sitting near the back.

"Special Agent Rick Reilly from the Hazardous Materials Response Team of the FBI has worked closely with the Behavioral Science Team to create a profile of the Chemist. This profile states that since he's been paid, he will no longer have any interest in harming our city. Is that right, Special Agent?"

Rick stood. "That's right. The Chemist is probably on his way out of the country right now. We've got teams at bus stations and airports—"

"Looking for a soaking wet man carrying a yellow bag," I interrupted. "The FBI profile is flat-out wrong, and I don't want anyone wasting their time with it. The Chemist is still in town. He's going to try to be at the reception. Maybe as a guest or an employee. Maybe he'll just watch from across the street. But he'll want to see it. I'll need people double-checking the guest lists, new hires, anyone hanging around who shouldn't be there, plus SRT members to run recon on the locations, to see if anyone is playing I Spy."

"The profile—" Rick said.

I finished for him. "Sucks. Rogers, Reynolds, divide up your people. Baker, put the teams together. Everyone extra, go where you think you can do some good. I want everyone on headsets. Alpha Team has the Cubs catcher—Baker, you're in charge. Taylor, you're leading Bravo Team, and you've got the Kent wedding. Charlie Team is Corndog Watkins—Collins, that's you. I'm heading up Delta and the Bains reception. Keep in touch, keep communicating, and if we find the Chemist, I don't want to hear any bullshit about letting the guy go."

Davy Ellis, looking like he'd just stepped off the Ralph Lauren runway, raised his hand.

"The mayor said—"

"The mayor said not to apprehend him during the money drop. The drop is over. Isn't that right, Superintendent O'Loughlin?"

All eyes locked on the super. Her voice radiated a lot more authority than mine did.

"If we find him, we grab him."

I adjourned the meeting, and began to work with Baker putting teams together. Rick came up, his prettyboy looks spoiled by a scowl. He took my elbow and edged me aside.

"Not very professional, Jack."

"About as professional as telling the super to take my gun."

"You were going to do something stupid."

At least he didn't deny it. But that didn't make it any less of a betrayal.

"I do a lot of stupid things," I told him, and let my eyes add extra weight to my words. Rick caught the implication and walked off. There would be no more footsie with Special Agent Hottie. Good-looking men were nice, but loyalty was a helluva lot nicer.

After my team was organized enough to roll, I tracked down the super, who was in a heated discussion with the PR guy.

"I need my weapons," I said to her.

O'Loughlin reached into her enormous jacket pockets, pockets so large they belonged on a clown or a mime.

"If you apprehend or kill the suspect," Davy said, "it could get out that the city knew about his plot, and that we paid him off. Think about the outrage, the lawsuits, the damage to Chicago's reputation."

"All I'm thinking about," I said evenly, "is getting him so more people don't die."

"It would be impossible to recover from—"

"I forgot to mention," I interrupted. "The last time I spoke with the Chemist, he asked me why we hadn't gone public about the money. I told him to take it up with Davy Ellis of Ellis, Dickler, and Scaramouche, that you were the one suppressing his story. He didn't seem happy."

Ellis turned a lovely shade of pale beneath his perfect tan. Peripherally, I saw the super's lips twitch, as close as I'd seen her get to smirking. I turned away, tucked my guns into both holsters, and then headed for Chateau Élan on North and Clybourn to ruin Captain Bains's joyous occasion.

CHAPTER 32

From the outside, Chateau Élan looked like it was designed by an ancient Roman architect with a column fetish. The facade boasted ten of them, thick and white and supporting a vaulted roof. Six columns graced each side of the building, and two held up the marquee on the front lawn, which proclaimed congratulations to Mr. and Mrs. Bains and Mr. and Mrs. Rothschild.

The valet seemed anxious to park my car, until he found out I was a cop and not going to tip. I parked in the valet area just the same—I'd done enough walking for the day. I was followed into the lot by a parade of cop cars, including the Mobile Command bus. When Bains showed up, he was going to have a stroke.

The lobby had a few marble statues, a fountain, and a lot of flowers and plants. I talked to a Hispanic cook, who led me to a comb-over manager named Bob Debussey. Bob appeared ready to cry when I laid out the story for him.

"Oh dear. This is horrible. Oh dear oh dear."

"Where do you keep the liquor?"

"Oh dear. There's a wine cellar, and the cooler. Both locked. Oh dear."

"Who has keys?"

"I do, and my assistant manager, Jaime. Oh dear."

Between *oh dears* I gleaned that there were no new hires recently, there haven't been any strange people hanging around, and they'd gotten their latest liquor delivery this morning.

"I was missing a case of champagne, and a bottle of Oban. The groom's father specifically wanted that scotch. The driver had the champagne, but had to go back for the scotch. Marty would have never messed up like that."

"Who's Marty?"

"The previous driver. Wonderful man. Died a few weeks ago. Heart attack, right after dropping off our order. Oh dear."

I directed the mob of police entering the lobby to ask questions, take names, secure the perimeter, and search for IEDs. Bob led me, Rogers, and a perky CSU girl named Patti Hunt over to the wine cellar. Hunt was lugging a large black ALS box, and Rogers had a kit similar to Hajek's. Bob fussed with the keys, shaking so badly I felt the wind. When he got the door open, he pointed out the stack of boxes in the near corner, sitting in front of a large wine rack that took up the back wall.

"This is presumptive, guys," I told the team, "not evidentiary. Get me some clues, and the court case can be built later."

Hunt found an electrical outlet for the alternate light source, Rogers dug out an aerosol can of ninhydrin, and I snapped on some latex gloves and eased a bottle of Perestroika vodka from the top carton.

"The driver today," I asked Bob. "Was he wearing gloves?"

"Oh dear. No, I don't believe so. He brought the boxes in on a dolly. I don't remember gloves."

"Is this the bottle of scotch he forgot?" I pointed to the Oban sitting on a wire rack.

"Yes. He brought that to me about an hour ago. Said he was sure he packed it the first time."

Rogers spritzed the Oban and the vodka, and Hunt switched on the ALS and pointed the silver wand at the bottles, bathing them in green light. Nothing fluoresced.

"It's at five fifty-five nanometers," Hunt said.

"Nini is a picky lady," Rogers said. "Try six hundred."

Hunt dialed up the spectrum, and the light went from green to orange. It also brought out a dozen yellow prints on the Oban bottle, and three on the vodka.

Rogers looked at them through a loupe.

"Gloves on the vodka, at least seven different prints on the scotch."

I took another bottle out of the top box, and a bottle out of the box beneath it. Then I went to the shelves and pulled a few random bottles. We did another spray and glow.

"All gloves on the new bottles, prints all over the old ones," Rogers concluded.

"The distributor doesn't wear gloves," I said, "and he packs the liquor himself. These should have prints on them, unless they've been wiped down or switched."

"But they don't look like they've been opened." Hunt

pointed at the cap on the Perestroika. "The safety seal is still on."

She was right. And the jet injector, powerful as it was, couldn't shoot through glass. I placed three identical bottles of vodka on the floor and looked at the fill levels. All of them were uneven by a wee bit. But was that the Chemist's doing, or were all liquor bottles slightly off?

I unscrewed the cap off of one.

"Lieutenant," Hunt said, "if you're thinking of taking a shot, that's a poor way to test for toxins."

Rogers raised his hand. "I'll volunteer to try it."

I squinted at the cap. There didn't seem to be any signs of tampering. I took a tentative sniff. Smelled like vodka.

"Rogers, pass me that loupe."

I held it to my eye and saw a tiny crystal winking up at me on the rim. I ran my pinky—my only finger currently lacking a decent fingernail—around the inside of the cap, and felt a bit of roughness.

"Unless the Perestroika master distillers use ground glass as a secret ingredient, I think we've found our toxic liquor. What else came with this shipment?" I asked Bob.

"Oh dear oh dear. A few cases of beer, and some pop. It's all in the cooler."

I ordered Rogers and Hunt to go with him, and I opened two more bottles, whiskey and rum. Each had overshot their recommended daily allowance of glass. I called the super.

"It looks like Bains is the target. It's the liquor. I'm going to shut everything down here."

"I'll talk to your captain. We can let the reception go on anyway, bait a trap for the Chemist."

"I was thinking about that, but it's too dangerous. There might be other things tampered with, and I don't think Bains wants to use his son's wedding for a sting operation."

"Agreed, Lieutenant. I'm glad I put you in charge of this case."

I was going to remind her that I wasn't her first pick, or even her tenth pick, but instead I said, "Thanks, but it isn't over yet."

I hung up and called the other team leaders to have them look for broken glass under bottle caps. Then it was huddle-time in the lobby for my team.

"We've found what we believe to be contaminated liquor bottles. Talk to me, Reynolds."

"Perimeter is clear. No IEDs, no sightseers for a block in all directions."

"Rogers?"

"Beer is bad. I looked at the bottle caps under high magnification, there are marks. Some two-liter bottles of soda have also been compromised."

"What else have we got?" I asked.

A cop named Mathers said, "Nothing out of the ordinary in the kitchen. They had a few deliveries earlier today, nothing strange about them."

Another named Parker added, "No strangers prowling

around. Staff is spooked, but that's to be expected. Everyone here knows everyone else, no newbies in the group. We did catch two Latinos trying to sneak out the back door, but that's because they thought we were Immigration."

"Okay, we're still going to shut the place down. Mathers, I want you to—"

"You can't close us!" This from the worrisome Bob, of course. "We've got two events today! These people have counted on us to make this the most important day of their lives!"

"Sorry, Bob. Can't risk it."

"But you said the kitchen was fine! It's only the liquor shipment that came today!"

"We can't take the chance."

Bob began to cry, then fled the lobby with his hands over his face, but not before running headfirst into a plaster reproduction of Michelangelo's David. It was more sad than funny. After thirty seconds of uncomfortable silence, I picked up where I left off.

"Mathers, get five guys to bag and tag the liquor bottles. We're going to have to clean out the pantry, and the staff needs to be tested for BT as a precautionary—"

Bob came galloping back into the lobby, with a large pan full of linguini. Noodles hung from his mouth.

He yelled, "It's fine!" or something similar. Hard to tell with all the food stuffed in his cheeks.

There were no heroic attempts on behalf of my people to tackle Bob and wrench the linguini from his starch hole. No one screamed, "Spit it out, you idiot!" We all just watched, silently, as Bob chewed, swallowed, and didn't die. When he finished, he held out both arms in a silent *ta-da!* No one applauded.

"I'm trying the soup next," Bob said, and trotted off.

Captain Bains chose that opportune moment to call, spitting vitriol and threats before I said word one. When he paused to take a breath I cut in, explaining how everything went down.

"And what's Bob doing right now?" Bains asked when I finished.

"He's standing three feet away from me, eating a bowl of wedding ball soup."

Bob nodded vigorously and gave me a thumbs-up.

"How does he look?"

"Crazed."

"Sick? Poisoned?"

"Not so far."

"Tell him if he tries everything on the menu and lives, we'll go on as planned. And also tell him to run to Costco and pick up a truckload of liquor. My side of the family likes to drink."

"I'll let you tell him that. How was the ceremony?"

"The flowers look like shit. One of the big arrangements fell over during the vows, and the ring bearer is still screaming in fright. I'm going to hang the florist by his green thumbs and have everyone in my District take turns beating him with hoses."

"I'm glad it went well."

"I'm on my way there. Let me speak to Bob."

I passed the phone over to the manager, and informed my team that we'd just confiscate the liquor and beverages for now. Then I conferred with Reynolds.

"Have you checked in with the SRTs at the other weddings?"

"They all seem to be clear."

"Call them over here. I want a watch on the property, and I want two undercovers inside checking the guest list. It looks like Bains is going to jeopardize hundreds of lives to make his son happy."

"Can't blame the guy. The bond between a father and a child is a powerful thing."

"Yeah," I said, conjuring up the image of me and my father in Grant Park. "Nothing can break that bond."

A few minutes later I had my phone back, Manager Bob was noshing on a Caesar salad with anchovies, and Bains arrived and in no uncertain terms told everyone to get the hell out. I might have put up a fight if it was anyone other than my boss, and I might have even put up a fight with my boss, but the double vision had returned and I was so tired I could fall asleep standing up.

Which is why I left Reynolds in charge and hopped in the car, ready to head home. It was only a little past noon, and I felt like I'd been awake for a year.

I doubted we'd pick up the Chemist today. If he did stop by, all of the police vehicles still in the parking lot would scare him off. But I felt pretty good that we would eventually catch him. He'd gone through a lot of trouble and risk to steal the case files from Records. There had to be something in there worth protecting. And though

Alger and his partner were dead, and those files were gone, the information they contained was still available if I dug deep enough.

This wouldn't end in a dramatic gun battle, or a climactic chase. It would end in a warrant and a quiet arrest. But it would end. I was sure of it.

I took 290, heading back to my house. I was making damn good time too, so good, I might actually make the trip in less than an hour. I would take a shower, maybe do a little napping, then visit Latham.

Which is why it was especially surprising to me when I exited on Harlem and headed north. Bensenville wasn't north. The hospital wasn't north. Elmwood Park was north. Elmwood Park, where Wilbur Martin Streng lived.

"This isn't a good time," I said to myself.

But I kept going, on my way to visit a man I thought died about forty years ago.

CHAPTER 33

*T*HE CHEMIST DRIVES PAST Chateau Élan, sees the police brigade camped out in the parking lot, and doesn't even slow down.

The cops figured it out fast. Very fast. But it doesn't matter. That's only a side bet. The big wager hasn't been placed yet.

He thinks about tomorrow. If everything goes according to the Plan, the death toll will be in the tens of thousands. And there will be drastic aftereffects as well. Panic. Riots. Widespread terror. Crime will spin out of control, with no one to stop it.

It's more than simple revenge. It will teach the world an important lesson.

And the best part of all is that no one will see it coming.

He heads home to make the final preparations.

CHAPTER 34

WHAT DO YOU SAY to a dead man?

I started with, "Hello."

Elmwood Park blended into Chicago on the west side. It was small but densely packed, predominantly white middle-class, mostly residential. Wilbur Streng lived in a small beige house on a small piece of property, bordered on either side by equally small houses, at Belden and Seventy-third. There was room for me to park on the street legally, but I chose a hydrant out of habit.

I didn't need to psych myself up, or check my makeup, or consider what I was going to say. I was on autopilot, acting without thinking. After parking, I walked up to his door and pressed the bell, and a minute later an old man answered.

I expected some sort of emotion on my part, some sort of internal dam breaking. But I felt nothing. The person standing before me didn't look anything like the memories, or photos, I had of my father. He was stooped with age, which put him at my height. More liver spots on his head than hair. Thick glasses, and a lot of loose skin on the face and neck. Slightly built, but with a small pot belly.

"Figured you'd come by someday. Might as well come in."

And then the dam broke. I'd forgotten what he sounded like. Is that odd? To forget a parent's voice? But when he spoke, I realized I hadn't forgotten it at all. I could never forget it. That voice had read me countless bedtime stories, had answered my questions about lions and thunder and airplanes, had helped me with my homework, had said *I love you* so many times. That same voice had bought me three ice creams and never gotten angry.

My father's voice. Dad's voice.

I felt my throat begin to tickle and my chest get heavy, but I stayed outwardly calm.

"You . . . know who I am?"

"Saw you on TV, many times. In the paper too. Your mother finally tell you?"

"She told me you were dead."

He nodded. "It was easier that way. You coming in?"

I wasn't sure if I wanted to. Still, my feet followed his into the house, and the door closed behind me with a surreal, otherworldly feeling.

The house was dark, clean. It smelled of lemon polish and cigar smoke. We passed a living room with a leather couch, a TV, an old hi-fi. Paintings on the wall, mostly of wooded landscapes, in heavy ornate frames that were popular in the '70s. Lots of wood paneling. Lots of wood everything. The kitchen was also done in brown, tile and wallpaper. Tidy, but without any overt personality.

"Would you like coffee? I have some from earlier."

He indicated the green percolator on the counter. I didn't want coffee, but I suddenly felt uncomfortable and I wanted to have something to do with my hands.

"Coffee is fine."

"Cream or sugar?"

"Black."

He grunted, like he expected that, and took a mug out of the drying rack in the sink.

"Got this machine about thirty years ago. Still brews a decent cup."

So he didn't abandon appliances, only families. He handed me the mug, and I was grateful for the warmth.

"Your mother tell you why?" he asked. He sat across from me at the kitchen table.

"She wrote a letter. You said you hated her, hated me, and didn't want to have anything to do with us ever again."

Wilbur grunted again.

"Is that true?" I asked.

"No. I was always fond of you, and your mother. It hurt like hell to leave."

"So why did you?"

"I had to."

I pushed down the anger, which was gathering like a storm in my head.

"Another woman?" I asked.

Wilbur laughed.

"No. If that were the case, I would have told your mother."

"So what happened? You woke up one morning, decided you no longer wanted the responsibility?"

Wilbur stared at me for a long time, and for a moment I wondered if he'd died with his eyes open. I was almost ready to reach out and feel his pulse, when he said, "How is your mother doing?"

"She's doing fine. And you're avoiding the question."

"I suppose I am. I've . . . thought about this moment. Many times. You, being here. Sometimes you're yelling at me, screaming. Sometimes you're crying. Sometimes you even pull a gun on me. I always start off by trying to explain how things were different back in the sixties. It's not like it is today. Men were expected to act like men. I could have done the easy thing. I could have stayed and lived a lie."

Some anger seeped out. "You're acting like leaving your family was courageous."

"You asked me if I no longer wanted the responsibility. I always wanted the responsibility." Wilbur's eyes got glassy. "The day you were born, I promised to—"

"Stop."

"—take care of you, forever. I made that same promise to your mother, on our wedding day."

"Which is why you abandoned us, left us with nothing." I folded my arms. "You never tried to contact us, never gave us a dime."

Wilbur stood up, walked to the percolator, and took a fresh mug from the cabinet. He poured himself some coffee, sipped it slowly.

"It was easier to walk out of your lives than have you and your mother deal with . . . everything. I had to play the bad guy."

"Why?"

"Because the truth would have hurt more."

"And what is the truth?"

Wilbur didn't answer. I decided I'd had enough of this. It was only making me angry. I stood up.

"Thanks for the coffee, *Dad.* Maybe we can do this again in another forty years."

"Jacqueline, wait . . ."

I left the kitchen, walked down the hall, and noticed some pictures hanging on the wall. One was a baby photo of me. I pulled it down and stared at it.

"Why do you have this?" I yelled. "You don't deserve to have this."

I wasn't sure if I should keep it or throw it across the room, when I noticed another picture on the wall, of my father and another man, both wearing tuxedos. By the size of the lapels, this was mid-1970s. Wilbur was smiling, and so was the other man, who had his arm around my father's waist.

And all of my anger vanished, as if a trapdoor had been pulled under it. I took the frame off the wall and walked back into the kitchen.

"You're gay," I said.

Wilbur opened his mouth, then closed it. He did this a few times, like a fish in a net, before he finally spoke.

"I think I always knew. But I spent the first thirty years of my life denying it. Fighting it. Unable to accept it. Homosexuality was considered a weakness back then. A lack of self-control. Or a disease."

Wilbur smiled, but it was tinged with pain.

"The University of Chicago had an experimental program at the time. I went once a week to get shocked. Electrocuted. Aversion therapy, they called it. They showed me gay images, had me read gay literature, and then gave me a jolt. Barbaric, by today's standards. So much has changed."

"Mom didn't know?" I asked softly.

"No. And I couldn't tell her. Not only because of the ridicule she would have gotten from her friends, her family. But it would have really hurt her. She would have felt like it was her fault, that she wasn't trying hard enough, that she made some kind of mistake. It would have been a much harder rejection for her than me leaving because I was an uncaring bastard."

I looked at the tuxedo picture again. Saw how happy he looked.

"Did you . . ."

"I never cheated on your mother. Not once. But I couldn't give her what she needed. If I'd stayed with you, I would have been living a lie, and we all would have been miserable as a result."

"But what about me?" I asked, my voice very small.

"Your mother told you I was dead. How could I visit you? I sent money, of course, kept sending it up until you graduated from college."

Now my eyes were glassy too.

"How responsible of you."

"I'm sorry, Jacqueline."

I turned away, unwilling to let him see me cry.

"When I got older. When I grew up. Why didn't you ever try to contact me?"

"I meant to. I always meant to."

I wiped my cheeks.

"I have to go now."

"Please stay."

I looked at him.

"Forty years, Wilbur. You missed out on my entire life."

"I can't tell you how hard it's been. At least you thought I was dead. I knew you were alive. I've spent more time thinking about you than most fathers actually spend with their children. Every morning I'd wake up and think about calling you, about talking to you."

"But you didn't call." The tears were really coming now. "I found out you were alive, and *I came*. You knew I was alive, and never came."

"Jacqueline . . ."

I whispered, "I wouldn't have cared that you were gay."

"Please stay . . ."

"Good-bye, Wilbur."

I walked out of his tidy little house, went to my car, and cried the entire way to the hospital.

Latham was asleep when I arrived. I held his hand and thanked the universe that he was most certainly heterosexual and decided that when we got married, I wanted to have my reception at Chateau Élan because the staff was certainly dedicated.

And when the wedding was over, I'd send Wilbur a picture of me in my dress and write *See what else you missed* on the back.

CHAPTER 35

THE DOORBELL WOKE ME UP. It was still strange to hear a doorbell, having spent my entire adult life in apartments. I peeked at the digital, noted it was almost nine a.m., and calculated that I'd gotten a full eight hours of sleep. After leaving the hospital late last night, I picked up a frozen pizza and a six-pack of Goose Island IPA and finished both of them, then ordered a bunch of crap from HSN that I didn't need. If memory served, one of the items was a vacuum cleaner that could suck up a bowling ball. This was incredibly important, as most homes in North America are just filthy with bowling balls.

Another doorbell ring. I peeled myself out of bed, wincing because everything hurt, including my head. I had on one of Latham's T-shirts, big enough to come down to my knees, and I deemed that suitable as greeting wear. That is, until I looked through the peephole and saw who was at the door.

"Hurry up, Jackie! I gotta use the can!"

Harry McGlade. Dressed in the traditional Harry outfit of an expensive suit, wrinkled beyond belief, and a Bogart hat. I rolled my eyes. I'd forgotten today was PoliceFest. Maybe if I didn't answer, he'd go away.

"I know you're in there. Your car is parked in the driveway. Open up or I'll piss in your mailbox."

I had no doubt he'd do it too. I opened the door.

"Jesus, Jackie, I just spent an hour on the expressway with an Ultra-Mega Big Gulp. My bladder is so full, it's putting pressure on my heart. Where's the bathroom?"

"Straight back, to the right," I told him. "Don't touch anything. Especially the towels."

I went into the bedroom and changed into some baggy button-fly Yanuk jeans, Nikes, and an oversized Gap golf shirt. Rather than futz with my hair, I opted for a Cubs baseball cap, pulling my ponytail through the hole in the back. I probably could have used a shower, but I was afraid to leave McGlade unattended in my home for any period of time.

After washing my face and carefully brushing my teeth—my lower lip was still sore—I found McGlade in the kitchen. Every cabinet was open, and he was poking through a Tupperware container, transferring a handful of something to his mouth.

"These are all you have to eat in this entire house," he said between bites, "and I think they're spoiled."

"Really? I just bought them last week."

"They taste like ass."

"The cat likes them."

He stared at the cat treats and frowned.

"This is cat food?"

"Yeah."

"Liver and onion?" he ventured.

"Liver and tuna."

He set the container down on the counter. "You got any mints?"

"No. Sorry."

"How about floss?"

"Bathroom cabinet."

He scurried off. I sniffed the treats, shuddered, and put them back in the cabinet. Then I closed all the other cabinet doors, poured a large glass of water, and drank it while silently dreading PoliceFest. Last year it had been held in Indiana, and I'd gone with Herb and his wife at their insistence. It was a crowded, hot, loud event, with carnival rides, face painting, pricey beer and hot dogs, and a lot of macho boxing and shooting contests. I snagged second place in one of the shooting contests, but that didn't mean I enjoyed myself.

Harry returned, scowling.

"Were you telling the truth about the cat treats?" he asked.

"No."

He seemed relieved. "They're not for cats?"

"Yes, they are. But they're not fresh. I bought them a year ago, and my cat hates them."

I heard a humming sound, and noted that McGlade had clenched his robotic hand into a fist. While he was annoyed, I hit him with more bad news.

"I'm driving."

"No way. I'm a guy. We can't let chicks drive. It's a form of castration."

"Well, pick up your balls. We're leaving."

I double-checked to make sure Mr. Friskers had food and water, and then walked past Harry and out the front door. He tagged along behind me like a puppy.

"I wanna drive."

"Not gonna happen."

"Did you see my Vette? It's fast."

"I bet."

"Why can't I drive?"

"Because I'm driving."

I got behind the wheel, and Harry sat next to me.

"Your car sucks."

"I know."

"Can I park the Vette in your garage?"

"Garage door is broken."

"Your house sucks."

"I know."

I pulled out of the driveway, and Harry began to mess with my radio. Better the radio than listening to him talk. Unfortunately, he switched it off after only listening to three bars of "Freebird" by Skynard.

"Your radio sucks."

"Let's try being quiet for a while, okay?"

He lasted a whole two minutes.

"I've started to write poetry," Harry said.

Lord help me.

"That's nice."

"It helps me deal, you know, with the pain."

"VD?" I asked.

"Of losing my hand. There isn't much physical pain anymore. It's on permanently. They did a bone graft. Carbon fibers. Want to see where it's attached?"

"No."

He showed me anyway, peeling up the latex covering,

pointing to his wrist where the scar tissue met the prosthesis. It wasn't as ugly as I imagined.

"Gotta keep rubbing antiperspirant around the edges, because the latex gets hot and I sweat like crazy. Inside the hand, along with the mechanical parts, are myoelectric sensors, attached to my nerves and muscles. If I concentrate on *open*"—I heard a mechanical whir, and Harry's thumb and fingers separated—"and *close,* the fingers move. Only three of the fingers are actually robotic. The ring finger and the pinky just go along for the ride. It's pretty strong, though. See?"

McGlade gripped my dashboard with the prosthesis, and his fingers punched right through.

"Harry!"

"Don't worry. I'm okay. It doesn't hurt at all."

I looked at the damage, realized it was no big loss, and turned onto I-190, passing O'Hare and heading for Skokie. Harry was mercifully quiet for a few seconds.

"So, do you want to hear some of my poetry?"

"No."

"A short one."

"No."

"It's really short."

"I don't care how short it is, I don't want to hear it."

A few seconds ticked by.

"Want to see my new phone?"

"No."

He tugged it out of his wrinkly blazer just the same.

"It's a phone, a camera, a PDA, and it can even surf the Internet."

"Have you been tested for ADD?" I asked.

He pressed a few buttons, and a loud feminine moan came from the device.

"This is a good Web site. BubbleBooty.com. It costs twenty bucks a month, but you get free fifteen-second previews of all their movies. So who needs to join?"

More moaning, and then the sound of a donkey braying.

"Or check this out."

He stuck the camera in my face, and there was a blinding flash.

"Jesus, McGlade!"

"High rez, 1500 dpi. Look at that clarity. I can count the pores on your nose. Well, I could, if I had all day."

"It's quiet time again," I said. "Let's see if we can be quiet for the whole rest of the ride, okay?"

Quiet time lasted less than a minute.

"Just like the old days, isn't it, Jackie? Cruising down the highway. Me and you. Young cops with bad attitudes. We had some fun times, didn't we?"

"Not really."

I watched peripherally as Harry tried to adjust the air-conditioning vent using his prosthesis, and snapped it right off. He pondered it for a moment, checked to see if I noticed, and then hid it under his seat.

"I don't regret quitting the force."

"You didn't quit. You were kicked off."

"I don't miss it. It's not like PI work. Someone hires me to do a job, I get paid, they're grateful. Not like being a cop. Too many people hate you. Like all the traps in that house the other night. Someone had to really hate the department to set all that up. I heard it was a cop's house too."

Something itched at the back of my head, but I couldn't quite scratch it.

"This guy has killed a lot of cops," I admitted. I thought about Sardina, and Roxy, and the two Cicero officers. Plus all of the incidental police officer poisonings; three died at the Sammy's, and twelve more became sick eating at various locations around the city. Hell, the Chemist even spread his toxins at the German deli only a block away from . . .

"The one-five."

"You say something?" Harry asked. He was using his prosthesis to touch himself in a private place.

"Can you not fondle yourself in my front seat?"

"Just making a minor adjustment. It's kind of strange, because it feels like someone else's hand."

"Shut up for a minute."

"Why?"

"I'm thinking. Just be quiet."

"I was being quiet. You're the one who started talking."

"Harry, shut the hell up."

"Boy, you're bitchy. Don't they have hormones for after menopause?"

I tuned him out, concentrating on all of the restaurants and grocery stores the Chemist had poisoned. As I ticked them off, one by one, I realized that there had been a pattern all along.

"Each store was within a block of a police station."

"Huh?" McGlade had gone back to adjusting himself.

"The police. The Chemist was targeting the police all along. Even the wedding—Captain Bains's son. Why the hell didn't I see it before?"

"Because you're functionally retarded?" Harry offered. "Going senile? Have Alzheimer's disease? Personally, I wouldn't mind Alzheimer's. You buy one magazine, and you're entertained for the rest of your life."

I drew in a sharp breath, having one of those rare moments where everything suddenly came together. If the Chemist truly wanted to hurt some cops, he needed to strike where there was a large concentration of us in a small area.

"PoliceFest," I whispered.

More than twenty thousand cops, plus another twenty thousand family members and visitors, all in the same place at the same time.

"I think I broke your radio," Harry said, handing me a knob with his rubber hand.

I jammed down the accelerator. While it wasn't enough to pin us to our seats, I was pushing eighty soon enough.

"What the hell are you doing, Jackie?"

"I'm praying," I told him. "Praying that I'm wrong."

CHAPTER 36

THE VILLAGE OF SKOKIE covered roughly ten square miles. It was one of Chicago's larger suburbs, with a population of over sixty thousand, bordering the city on the north side.

I was burning some serious rubber, edging the car up into the nineties, and then I had to stop very quickly. Traffic had gone from open to insane. The Touhy ramp off of I-94 was backed up for at least a mile, bumper to bumper. All because of PoliceFest.

"McGlade, grab my cherry—"

I regretted saying it as soon as it breached my lips, but before I could qualify it he'd already answered, "I think I'm about thirty-five years too late for that, Jackie."

"The red and blue light, smart-ass. In the backseat, on the floor."

He fished around for it and set it on his lap.

"They still use these things?"

"The classics are still the best. Plug it in and stick it to the roof."

McGlade put the cord into my cigarette lighter, and it turned on and began to spin, flashing colors.

"My key chain light is brighter than this stupid thing."

"Just put it on the roof."

"What is that? Is that a suction cup?"

"The roof, McGlade!"

I hit the gas and pulled onto the shoulder, spraying gravel. McGlade leaned out the window and attached the cherry to the top of my car. When he finished, he sat back down and buckled his seat belt.

"Where's the siren?" he asked.

"No siren."

McGlade seemed to consider it.

"Want me to stick my head out the window and go *woo-woo-woo*?"

I hopped back onto the street, buzzed through the red light, and swung east onto Touhy, missing a pickup truck by a good two feet.

"Did you pull down the little lever on the suction cup?" I asked, swerving to avoid the SUV ahead of me.

"There was a lever?"

I tapped my brakes, and the cherry bounced off my hood and onto the sidewalk, where it hit a mailbox and splintered into a million little red and blue pieces.

"Hell." I frowned. "That thing was vintage."

"Don't worry about it. You can hire a midget to sit on your roof and hold a lava lamp. You'd get the same effect."

I passed a Jeep, hit the horn, and took a right onto Lincoln.

"How old is this car?" McGlade asked. "It's a model made before airbags, isn't it?"

"Just go limp at impact. It's the same thing."

I heard a whirring sound, and chanced a look. McGlade had locked his hand onto the door grip. I smiled, and pinned the speedometer.

"McGlade, what street is the festival on?"

"Pratt and Central Park Avenue. You could drop me off wherever, though. Up here is fine. Or here. Or at that nail salon. I was thinking about doing my nails."

I zipped past the nail salon, breezed through a yellow light, and hung a left onto Pratt. Then I hit the brakes.

Yellow sawhorses blocked off the street, a thick wall of people milling around behind them. Thousands of people.

"Parking is going to be a bitch," Harry said.

He was right. And because a lot of these folks were cops, all of the hydrants were already taken. I stopped in the middle of the street, dug my ankle holster—complete with AMT—out of my purse, and put my leg up onto the steering wheel to strap it on. Naturally, McGlade had to comment on this.

"You're pretty flexible for an old chick. Can you put your foot behind your head? I dated this girl once. Well, not really *dated.*"

I grabbed my purse, hopped out of the car, and waded into the crowd. It was elbow to elbow, a carnival that seemed to go on forever, complete with music and rides and plenty of food. Besides the prerequisite amount of coptosterone, there were also plenty of women and children, and every third person was eating or drinking something. Beer. Lemonade. Corn on the cob. Hot dogs.

Nachos. If the Chemist was going to unleash his toxins at this event, a lot of people would die.

I pushed my way up to a popcorn vendor and asked who was in charge. He had no idea, but offered me a program. I folded out the map and studied the gigantic layout. The information booth was dead center. I moved as fast as I could, which wasn't very fast at all. I literally had to force my way through people, enduring a slew of unhappy stares and a few off-color remarks.

"So what's the rush anyway?" Harry had somehow caught up and was right behind me. "You think this poison guy is going to try something?"

"I don't know. There's a good chance he did something. This guy hates cops, and here's a chance to kill a bunch at once."

"Think he did something to the soft pretzels?"

"I don't know."

McGlade shoved a large pretzel under my nose.

"Take a bite, tell me if it's safe."

I knocked it aside, pushed over to the edge of the crowd, and walked along the perimeter, which was much quicker.

"Lots of people," McGlade said. He'd risked it; his mouth was full of pretzel. "Whaddaya think? Thirty thousand? Forty? Be tough to poison this many people."

Harry had a point. So many different vendors, it would be an impossible feat to hit all of them, or even half of them. If I wanted to kill a bunch of people here, how would I do it? Gas? I spied a helium tank being used to fill balloons. I also noted a cooling-off station, which sprayed a fine mist of cool water onto people who walked beneath it. The problem with either was speed. The poison would have to be slow-acting, so as many people as possible could become infected before panic made the rest flee, or instantaneous, getting as many people as possible at once.

"How about a crop duster?" McGlade said. "He could swoop down, trailing gas."

Harry pretended his fake hand was an airplane and made zooming sounds as he flew it around. I double-checked the map, decided that this was the midpoint, and forced myself back into the masses. The information booth was appropriately crowded, and I marched to the front of the line and said, "Who's in charge?"

The guy behind the counter folded his arms.

"This isn't the end of the line, lady."

"I'm a cop," I told him.

"It's PoliceFest. Everyone here is a cop."

The people I'd cut in front of echoed the statement.

"Look," I said, lowering my voice. "I'm on the Chemist case. Have you heard of it? I think he's here, and he's going to kill a bunch of people. Now, who is in charge?"

"Jim. Jim Czajkowski. I'll call him."

He used the walkie-talkie attached to his belt buckle. A minute later a short, slightly pudgy man with a waxed handlebar mustache stepped into the booth.

"I'm Jim, Skokie PD. What's going on?"

I leaned in and spoke softly. "We have reason to believe that this festival might be the target of a terrorist attack. Have you noticed anything unusual?"

"Not really. I mean, setting up an event like this is a nightmare. There are always snags."

"What kind of snags?"

"Well, the music tent has collapsed twice. The garbage cans are filling up faster than expected. Some moron drank too much and cracked open his skull."

"Are you sure it was alcohol?"

"I'm sure. He got into a drinking contest with his buddies."

"Anything else out of the ordinary? Problems? Complaints? Maybe from before the festival started?"

"There's that damn portable toilet truck."

Where had I recently heard about portable toilets? Herb. He was searching for a stolen truck.

"What about the truck?"

"Parked here real early this morning, right in the middle of everything, but didn't unload. All of those Porta Potties are sitting up there, just taking up space. We can't even take them down ourselves, because they're wrapped up in chains."

"Show me."

Jim led the way. Harry once again fell into step behind me, this time eating a hot dog. We walked past a Tilt-A-Whirl, a ring toss booth, and the aforementioned music tent, which appeared to have collapsed again. Eventually, we wound up behind a row of carny game booths on a small patch of dirt, next to a semi with a flatbed trailer attached. Stacked on the trailer were thirty-six portable toilets.

"Yipes!" McGlade said. "Johns!"

Jim spit onto the grass. "Someone just drove them up and left them there. And look at the way they're chained together."

I moved closer and agreed it went above and beyond simply securing them to the trailer. The heavy gauge chains formed a net around the toilets, and there were thick padlocks wherever two chains intersected. It would take an hour just to unlock them all.

I pulled out my cell phone and called Herb.

"Hi, Jack. I heard about the Bains wedding. Nice work."

"Thanks. That stolen Porta Potti truck, was it a flatbed, red Peterbilt cab?"

"Yeah."

"Are you at the fest?"

"Bernice and I are in the music tent, watching the volunteers wrestle with the collapsing canvas. Why?"

"I think I found your truck. I'm to the west of you maybe fifty yards, behind the Tilt-A-Whirl."

"I'll be right there."

McGlade had climbed up to the driver's side of the cab and was peering in the window.

"Hey, Jackie. Maybe you should take a look at this."

"What is it?"

"It's a clock."

"Most trucks have clocks, McGlade."

"This one is counting down. It's at 18:52 . . . 51 . . . 50 . . ."

That didn't sound good. Not at all. I turned to Jim.

"We need some tools. Bolt cutters, a saw, anything to get through these chains. Is there a PA system?"

"There's one in the music tent."

"Use it. Get some bomb squad guys over here."

Jim made a face. "If I go on the mike and say we need the bomb squad, people are going to panic. You ever see a human stampede?"

"Announce that it's time for the Bomb Squad Beer Keg Defusing Contest or something stupid like that. Snag the first guy that shows up."

Jim trotted off, and I pulled myself up onto the flatbed and cautiously approached one of the portable toilets. It was an aqua green color, made of fiberglass, about seven feet tall, and had a padlock on the door. The thing wouldn't budge, even when I leaned into it, hard. I wrapped my knuckles on the side and there was a dull thump, like it was full of something. I knelt down and tried to pry away the door using the lower corner. I couldn't get my fingers in the crack.

But I knew who could.

"McGlade! Come here!"

"Where are you?"

"Next to the toilets!"

"I don't have to go right now."

I clenched my teeth, remembered that he had the emotional maturity of a three-year-old, and forced myself to relax.

"Harry, you *do* want me to talk to the mayor, right?"

He sauntered over and stared up at me.

"What do you need, baby? Moral support?"

"You think you can crack one of these things open using your hand?"

"Maybe."

He tried to pull himself onto the trailer, but couldn't get a leg up over the edge. I had to help him.

"Whoa. I need to rest for a minute. Be a good girl and run get me a lemonade."

"Dammit, Harry, we don't have time for you to play around. See if you can open up one of these."

He sighed, crawled over to the toilet, and rolled up his sleeve. I watched, both fascinated and revolted, as he peeled off the flesh-colored rubber, revealing a curved metal claw with one lower thumb and two upper fingers.

"Here, Jackie. Hold my hand."

He tossed me the rubber cover, and I flinched and it fell at my feet. McGlade didn't notice. He'd gripped the lower corner of the Porta Potti and I saw his lips whisper, *"Close."* The fiberglass made a cracking sound, then splintered inward.

"Aw, Christ. That's disgusting. Open."

When McGlade retrieved the claw, it was covered with a brown, pasty goop. He stared at it, scowling, and then tentatively brought it under his nose.

"What the hell is this stuff? Smells kind of like gasoline."

I walked up to him, though I could honestly say it was the last thing in the world I wanted to do. The stuff on his hand had the consistency of toothpaste, and was a brownish gray with various-sized flecks of white and silver.

"Taste it." Harry stuck his claw under my chin. "Lemme know if it's poisonous."

I shoved him aside and bent down to look into the hole he made. The smell of gas was even stronger, and some of the stuff had poured out onto the trailer. Mixed in with the gunk was a one-inch nail.

"Don't touch it!"

McGlade and I looked behind us. Jim was hurrying over with a tall black guy wearing a T-shirt that said *If I Get One More Restraining Order I'm Gonna Kill Someone.*

"What is it?" I asked.

"I'm Murray. CPD, bomb squad."

Murray hopped onto the trailer with much more ease and grace than McGlade, and crouched down next to me. He peered into the hole.

"This is ANFO. Not commercial quality. Looks homemade. But competent. There's aluminum in here. An accelerant."

"It also has nails in it," I said. "Shrapnel?"

"Probably. Shit, that's bad."

"Question." McGlade raised up an arm. "What's ANFO?"

"It's a high explosive. Ammonium nitrate fertilizer mixed with fuel oil. It's what Timothy McVeigh used for the Oklahoma City bombing in 1995."

"Oh my God," McGlade said. He put his good hand on my shoulder. "I'm *so* glad we took your car."

I thought about the last thing the Chemist said to me on the phone. *I had a blast.* When he told me he wasn't going to poison anyone else, that had been the truth.

"Isn't this hard to get?" I asked.

"A few states have restricted policies for buying ammonium nitrate, and some require additives that make it difficult to weaponize. Unfortunately, Illinois isn't one of those states. The process isn't very easy, and it isn't very well-known, but anyone can learn how to make ANFO on the Internet. Luckily, most people get the proportions wrong and blow themselves up."

Murray knocked on the next toilet over, and then the one behind it.

"Are all of these full?"

"We haven't checked. But there's a timer in the cab."

"What's the timer at?"

"Probably about fourteen minutes left."

He hopped off the trailer bed. I followed him.

"Can you jimmy open a truck door?" I asked.

"Yeah."

Murray picked up a concrete block being used as tent ballast and crashed it through the driver's-side window. A moment later he was in the cab, cradling the timer in his hands.

"Bad news. This isn't the timer. It's just a countdown clock, probably synched to the timer, to show the detonation time to the driver. I'm guessing the real timer and detonator are buried in one of those porta stanks."

McGlade laughed. "Heh heh. *Porta stank.*"

"Can you disarm it?" I asked.

"Maybe, if we could find it in time. It might be nothing more than a few sticks of dynamite and a blasting cap. But it's buried in one of those things. Opening all of them up, digging through them, could take hours."

"So what should we do?"

"We have to get everyone out of here."

"Evacuate?" Jim said. "There are over forty thousand people at this festival."

"Well, we need to get all of them away from here within the next thirteen minutes and forty-three seconds."

"How bad is this?" I asked.

"As bad as it gets. When this thing blows, it's going to kill everyone in a one-mile radius."

CHAPTER 37

14 MINUTES

DID YOU SAY a one-mile radius?"

Everyone turned to look at Herb Benedict, who was standing behind us. He wore a blue Hawaiian shirt and khaki shorts, and his plump wife, Bernice, was at his side, equally attired.

"Don't worry, fatso," McGlade said. "You'll probably bounce free of the explosion."

Herb reached for his hip holster, but his wife held his arm back.

"We need to get everyone away from here." On impulse I looked around. People everywhere, at least a mile thick. To get all of them a safe distance was—

"Impossible," Jim said. "We'd never get them all away in time. And if we tried, hundreds would get trampled trying to get away."

Murray looked scared, which scared me, because bomb guys weren't supposed to look scared.

"No one will get away in time." Murray's voice was soft and low. "A pound of ANFO can make a crater a yard deep and kick debris ninety feet away. We've got about eighteen tons of ANFO here. This thing is maybe ten times the size of the Oklahoma City bomb, and it's out in the open with nothing to damper the blast but people. Human tissue won't do much to stop nails moving at thirty-five hundred meters per second."

Everyone leaned away from the truck, and Jim actually took a few steps back.

"Someone drove it in." I forced myself to touch the trailer. "Maybe we can drive it somewhere safe. Anyplace around here that might work? Jim, Skokie is your town."

"I . . . I don't know. Look, we all should leave." Jim was sweating, and he looked ready to bolt. "When this thing blows—"

"Answer the question." Herb's voice was hard.

"There's . . . um . . . there's a few golf courses . . ."

"What's around them?" Murray asked.

"Um . . . houses. Residential areas."

McGlade snorted. "This entire town is one big residential area. If you're going to dump this someplace, at least pick a rich neighborhood. They're insured."

Herb scowled at him. "You got any better ideas, Lefty?"

"Lake Michigan," Harry said. "The water absorbs the energy of the blast, and it also creates some new beachfront property."

Jim shook his head. "The lake is too far away. You won't make it in time."

"Rivers?" I asked. "Big holes? Tunnels? Stadiums?"

"Bomb shelters?" McGlade added.

"A river would be good," Murray said. "ANFO isn't

water resistant. If it's soaked, it might limit the force of the blast."

"How close is the Chicago River?" Herb asked.

"It's about—wait . . . the plant. The Northside Water Reclamation Plant."

"What is that? Sewage treatment?"

Jim nodded. "Yeah. It's about two miles away. It's big. And it's all concrete. Some of those settling tanks are deep too."

"What's around it?" Herb asked.

"Some offices, south of Howard Street. On the west, homes, but not too many. North is a country club, east, a factory, but it will be closed today. So will the offices."

"Okay, Jim, listen carefully. You need to get in touch with the plant, clear them out, and have someone from there call me. You also have to warn the country club and the residents in those houses. Evacuate them, or have them get in their basements."

I gave Jim my phone number, and he programmed it into his phone and began making calls.

"You're the one going?" Herb's chubby face was pinched with anger.

"Yeah," I said.

He folded his arms. "Since when can you drive a semi?"

"How hard can it be?"

"Can you even drive stick shift?"

Now I folded my arms. "I've seen other people. I think I can figure it out."

Harry shook his head. "Even if you can drive stick

shift, a truck is an entirely different animal. It's a ten-speed manual transmission, and it's not synchronized like a car."

"Can *you* drive this semi?" Herb asked him.

McGlade waved his robotic hand in Herb's face.

"Sure I can, Einstein. I'll shift gears with my ass."

"How about you use that big mouth of yours instead?" Herb said. "I bet it's been on quite a few gearshifts in the past."

McGlade's eyebrows creased, and then he started to laugh. "That one was actually pretty good."

I put my hand on Harry's shoulder, drawing his attention. "What if I helped you shift?"

"It's too hard, Jackie. You have to match the engine revs with the transmission revs. There's a rhythm to it. You mess it up, you can stall out, or even strip the gears. Plus steering the damn thing is a bitch."

Herb said, "You're a coward."

McGlade nodded. "There's also that."

"Harry, if you save forty thousand people, half of them cops, I'm sure the mayor would let you have a liquor license in the middle of the goddamn Lincoln Park Zoo."

A sly grin formed on Harry's unshaven face. "In the zoo? You think?"

"I've done some calculations." Murray had a calculator in his big hands. I guess bombies didn't travel without one. "You'll need to be a mile away after you leave the truck, so if someone follows you in a car, you'd need at least ninety seconds to get out of there to have a chance at surviving."

Herb nodded. "I can do that."

I asked, "Do what?"

"I'll meet you guys there, drive you to safety."

"Herb . . ." Bernice and I said in unison.

"If you two can get the truck to the plant, I'll be there to pick you up." Herb kissed his wife on the forehead. "It'll be okay, dear."

Bernice put her hands on his cheeks. She'd begun to cry.

"I'm warning you, Herb Benedict. If you get yourself blown up, I'm going to date younger men."

McGlade raised his hand. "I'm younger. And with me, there's no risk of smothering to death."

"How safe is this stuff to haul?" I asked, eyeing Herb to make sure he didn't shoot McGlade.

"ANFO is pretty stable," Murray said. "It won't ignite even if you fire a few bullets into it. It should be safe to transport. Just try to avoid any major collisions."

"We'll try our best."

"Is there anything else I can do?" Murray asked.

"Clear a path from here to the street. We need to get these people out of the way so we can get through." I looked at Harry. "Are you out or are you in?"

"You sure I'll get a liquor license?"

"I guarantee the mayor will be there for the ribbon-cutting ceremony."

McGlade grinned. "Ten-four, good buddy. Let's get it into gear and put the hammer down."

"Okay, it's a go." I looked at the cab and frowned. "Does anyone know how to hot-wire a semi?"

CHAPTER 38

9 MINUTES

WE WASTED TOO MUCH TIME trying to start the truck. McGlade tore open the steering column housing and tried crossing several different wires, but all he accomplished was turning the dashboard lights on and off.

Herb stuck his head in the door. "It's the red wires."

"I'm crossing the red wires. It isn't doing anything."

I watched the timer count down and felt myself getting sicker and sicker.

"Are you sure they're crossed?" Herb said.

"They're crossed! You want to squeeze your fat ass up here again and take a look?"

"You've got the truck in second gear."

"It's supposed to be in second gear. If you don't stop bugging me, I'm going to stick my claw so far up your—"

From behind us: "Is there a brown wire?"

Someone else had joined the party. A tall woman, young, brunette, tattoos on bare arms, named Renée Davidson. Bernice had apparently gone off and brought back someone who knew what the hell she was doing.

"Yeah," McGlade said. "There's a brown one."

Davidson climbed onto the foot platform, next to the driver's-side door.

"The red ones are the ignition wires, the brown one is the starter wire. Strip the brown one and touch it to the reds."

"Stripping is kind of a problem one-handed. Porky had to strip the other ones, and he almost got stuck."

"Let me give it a try," Davidson offered.

"Sure. We won't have to grease your hips first."

McGlade scooted over. Davidson removed the folding knife clipped to her belt, bent under the steering wheel, and five seconds later the truck coughed and roared to life.

"The steering column is still locked," she said. "You won't be able to turn unless you break the mechanism. It's in the ignition."

"That I can do," McGlade said. He held his claw over the key switch and said, "Close." His hand crunched down on the mechanism and cracked it off.

"Can you drive a truck?" I asked Davidson.

Her shoulders slumped. "I'm here with my kids. I can't take the risk. I'm sorry."

She didn't look too sorry, but I really couldn't blame her. I thanked her for the help and watched her jog off. Herb checked his watch.

"I'll meet you there, Jack. My car is parked about three blocks away. I have to get moving."

"Good luck," I told him.

He nodded, and then hurried into the crowd.

"Don't run!" McGlade called after him. "Don't risk the heart attack!"

I ran around to the passenger side, grabbed the side bar, and swung myself up in the seat. I considered putting on my seat belt, and decided there was no point when I had forty thousand pounds of high explosive five feet behind me. Harry closed his door, adjusted his seat, then played around with his side mirror. He glanced over at mine.

"Jackie, can you tilt your mirror forward just a bit?"

I cranked down the window, reached for the mirror, and froze. There, plain as day, was a perfect latent fingerprint, gracing the lower right-hand corner of the mirror glass. The Chemist's? He'd been fanatical about not leaving prints, but had he gotten a little careless? Especially since he figured the truck would be obliterated in the explosion?

"Jackie, the mirror."

I held the back and nudged it forward an inch.

"Is that better?"

"I have no idea. Your big gray head is in the way."

"Just get moving, McGlade." I fished through my purse, looking for my eye shadow.

"Sure. Get moving. Okay. Let's see. Gas . . . bring up the RPM . . . clutch . . . neutral . . . neutral . . . dammit, Jackie, help me get this into neutral."

He was trying to use his fake hand, and his claw kept sliding off the shifter ball knob.

"Where is it?"

"The middle."

I fought with the stick and popped it into the center.

"Okay, I'm hitting the clutch, put it into first."

I did, and the truck jerked and then began to groan and shudder without actually moving.

"Oops, I'm doing something wrong."

The truck wasn't moving, but the engine revved into the red zone and the cab began to bounce.

"McGlade, it's probably not a good thing to shake up the bomb."

"I'm thinking . . . Hold on . . ."

"Harry—"

"Shit! The trailer hand brake." He gripped another stick, pulled it back, and the truck lurched forward. "My bad."

He drove us off the patch of dirt and down the path Murray had cleared, into the throng of people. I found my eye shadow and dabbed the applicator into the purple powder. I was lightly dusting the latent print on the mirror when a tremendous piercing sound shook the floorboards, almost causing me to drop my brush and wet myself. It was McGlade, tugging on the pull cord for the horn.

"Dammit, Harry, I thought we blew up."

"These people need to get out of my way."

I peered out the front window and saw a man in a wheelchair in our path, twenty yards ahead.

"Watch out for the disabled guy."

"I see him."

We closed to within ten yards.

"You're heading right for him."

"He needs to move."

Five yards. McGlade blared the horn again.

"HARRY!"

We bumped the man, and he went careening off to the side at a very high speed.

"Jesus, McGlade! You hit him!"

"He should have moved faster."

"He was handicapped!"

"It's not like I did anything to make his life any worse. He already couldn't walk."

My cell phone buzzed, and I picked it up.

"Daniels."

"Jim Czajkowski told me to call you. I'm Dalton Forrester from Northside Treatment. You're bringing a bomb to my plant?"

"That's the idea, Dalton."

"We supply close to two hundred thousand homes and businesses with fresh water. If you blow up the facility, they could be without water for weeks."

"Simple math, Dalton. People without any water is a better deal than water without any people. Have you evacuated your staff?"

"Yeah. I was the last one to leave. I'm heading home to my family, five miles away. Is that far enough?"

"It should be. What's the best place to drop off this payload?"

"It's a truck, right? Avoid the settling tanks. Those are the round ones. They aren't very deep, and there is skimming machinery that you could get stuck on. You should sink it in one of the aeration pools. They're square, about an acre wide, twenty feet deep. That's where the microorganisms eat all the organic solids. When you turn into the plant off of Howard, go left, to the west. And good luck getting here—the roads are all blocked off."

Czajkowski moved fast. I thanked Dalton, hung up, and went back to dusting. McGlade hit the horn again, and I heard someone scream.

"Old lady," Harry said. "I think I missed her. Mostly."

"McGlade, you need to—"

"Turning onto Pratt. It's going to be tight. Hold on."

The truck smacked into two parked cars—sending them off into opposite directions as if they were toys—jumping the curb and screeching onto the asphalt, beelining for an office building straight ahead. McGlade wrestled with the steering wheel, and we kissed the brick wall, pulled past, and then straightened out onto the street.

"Okay, I'm going to turn onto Hamlin. Get ready to shift. Ready?"

I had turned my attention back to the latent on the mirror. The eye shadow wasn't fingerprint powder, but it had done a fair job clinging to the oils and making the ridges stand out.

"Jackie! You with me?"

"Yeah, Harry. Say when."

"Okay, gas . . . clutch . . . neutral . . . shit!"

Ahead of us on Hamlin was a gridlock of cars, none of them moving.

McGlade hit the brakes, and the tires squealed, but the truck groaned and didn't slow down.

"The hand brake!" he yelled, his claw bouncing off the stick.

I looked out the side window and watched, horrified, as the trailer kicked out to the side and the truck began to jackknife.

CHAPTER 39

6 MINUTES

SERGEANT HERB BENEDICT, gun in hand, jogs up the sidewalk, past one idling car after another. His own car is pinned between three others, impossible to drive. The streets are jammed, and nothing is moving. It's like all of Skokie has become a giant parking lot.

He's looking for a car, any car, that isn't trapped, but even the intersections are completely congested. A hundred horns are sounding off around him, coupled with angry shouts. He's still two miles away from the treatment plant, and if he doesn't find a vehicle quickly, Jack and McGlade are going to die. In McGlade's case, it's no big loss. But Jack is like a sister.

Switching to Robbery had been the hardest thing Herb had ever done. He felt like he was betraying, and abandoning, his best friend. He had hoped that Jack would recognize how ridiculously dangerous their job had become, and would follow him. But she didn't.

She keeps on risking her life for the Job, Herb thought, and here I am, yet again, running toward danger rather than away from it, to try and save her life.

An engine, behind him. He stops and turns, sees a

car has gotten sick of the traffic and driven onto the sidewalk. Something older and sporty, a Challenger or a GTO. Perfect. Herb tucks his 9mm into his hip holster and holds up his badge. He can commandeer this car and—

The car accelerates. The driver either doesn't see him or doesn't care. Herb yells, but his voice isn't audible above all of the honking. He realizes the car is going to hit him, and he tries to step to the side.

At the last possible moment, the car swerves right, but it isn't fast enough, and the back end clips Herb and sends him spinning into a storefront window. He bounces off the glass and slams onto the pavement, where he lies, unmoving, in a growing pool of blood.

CHAPTER 40

5 MINUTES

PUT IT IN GEAR!" McGlade screamed, an octave higher than his normal voice. I helped him tug the shifter into second, and the cab shook and then jolted forward. Behind us, the trailer rocked from side to side, but quickly straightened out. This saved us from jackknifing, but didn't save us from the line of cars fifty yards ahead and closing.

He tugged the wheel to the right, forcing the truck up onto the carefully maintained lawn of an office complex. Harry continued to turn, winding up behind the building in the back parking lot, heading straight for a fence.

"McGlade . . ."

"Don't worry. I do this all the time in Grand Theft Auto."

"That's a video game."

"Pac-Man is a video game. GTA is a way of life."

The semi plowed through the fence with almost no resistance, and then we were in a factory loading area.

"Gear down on three. One . . . two . . . three."

I helped him shift into first, and the truck slowed down, allowing McGlade to navigate a sharp turn. We bounced over a curb and wound up on Morse going east. I looked at the countdown clock and felt ill. We were still over a mile away from the treatment plant and heading in the wrong direction.

"Train tracks ahead," Harry said. "I have an idea."

McGlade swung the truck left, and we ran parallel to the tracks on the gravel. There was a slight grade, maybe five percent, but the truck didn't tip.

"Let's go to second . . . now."

The truck picked up speed, and I listened to the RPMs and was able to gauge when to put it into third, and then fourth. The ride was bumpy, and tilted, but we were making good time, and there were no cars blocking our way. McGlade hummed the song "Convoy," off-key. I once again turned my attention to the latent on the mirror.

"Gimme your phone," I told him.

"My new one? Why?"

"Just do it."

"It's in my right pants pocket. Help yourself."

I reached for his lap, then hesitated. It was like willfully sticking your hand into a mousetrap. Not having any other choice, I slipped a finger in, shuddering.

"It's at the bottom. Reach around for it."

I was about to go deeper when I realized the obvious.

"How could you put anything in your right pocket with a mechanical hand?"

He smiled, sheepish.

"Caught me. It's in my jacket."

I muttered *asshole* under my breath and quickly found the high-tech phone in his jacket.

"How do I use the camera?"

"Go to the menu first."

I stared at the device, which looked slightly more complicated than the helm of a nuclear submarine.

"Is this a touch screen?"

"There's a menu button in the center of the keypad."

"What's it look like?"

"It looks like the menu button. It says *menu* on it."

"There are six thousand buttons."

"Give it to me."

"Harry, keep your eyes on the—"

The wheels caught on the tracks and hopped them, jerking the whole truck to the right. We hit one railroad tie after another in rapid succession, each feeling like it would rip us apart.

"Downshift!" McGlade screamed, while he reached lefty for the hand brake. I fought the ball knob into neutral, then tried to steady the wheel as we slowed down, and finally stalled.

I checked my mirror, and miraculously the trailer was still attached.

"Look." Harry tore the phone from my hand and pressed something. "There's the damn menu button. Happy now?"

"I'd be happier if we got moving. We've only got—"

A whistle cut me off. It was followed by a familiar *ding ding ding* sound, coming from the intersection up ahead.

"No way," Harry said. "No fucking way."

I squinted into the distance and saw the small black dot of a train.

CHAPTER 41

4 MINUTES

Start the truck, McGlade."

"You think?"

I cursed myself for not telling Jim to also stop all train traffic, but hindsight is always 20/20. Harry stuck his butt in my face and bent under the steering column, fussing with the wires.

"It was brown, right?"

"Yeah, touch the brown to the red."

"It's too dark. They're all brown. Hold on."

He dug into his pocket—his left one—and removed a set of keys.

"Damn. My key chain light is out."

"Open the door, McGlade. Get some sunlight in here."

"This thing had a five-year warranty."

"McGlade!"

He opened his door and climbed onto the foot stand. I chanced a look at the oncoming train. I'm not a good judge of distance, but I estimated that we had roughly thirty seconds before impact. I had an irrational urge to jump out of the cab and run for it. Or maybe it wasn't irrational. It was, however, pointless. Frightened as I was, I wouldn't be able to run a mile in thirty seconds.

I wondered if anything poignant should be playing through my head, about my life or my past or my dreams, but the only thing I could focus on was the fingerprint. If I died, I wanted the Chemist caught. I fumbled with the phone menu until I found the camera selection, and then I held it up to latent, using the WYSIWYG screen to make sure I framed it well.

"I'm touching the wires. Nothing is happening."

Another train whistle, louder and deeper.

"Are we in second gear?" McGlade asked.

I clicked the picture, then hit menu to access e-mail.

"Jackie! Put it in second!"

I looked up at the train. Real close now. I could see it was Metra—a commuter—probably loaded with people. I grabbed the shifter, but it didn't move.

"The clutch, McGlade!"

He hit the clutch with his hand, I popped it into second gear, and the truck roared to life. We had maybe ten seconds before the big bang. I heard a painful screeching of the train hitting the brakes, McGlade pulled himself up behind the wheel and revved the engine, and we shifted into first. The truck jerked forward, Harry hit the gas, and he muscled it over the tracks and down the incline, toward the street. The train squealed past.

"No problem," he said, turning onto St. Louis Drive. "That missed us by at least six seconds."

I tasted copper. I'd bitten the inside of my cheek hard enough to draw blood.

St. Louis was free of cars, and it was a straight shot to the treatment plant, only a few blocks ahead.

"Your fat partner better be there."

"He'll be there."

I finished typing in Hajek's e-mail address, which I remembered from the other day, and sent him the fingerprint picture with a note saying *Chemist*. Then I called Herb. A recording answered.

"The cellular customer you are trying to reach is currently unavailable. Please try your call again later."

I tried again. Same result. Third time wasn't any different. I checked the clock. A little over two minutes left.

Not enough time for us to get away.

If Harry left now, maybe he could find another car to escape the blast in time, or some kind of shelter like a basement.

"You need to get out, McGlade."

"Get out of what?"

"The truck. I can't get in touch with Herb. If all the streets are as backed up as Hamlin, he's not going to be there on time."

Harry looked at me.

"So we just leave the truck here, in the street?"

"No." I swallowed. "I'm taking it to the plant by myself."

"Gotcha. Nice knowing you, Jackie."

He swung open his door.

Two seconds passed. Five. But he didn't leap out.

"Dammit, Harry, get the hell out of here."

I shoved him. He didn't budge.

"Harry! Go!"

McGlade closed the door.

"Fatso will show up. I can't stand that guy, but he'll find a way."

"What if he doesn't? Don't you want to live?"

McGlade drummed his fingers across the top of the steering wheel.

"Remember the end of *Butch Cassidy and the Sundance Kid*? Where they both run out of the building to face the entire Bolivian army, and then the movie freeze-frames because you know they're both going to die?"

"Yeah," I said.

"Wasn't that the coolest?"

I understood what he was saying, and found myself getting a little choked up. "It was pretty cool, Harry."

McGlade turned to me, and winked.

"Last stop just ahead, Butch."

Harry turned right onto Howard Street, and we faced the sprawling sewage treatment complex. At least half a mile long, and maybe three-quarters of a mile wide, on a big patch of very green land.

We hung a left onto the access road, passing two towering brick buildings connected by a massive black air pipe, which stretched over our heads and into the distance like a monorail. The entrance was surrounded by trees, probably planted there to disguise the community eyesore. They should have planted flowers instead. The smell of sewage and waste overpowered us when we pulled onto Howard, and steadily increased the closer we got. *Ripe* was a good word. *Revolting* was even better.

"You think we got it bad?" Harry said. "At least we don't have to work here."

"Go left. We're looking for the aeration tanks."

"Those round ones?" McGlade pointed to a group of eight settling tanks on our left, each the size of a large swimming pool.

"No. Ahead of us. That big one."

It looked like a small, filthy lake, except it was a perfect rectangle, and the stuff floating on the surface wasn't algae.

"What should we do?" Harry asked. "Jump out and let the truck coast in?"

"That's probably the best way."

"Should I slow down?"

I noted we were going about twenty miles an hour.

"Why bother? If we hurt ourselves, we won't feel it for long."

McGlade aimed the truck for the water, and we both opened our doors.

"If there's an afterlife," he said, "you owe me some sex."

I looked down at how fast the ground was moving, reminded myself that fear didn't matter at this point, and jumped from the cab at the same time as Harry.

CHAPTER 42

90 SECONDS

I HIT THE PAVEMENT like a paratrooper, ankles tight together and knees bent. It did nothing to cushion my fall. I skidded across the pavement like a skipping stone and then turned a cartwheel or two onto the grass. When the world stopped spinning, I knew I'd done something bad to my right ankle, and I had a scrape across my left palm that looked like I'd taken a belt sander to it.

I sat up, my head screaming at me. It took me a few seconds to find the goose egg, near my crown, leaking blood. I'd lost my Cubs cap.

Gagging screams to my left. McGlade, pulling himself up out of the aeration tank. He looked like a mud monster, rising from the swamp. He lumbered toward me, spitting out brown water, and as he got closer I noted he had several multicolored things stuck to his body.

"You've got a . . . condom on your shoulder."

He looked at it, and flicked it off with his claw.

"Yuck. And what the hell is this plastic thing?"

"It's an applicator."

"Do I want to know what it applies?"

"Probably not."

The truck had almost completely sunk. Bubbles were still coming up from the cab, and the impact waves had disturbed the entire pool, sloshing filthy water up onto the land. Mission accomplished. But I was having a hard time feeling any sense of accomplishment. Even dampened by the water and the concrete, the blast would destroy this entire plant. We were as good as dead.

McGlade rubbed some muck off his face and gave me a lecherous grin.

"So . . . about that sex you owe me."

I checked my watch. "We've only got fifty seconds left."

"I only need thirty."

"Sorry, Harry. Not even if you weren't covered with human waste."

He pouted.

"Come on, Jackie. I've always known you had a little thing for me."

I started to laugh. "You're the one with the little thing."

McGlade started to laugh too. And then we were hugging each other, laughing like fools, and I noticed he was angling me toward the truck, like a shield, which made me laugh even harder.

"You're such an asshole, McGlade."

"You love me. Admit it."

"I admit nothing. I—"

A sound, to the south. Mechanical. Rumbling. Growing louder.

"A helicopter." McGlade shielded his eyes from the sun and peered into the distance. "Son of a bitch."

"I'll second that."

As it came into focus, I saw it was a Chicago police chopper, coming at us fast. Real fast. I looked at my watch. We had fifteen seconds left.

"WE DON'T HAVE TIME TO LAND!" the megaphone boomed, and I'd recognize that voice anywhere.

Herb.

"GRAB THE LADDER! WE CAN ONLY MAKE ONE PASS!"

Harry and I watched as a rescue ladder unfurled below the landing skids. The bird swooped in low, the bottom of the ladder sparking against the pavement. It was coming so quick, it would knock out our teeth, or yank our shoulders from our sockets. I decided I could live with either.

At nine seconds until detonation, the ladder hit us with the force of a car wreck. I'd been aiming to get my arm in between the rungs, and I did it, getting a smack in the chest that knocked the wind out of me and probably broke a few ribs. I was jerked off my feet, and so was Harry. The helicopter began a rapid ascent, but it was too fast, too much G force, too much wind resistance, and I just couldn't hold on.

My grip failed, and as I began to fall I wondered what would kill me first, the ground or the explosion.

CHAPTER 43

4 SECONDS

I DIDN'T FALL.

McGlade—stupid, offensive, obnoxious McGlade —wrapped his legs around my waist in a fireman rescue, and I squinted through the rushing air and saw his mechanical hand locked tight onto a ladder rung.

We climbed even faster, the treatment plant getting smaller and smaller until the cloud cover made it disappear. I held on to Harry's waist, and looped an elbow around the ladder.

And then the world exploded.

It wasn't a *bang*. More like a *whoomp*. Beneath the clouds came a searing flash of light, and then a wall of hot air and detritus, which rocked the whirly-bird like a toy boat in a hurricane. We tilted to the side until the ladder was actually higher than the propeller, back the other way, and into a spiral that once again broke my grip, but not Harry's. I squeezed my eyes shut, unsure which way was which, only that I was alive for a little while longer and damn grateful for it.

Then the storm passed. The chopper regained control and began a steady descent that took a tremendous amount of strain off of my muscles and joints, making hanging on almost child's play. We crept down past the clouds, and I looked toward the treatment plant and saw a giant column of smoke where it used to be. But the houses to the west, and the businesses to the south, seemed intact. It was strangely quiet, and I realized the explosion had knocked out my hearing, which for some reason was more peaceful to me than frightening.

We landed on the country club green, though it wasn't actually green anymore. Sludge and waste and debris was spewed across the golf course, making it look like a dump. It was still coming down from the sky too, a foul black drizzle mixed with smoke and tiny bits of dirt.

When my feet touched land I cried out in pain from five different places at once, but I was in better shape than McGlade. His prosthesis was soaked in blood, which had leaked from where it was attached to his stump, and his shoulder was noticeably dislocated. Eyes closed. No movement at all. But his legs remained locked around my waist.

"Harry!" I yelled, barely able to hear my own voice.

A dozen things flashed through my mind. Had he been hit by some shrapnel? One of the nails from the bomb? Some sort of internal injury? A fast-acting disease from the raw sewage he'd flopped around in?

I gave McGlade a shake, and one eye peeked open.

"Is it over?" he asked.

I nodded.

"Did we live?"

I nodded again.

He smiled. "For a moment there I thought we were in trouble."

I smiled back. "Nice work, Sundance."

"You *so* owe me some sex."

I disentangled myself from Harry and managed to stand up, albeit painfully. A few yards away, the helicopter powered off and a beaten-up Herb hopped out. He hobbled over to us, his face awash with concern.

"Jack! Are you okay?"

He came to me, approaching slowly, and I threw my arms around his shoulders and hugged him.

"Thanks, Herb."

I felt his strong arms patting my back. "Somebody's gotta save your ass."

After the male-bonding, I pulled away and sized him up. Herb didn't look much better than I did— skinned knees, bleeding head, torn shirt.

"What happened?" I asked.

"A little car trouble. Nothing serious. I was lucky my phone didn't break; I wouldn't have been able to call for the chopper."

I heard a very faint sound. It was music, some heavy metal song from the eighties.

"Speaking of." Herb pointed. "Your pocket."

I stuck my hand in and pulled out Harry's phone, surprised it had survived. I'd have to pick up one of these things.

"Daniels," I answered.

"Lieutenant? Is that you? It's Hajek, at the crime lab. Are you the one that sent me the fingerprint from this phone?"

"Yeah. What have you got?"

"I got a trace. It belongs to a postal worker named Carey Schimmel."

I knew that name.

"He was the guy who delivered the extortion letter to the superintendent's office, the one covered in BT."

And it suddenly made sense why the Chemist was so paranoid about leaving prints. Postal workers are government employees, and they get fingerprinted when they're hired. Schimmel's prints were on file. I remembered his brief statement, and then wanted to kick myself.

"He said he wore gloves. But there were no other prints on that letter, other than from people at police headquarters. Dammit, how did we miss that?"

Hajek groaned. "It was staring us right in the face. A dozen people in the post office would have touched that letter, left some prints. But none of them did, because Schimmel was the only one who handled it. Did we even check to see if headquarters was on his route?"

"No," I said, feeling like an ass. "Does he have a record?"

"No, he's clean. But I've got his current address. He lives in Forest Glen."

That was a Chicago neighborhood on the north side, only a few miles away.

"Call the super. Get a warrant. We'll be there in two minutes."

"Hold on, I'm sending you a JPEG of his driver's license picture."

I shared the information with Herb, and the chopper pilot, a woman called Leaky. She radioed base to get coordinates. Next, I approached Harry, who appeared to have successfully snapped his shoulder back into place, but not without consequences. He was moaning, and tears had left some clean trails in the filth on his cheeks.

"Got any morphine on you, Jackie? Or crack?"

"You'll get some help soon, Harry."

"Going to drop me off at the hospital?"

"No. You're staying here."

"No I'm not."

"We'll send an ambulance for you."

"I'd like that, but I have to come with." He pointed to his mechanical hand, still locked on to the ladder rung. "It won't come off."

Against Herb's protestations, we helped McGlade into the bird.

"No grab-ass," Harry warned him.

"I'll try to restrain myself."

"No reach-around either, Sir Eats-A-Lot."

"I did save your life. How about a thank-you?"

"Be honest. The reason you came charging in here so fast is because you thought I had a cruller in my pocket."

"God, you're an asshole."

Once we were airborne, I played with Harry's phone and managed to access the Internet. After sifting through an extraordinary number of e-mails that involved porn, much of it the *chunky booty* variety, I found the picture from Hajek. Carey Schimmel was an average-looking white male, thirty-five years old, dark blond hair, and brown eyes. I remembered those eyes. They were the same eyes I saw in Records.

I Googled "Carey Schimmel" and got a hit that referenced a lawsuit from five years ago. An old newspaper article:

SLAIN WOMAN'S BOYFRIEND LASHES OUT

Merle and Felicity Hotham of Cicero settled out of court today in a wrongful death suit brought against the city of Chicago. The Hothams claimed the police department's late response to a 911 call resulted in their daughter's death.

Tracey Hotham, 29, died last August at the hands of convicted murderer Martin Welch, during an attack that lasted over fifty minutes. Hotham reportedly dialed the 911 Emergency number just as Welch entered the Chicago apartment she shared with her fiancé, Carey Schimmel. She was beaten, raped, and strangled in a 53-minute ordeal that ended just before the police arrived.

Sources say the settlement, an undisclosed sum, was well below the two million dollars in damages originally sought. Schimmel was reportedly outraged at the announcement, calling the parents "cowards," and was removed from the courtroom when he began to chant "the system doesn't work."

Welch, sentenced to life for the attack, is currently serving time in Joliet State Prison.

I shared this with Herb.

"I'd be pissed too," he said. "But not enough to poison half the city and try to blow up forty thousand people."

We set down a block away from Schimmel's house, in an empty public baseball field. I checked my ankle holster, which still held the AMT. Leaky unlocked the helicopter's anti-riot arsenal, and offered Herb a 40mm multi-launcher with ten nonlethal beanbag rounds. The large silver canisters were packed with gunpowder, but instead of a lead bullet or buckshot, the projectile was essentially a small, woven Hacky Sack. It hit with enough velocity to knock down a three-hundred-pound linebacker.

"You sure you're ready for this?" Herb asked. "You look pretty banged up."

"I'll manage. How about you? This is a long way from Robbery."

"I wouldn't miss this for the world." Herb dropped the final cartridge into the weapon's cylinder and snapped the breach closed. "You think he's still in town?"

I thought about the Chemist, hating the police so much that he spent years planning this elaborate revenge scheme.

"I'm sure of it. He needed to hear the *boom*."

"How about the warrant?"

"Probable cause. We believe that retired CPD officer Jason Alger is being held inside Schimmel's residence against his will."

"That works for me." Herb grinned. "Partner."

He helped me out of the chopper, and we went to go pay the Chemist a visit—one he wasn't expecting, and definitely wouldn't enjoy.

CHAPTER 44

THE EXPLOSION IS SPECTACULAR. Standing in his backyard, Carey Schimmel actually feels the ground shake beneath him, and he's seven miles away. The Chemist has been dreaming about this day, this moment, for so long, and it has finally arrived.

After six years, three months, and fifteen days, he's finally fulfilled.

He watches the smoke cloud drift upward for several minutes, then goes back into the house and turns on the television to see the devastation up close.

The first reports are sketchy, but he expected that.

"Something has exploded in the village of Skokie. We'll have more information as reports come in."

There is much speculation. A gas line? Terrorists? The first cameras on the scene show smoke and wreckage. He microwaves some popcorn and waits expectantly for the video of the slaughter to be broadcast.

CNN has a special report. So does Fox. Channel 5 and channel 9 interrupt the regularly scheduled programming with breaking news. But no one knows anything. He wonders if he should call, help them out. Maybe he'll do that tomorrow, from the cabana he's renting in Mexico. Reveal everything about the Chemist, and what Chicago has covered up.

"I got them, Tracey," he says. "I got them good."

This is how revenge tastes, and it is delicious.

Just in, the source of the explosion has been pinpointed to the Northside Water Reclamation Plant, on 3500 West Howard Street. So far, there have been no reported casualties.

The smile freezes on Schimmel's face. What is this, a cover-up? A government conspiracy?

He watches it, live. There's the plant, blown up. The debris, scattered all over the street. Is this some kind of old footage, used to spin the truth?

No. These are definitely pictures of Skokie, and it's happening right now. But how could they have figured it out? How could they have—

There's a banging on the front door. "Carey Schimmel, this is the Chicago police!"

Schimmel doesn't think, he acts. He assumes they're also covering the back door, so he enters the kitchen, climbs onto the sink, opens the window, and crawls out face-first. The money is still in the house, but he isn't considering the money. Escape is not an option. He means to kill as many cops as he can before they take him down.

He rolls onto the lawn and runs to the greenhouse. To get his jet injector. To make his last stand.

CHAPTER 45

FREEZE!"

Schimmel didn't freeze, and I didn't fire; he was ten yards away and moving fast, and with the short-barreled AMT I'd just be wasting bullets. The quick glimpse I caught didn't reveal if he had any weapons or not.

"Herb! Around back!"

I limped in pursuit. My ankle was swollen from the truck leap, but the pain was minimal compared to my resolve. I wasn't going to let this guy get away.

He stopped in front of the greenhouse—a large glass structure that took up much of his backyard—and fussed with the door. I closed to within twenty feet and yelled, "Hands in the air!" He didn't comply, and I fired twice, but he was moving fast and crouching down, and I missed both shots. He was inside his garden of death before I could adjust my aim.

Herb met me at the greenhouse entrance, told me to stand back, and pumped two beanbag rounds through the locked door, shattering the glass. I went in first, my weapon in a two-handed grip, and was enveloped by moist heat.

It was big, bigger than it seemed from the outside.

About the size of a small house, with opaque plastic partitions serving as walls. All around me were plants, rows and rows of plants, some of them as high as the glass ceiling. Flowers, in every imaginable color, trees, vines, even a table covered with brownish moss. It smelled fragrant, tropical, and the sweat had already broken out on my brow.

There were plenty of places to hide. The safe thing to do would be to wait for backup. Or maybe burn the entire structure to the ground. The foliage looked harmless, but I knew better. Each lovely bit of flora promised a different, horrible death.

I moved slowly, keeping my elbows tucked in, trying not to touch anything. Herb lumbered in a few steps behind me, and he went left while I stayed right. We would work the perimeter first, moving in opposite concentric circles until we reached the center.

I crept past a bed of striking red flowers, but restrained myself from gathering up a bouquet. Beyond them was a large compost heap, a refrigerator, a workbench, a pallet of stacked brown boxes—

I froze, my feet growing roots.

"Oh, Jesus."

Those weren't boxes. They were beehives. And the bees noticed my arrival, several hundred of them swarming out of the box and over to me, to investigate the intruder.

I tried to remember everything I'd ever learned about bees, and I'd learned a lot since almost dying from that sting years ago. They were attracted to sugar, and perfume. They attacked the color black. They attacked when provoked. They hated sudden movements, or loud noises. After a bee stung you, its stinger pulled out and it died, but the stinger continued to pump poison into your body. Bees were attracted to CO_2, to your breath. Each year, a hundred people in the United States were killed by bees, mostly because of allergies like mine. Once a bee stung you, it released a pheromone that made other bees sting in the same spot. But all the experts agreed that if you don't bother them, they won't bother you.

All of these things swirled through my head as the bees buzzed around me. One landed on my bare arm. Another flew into my face, bouncing off my nose. I held my breath, shut my eyes, and tried to stop trembling. I needed to back up, to get out of there, but my feet wouldn't move. This was so much worse than the cockroaches. This was worse than anything I'd ever encountered. I was too scared to even speak.

Buzzing, so close to my ear that I flinched. Bees on my hands now, on my neck, on my face. Some of them crawling. Some of them content to just stay there and find the best place to sting.

"Afraid of bees, Lieutenant?"

I squinted, saw the Chemist standing next to the hive, about eight feet away from me. He had a jet injector in his hand. I raised my gun.

"If you shoot, they'll sting you," he said. "These are very ill-tempered bees. I don't like keeping them around, but pure honey has quite a lot of botulism spores in it. It's not the easiest bacteria to culture. Required a lot of trial and error. Years of it, in fact. I've been stung dozens of times. Painful. Normally I don't come in here without my netting on. Why are you so frightened? Are you allergic?"

I was trying to aim at his center mass, but my arms were shaking too badly and I couldn't steady the gun. I was completely, utterly helpless. A bee landed on my lip and tried to crawl up my nose. I flinched, and almost started to cry.

"Allergic, I bet. You look absolutely terrified. Quite a change from the tough cop on the phone. I tell you what—I'm going to do you a favor."

He took a slow step toward me, and I felt my knees begin to buckle.

"This is loaded with ricin"—he held up the jet injector—"derived from the castor bean. It will kill you quickly. I can't promise it will be painless, but it is a much better way to go than anaphylactic shock, gasping for breath."

Another step closer. Now my knees actually did give out, and I fell onto my butt. The bees didn't like the sudden movement, and their buzzing became louder.

"What did you do?" the Chemist asked me. He seemed oddly calm. "Did you drive the truck out of the festival, to the plant?"

I nodded, forcing myself to do something. I thought about bravery. I'd been afraid many times before, but never to the point where it had incapacitated me. Even while in the truck, facing certain death, I'd been able to function. Why should a few lousy bees turn me into an invalid?

"Where is the rest of your squad? I only saw the fat guy. Only two of you came for me?"

I said, "More are coming," and surprised myself by how strong it came out.

"I'd better hurry then. I was thinking this was a final siege, an Alamo. But if it's only you two, then I can kill you both and get away. Then I can start all over again."

He raised the jet injector and took another cautious step forward. I brought up the AMT. My hand was no longer shaking. If I died, I died. Once I accepted that, a lot of the fear went away.

Schimmel paused, looking unsure.

"If you shoot me, they'll sting you."

"Fair trade," I said, my teeth clenched.

"Jackie! Duck!"

I looked to my left, and saw McGlade standing a few yards away, holding a semiautomatic in his left hand. He fired six times. Predictably, all six shots missed Schimmel, the bullets burying themselves into the stacked wooden beehive.

The bees weren't happy. Innately sensing their attacker, they swarmed on Harry.

I rolled backward just as Schimmel sprayed a cloud of ricin at the space I used to occupy. He jumped to the right, then scurried away to the rear of the greenhouse.

I continued to crab-walk backward, to get away from the bees, but they pretty much ignored me, focusing their wrath on McGlade. He ran past me, a cloud of bees around him, and then doubled back and went in the opposite direction, the whole time screaming,

"THEY'RE BITING ME! THEY'RE BITING ME!"

A *BOOM* to my right, and a sharp cry. Beanbag rounds were used to induce what law enforcement officers called "pain compliance." They weren't lethal, but they hurt so badly you wished they were. I limped after the sound and saw Schimmel writhing around on the ground, next to a small aquarium. The jet injector lay a few feet away. Herb was standing over him.

"Where'd you hit him?" I asked.

"Stomach. Want me to peg him a few more times?"

"No need. I think he's been subdued."

Schimmel moaned, doubling up into the fetal position.

"You got cuffs?" Herb asked.

"No. You?"

"No. There's probably something back in the chopper. I'll—"

The Chemist rolled up to his knees and reached for the aquarium beside him, lifting. Before he had a chance to throw it at us, Herb fired another beanbag into his legs.

Schimmel fell, the aquarium crashing down on top of him, dumping water and rocks and brightly colored shells onto his body.

He gasped once.

And then he began to scream.

CHAPTER 46

I FOUND OUT LATER that the brightly colored crea-
tures in that aquarium were called cone snails, and
their toxin was among the most poisonous in the animal
kingdom.

The snails apparently hadn't liked their environment
being disturbed in such a rough fashion, and moments after landing on Schimmel, they showed their disapproval.

First came screaming. Then convulsions. Then spitting blood.

Carey Schimmel died right before the ambulance
arrived, but I think their four-minute response time
would have pleased him.

Along with the ambulance, the police arrived in full
force. Crime scene units. The SRT. K9 units. I think they
came for closure more than anything else, to see the
corpse of the man who had caused them so much pain.
Though the police dog did sniff out a corpse in Schimmel's compost heap—one that was quickly ID'ed as retired cop Jason Alger, as evidenced by his missing fingers.

As the paramedics loaded a very puffy-looking
Harry McGlade into their truck, I asked them to wait a
moment so I could speak to the annoying guy who once
again wound up saving the day.

"Nice job, McGlade."

"Thankth."

His pronunciation wasn't too good, because while he was running around screaming, a bee had flown into his mouth and stung his tongue.

"Where'd you get the gun?" I asked him.

"Chopper. Took it from the cockpit when you guys were playing around with the launcher."

"So your hand wasn't stuck on the ladder?"

He smiled, looking a lot like a lumpy pumpkin. "I knew you'd need my help."

I patted him on the shoulder. "I'll speak to the mayor as soon as I get back to the office. I'll make sure you get your bar."

He shook his head. "No bar."

"I thought you wanted a liquor license."

"I'm not a bar owner," Harry sputtered. He stared at me, hard. "I'm a private eye."

I grinned. "What happened to being a poet?"

"I'm that too. Want to hear one?"

"If it's quick."

"This one is called 'Grandma.' Ready?"

"As I'll ever be."

"My grandma wears a diaper. I really hate to wipe her."

He waited for my reaction. "Stick to private investigation," I told him, then went off to find Herb. He was just getting off the phone with his wife.

"What's the verdict?" I asked.

"Starting tomorrow, I'm back in Homicide. Bernice said it would be selfish of me to waste all of this talent in Robbery."

We embraced. It felt good.

"Welcome back."

"She also said there were zero casualties. The plant and the water absorbed most of the blast. The mayor of Skokie is giving her, me, you, and that idiot McGlade keys to the city."

"I'd settle for a new purse. Mine blew up in that truck."

"It could have been a lot worse."

"Are you kidding? That purse was a Gucci."

Herb offered to share a cab back to Skokie, to pick up our cars, but I couldn't pick up my car without my car keys, which were in my purse. Along with all of my cash and credit cards.

"Can you even get in your house?" Herb asked.

"No."

"You want to stay with us tonight, until you get everything worked out?"

I looked past Herb to Special Agent Rick Reilly, who was headed in our direction.

"No need," I said. "I know someone who won't mind giving me a ride and putting me up for the night."

"You sure?" Herb asked.

I thought about it. Thought about it really hard.

"Yeah. I'm pretty sure."

"Okay. I'll see you soon, partner."

"Bye, Herb."

He waddled off, and I waited for Rick to approach.

CHAPTER 47

THANKS FOR CALLING ME. I know we didn't part on exactly the best of terms."

The Eisenhower Expressway was packed as usual, even on a Sunday. But rather than frustrate me, the stop-and-go traffic had a rhythm to it that was kind of soothing.

"This doesn't mean anything," I told him. "I just needed a ride and a place to sleep."

"I understand."

We were silent for a while.

"Are you hurt?"

"A little. Twisted my ankle, got a bump on the head."

He took his right hand off the steering wheel and went to touch my head. I flinched away from it.

"Sorry," he said.

"It's . . . too soon. We need to take this slow. I'm not even sure if this is the right thing to do." I laughed humorlessly. "Mom is going to hate me."

Wilbur smiled. "Your mother is a tough cookie, but she could never hate you."

"She sure hates you."

"Staying would have been bad for her. She wasn't getting the love she deserved, and I was holding her back."

"How do you mean?"

"She always wanted to be a police officer. Talked about it when we were dating. But when we got married, she dropped the subject. *Married women don't have careers,* she said. *I'm a wife and a mother now.* When I left, I offered to support both of you. Your mother took child support, but she wouldn't take alimony. Proud woman. Strong. Like you."

"Wilbur, I'm really not comfortable with you talking about me like you know me. How do you know I'm strong?"

"I know."

I turned away from him, closed my eyes until we arrived at his house. I thought about Rick, about his final attempt at the Schimmel residence to make a play for me, and how empty it felt. Then I thought about Latham, about the opportunity I'd blown by not immediately saying yes to his proposal, and if there was anything I could do to make it up to him.

I must have dozed off, because the next thing I knew the car door was opening. Wilbur held the door, grinning foolishly.

"Are you sure this is okay?" I asked, and immediately regretted it. I didn't want to seem grateful.

"It's a pleasure. Are you hungry?"

"No. Just tired."

"I have an extra bedroom. It hasn't been used in a while, but I have some clean linen in the closet."

I restrained myself from saying thank you, and followed Wilbur into his house.

"It's the last door at the end of the hall. Let me get you some fresh sheets."

I frankly didn't care if the sheets were fresh or soiled, as long as they weren't covered with bees. I was so tired I could sleep on anything. But when I entered the room and flipped on the switch, all of my exhaustion disappeared.

There were three large picture frames on the wall, each containing dozens of photographs in individual borders. And I was the subject of every picture.

The first frame was all from my youth. Baby pictures. School pictures. I'd seen most of them before, in my mother's photo albums.

But the second frame contained entirely new pictures. New to me, at least. They were from my teenage years. I wasn't posing for any of these; they'd been taken from the side, from behind things like cars or trees, or from a distance using a long lens. There were a few closer, clearer shots; pictures of me at my high school graduation, college graduation, police academy graduation, shaking the mayor's hand.

In the third frame, my wedding. My eyes welled up. I had no wedding pictures, and to see me in my wedding dress was an unbelievable gift. It was a little blurry, as if taken in a rush, but I touched the glass and a sob escaped my throat. Next to it, me walking down the aisle, with Mom. Exchanging rings with Alan. Even one of us kissing.

"Oh, my. I'm sorry, Jacqueline. I should have told you about those."

I looked at Wilbur, standing in the doorway with some folded sheets. "You were . . . at my wedding?"

"I had to stay in the background. I didn't want your mother to see me. Jacqueline, I don't want you to think that I'm some kind of crazy stalker—"

"And at my graduations?"

"Yes. I didn't mean any harm. I was so proud of you and—"

I opened up my arms and held him, held him so tight, I thought I might break him.

"You actually do care, don't you?"

"Of course I care. You're my daughter. I never stopped loving you."

I sniffled, rubbed my eyes, regained a little composure.

"I missed you at my wedding."

"I was there. Hiding in the shadows."

"I missed dancing with you. I remember thinking, at the reception, that there was no father-daughter dance, and it made me sad."

Wilbur said, "Hold that thought," and then turned on the clock radio next to the dresser. An oldies station came on, a classic Sinatra tune. Wilbur bowed.

"May I have this dance?"

I giggled, suddenly feeling like a little girl again. "I think I can squeeze you in."

He was a better dancer than I was, and after a few failed attempts at spins, we settled for holding each other and moving in small circles.

"You know," I said, "I'm seeing someone else now."

"Who?"

"His name is Latham."

"The accountant? The one from the Gingerbread Man case?"

I held him at arm's length.

"How do you know about that?"

"Want to see my scrapbooks with all of your press clippings?"

I laughed, hugging him again.

"Maybe later, Dad."

"Really?"

"Yeah," I said, putting my head on his shoulder. "Later, for sure."

I WATCHED LATHAM FROM BEHIND. He was standing between a set of parallel bars, his effervescent physical therapist urging him to take another step. He did, followed by another, and another, until he reached the end of the bars and had to turn around. I walked up behind him and kissed his cheek.

"Hi, honey."

"Are you here to save me, Jack? It's like a prison camp. Terrible food, unbearable torture."

"Can I borrow him for a minute, Julie?" I asked the therapist.

"Just for a minute. Then we have to do our sets."

Latham rolled his eyes in mock horror. "God, I hate sets. Carry me out of here, Jack. I don't need to walk anymore. Walking is overrated."

"Latham, I need to be serious for a moment. Can you do that?"

"Sure."

I breathed deep, let it out slow.

"I know we said we weren't going to talk about engagements and marriage until you're a hundred percent again. But that's not working for me."

Latham stared at me so deeply I felt he could read my thoughts.

"What are you saying, Jack?"

I clapped my hands once, and the mariachi trio entered, filling the hospital gym with music. Latham grinned at me when I got down on one knee. I was much more nervous than I thought I'd be.

"Latham Conger, I care about you more than any man I've ever met, and I don't want to wait to be engaged because every minute we're not together is a minute I'm dying inside."

"Really? Dying inside?"

I took his hand and tugged the ring out of my pocket. A gold band with a single diamond set inside. I was scared, but if I could handle bees crawling all over me, I could handle anything.

"Will you—"

"Wrong hand, Jack."

I grabbed his other hand.

"Will you—"

"Wow, that's a nice ring."

"Latham Conger," I said, loudly so he wouldn't interrupt me again, "will you marry me?"

He smiled at me, and my heart melted.

"Yes. I will."

Acknowledgments

FOR MY THIRD JACK DANIELS THRILLER, *RUSTY NAIL*, I was on tour for more than three months. I visited over six hundred bookstores in twenty-seven states, and drove 13,500 miles. While touring, I met more than eleven hundred wonderful booksellers, and promised I would thank them in the acknowledgments of this book. After all, you do all the work!

If your name was accidentally omitted or misspelled (it's not my fault, I swear!), e-mail me through my website, www.JAKonrath.com, and we'll fix it for future editions of *Dirty Martini*.

Thank you so very much for all of your help. Without you, I wouldn't be where I'm at today. Booksellers rock!

BOOKSELLERS:

Trish Abood, Cynthia Abraham, Al Abramson, Marsha Acevedo, Jen-na Acree, Matt Adair, Monica Adams, Nikki Adams, Starr Adamson, Mary Adkins, Jamie Agnew, Robin Agnew, Doris Ahrens, Augie Aleksy, Tracy Aleksy, Betsy Alexander, Gretchen Alexander, Timothy Alexander, Irwin Alexis, Manuel Aliceq, Jessica

Allen, Nicholas Allen, Alex Almieda, Ashley Altadonna, Sam Altman, Sara Alton, Terry S. Amstutz, Deborah Andalino, David Anderson, Jamie Anderson, Norman Anderson, Stan Anderson, Susan Anderson, Sonna Andrews, Carolyn Antolin, Nicole Aquilino, Coleen Archer, Marta Armata, Odessa Armstrong, Yanira Arriaga, Nevart Asadoorian, Sandy Aston, Rebecca Atchley, Pauls Atwell, Marti Auner, Joel Baer, Ruth Bagel, Jessica Baker, Stephanie Baker, Trace Baker, Lisa Bakke, Jessica Balbuena, Agnes Baldwin, Bob Baldwin, Kelli Ball, Matthew Ballard, Eddie Banchs, Linda Bantz, Cindy Barbour, Brian Barrett, Jessica Barton, Scott E.C. Baseler, Fress Bass, Brandon Baum, Melissa Bay, Nikki Beane, Laurie Beaster, Joi Bechett, Pam Beck, Kevin Becker, Alex Beguin, Nancy Bender, Pat Benham, Kathleen Benjey, Carolyn Bennet, Joe Benninghoff, Don Berg, Sarah Berger, Nina Bernard, Shannon Berndtson, Adrienna Berrien, Mark Berthiaume, Monica-Sabrina Bharoocha, Mark Bibler, David Biemann, Holly Biggs, Scott Bihorel, Terri Bischoff, Thomas Bishop, Tom Bisker, Isabel Luque Black, Peter Black, Emily Blackburn, Jody Blair, Courtney Blake, Melissa Blanchette, Alisha Blanding, Donna Blomquist, Kara Blood, Matt Bloom, Lesley Bodemann, Sharon Bodnar, Zack Bonchack, Nicola's Books, Kim Borcoman, Jen Borror, Joyce Botie, Allen Bouchard, Ron Bousquet, Amy Bovin, Pat Bowling, Anne M. Bowman, Patrick Boyle, Nancy Boyles, Dorothy Brackett, Anne Bradley, Barbara Brallon, Brennan Brammer, Julie Brandt, Vincent Brantley, Wendy Brault, Laura Brauman, Beverly Breeger, Kim Brei, Pamela Brent, Wendy Brewer,

Kerry Breymann, Colleen Briggs, Beth Bright, Allan Brightman, Karen Brissette, Kathryn Britto, Krystal Brium, Connie Brodovicz, Donald Brooker, Kay Brough, Bill Brown, Rosie Brown, Erica Bruns, David Bryce, Donna Buchignani, Stacey L. Buckland, Randell Buckler, Kristinia Buckwalter, Marquietta Buffaloe, Valerie Bullaughey, Loren Bunjes, Jacen Burchfield, Amanda Burgess, Bill Burlew, Bev Burris, Mike Bursaw, Kim Bushy, Diane Butler, Penny Byrd, Robert Cain, Jonell Caldwell, Mark Cameron, Patty Campbell, Pat Caniff, Amy Capobianco, Jonita Carder, Joann Carey, Becky Carigaan, Carrie Carlson, Erik Carlson, Marianne Carlson, Sue Carpenter, Carol Carr, David Carter, Judy Castell, Nicole Castelli, Emma Cawley, Randal Cefalli, Gerry Champagne, Joe Champion, Sherri Chavez, Lea Chisum, Michael Chovanes, Joanne Cilento, Ashley N. Cipollone, Ami Clare, Larry Clark, Tom Clark, Carol Cleaves, Jeremy Clegg, Jasmine Clemente, Virginia Cochran, Catalin Codescu, Julianne Cody, Harry Cohen, Jen Cohen, Liz Cohn, Peter Colatarci, Jason Cole, Lauren Colgan, Marion Collentine, Kari B. Collier, Andrea Collins, Peggy Coltus, Pat Comerford, Hillary Compton, Paul Concannon, Bob Connolly, Patrick Connolly, Carmine Consolazio, Barbara Cook, Sarah E. Corban, Erin Corbitt, Rebecca Coste, Cindy Coughlin, David Courtney, Siusan Cox, Tom Cox, Diane Cramer, Cheryl Crimmins, Dawn Crofoot, John and Toni Cross, Sarah Crook, Christopher Croser, Bart Crouch, JoAnn Crue, Kelly Crum, Sharon Curtis, Cyndi Custer, Guy Dabis, Amanda Dahling, George Daly, Kayto Daly, Mike

Danilowicz, Debbie Darrisaw, Merv Darter, Elizabeth
Dashiell, Sheryl Daughenbaugh, April Davis, Barb Davis,
Douglas Davis, Mark Davis, Peggy Davis, Jeremy Day,
Linda Day, Antonio De La Fuentes, Ariana de la Concha,
Lori De Almeida, Jim Dean, Nancy Dean, Marissa
Deaver, Mark Dec, David Dedin, Timothy Deerig, Di-
anne DeFonci, Derek DeMello, Mary Denaro, Jeffre
Dene, Tina Denson, Kerri Deoyelle, Dennis Detweiler,
Doug DeWeese, AJ DeWitt, Mary Anne Diehl, Mark
Diller-Lancaster, Bill Dinkins, Elaine Dixon, Jesie Do-
bies, Brain Dodl, Victoria Doherty, Mary Donlon, Linda
Dorsey, Dawn Doud, Bob Downing, Dan Doyle, Russ
Doyle, Joe Drabyak, Michele Droga, Monique Duci,
Heather Duesler, Charles Duhesi, Derek D. Dunbar,
Michael Dunn, Kathleen Duplinsky, Jenne Duprez,
David Durkit, Lola Durodola-Alston, Jessica Dyer,
Dawn Dyste, Elizabeth Earhart, Becky Eblen, Nicole
Eckersly, John Eckhoff, Joyce Edelin, Eliot Edge, Alex
Ehret, Benjamin Ellis, David English, Richard Erb,
Michelle Erwin, Beth Esser, Jennifer Etchason, Suzanne
Eversen, David Factor, Ann Fadze, Carolyn Falcone,
Melinda Fant, Annette Farrell, Amanda Fath, Chuck
Fath, Chris Feighner, Wanda Feleciano, Kelly L. Fenech,
Pat P. Fenning, Rebeca Ferreira, Cindy Ferris, Dwayne
Fields, Robert Figel, William Fike, Dick File, Marylin
Filipowicz, Charlene Fink, Jill Fische, Marilyn Fisher,
Sarah Fisher, Nancy Fitzgerald, Kate Fitzgerald-Lewis,
Nancy Flanagan, David Fletcher, Kim Fletcher, Cheri
Flood, Gabriel Flores, Jane Flowers, Kathy Forbes, Jessica
Ford, Nancy Foust, David Fox, Christina Foxley, Cathy

Frashuer, Zack Frederick, Becky Freed, Maria Frick, Al Friscia, Alfonso Friscia, Barb Frivance, Joyce Frommer, Branden Frost, Taryn Fry, Pam Fullord, Bill Fulton, G.K., J.W. Gaberdiel, Paul Gagne, Wendy Gale, Deb Galloway, Mary Ellen Gan, Geoff Gannon, Daniel Garcia, Emily Gardner, Gary Garletts Jr., Charlie Garnet, Natalie Garofalo, Mary Garst, Vivian Gatti, Ashley Gaus, Laurel Gauthier, Sarah Gay, Cheryle Wasson Geeding, Josh Gerding, Alicia Giacin, Joy Gibson, Sarah Gielhoff, Nora Gilchrist, Doc Gillespie, Jon Gingery, Wgwen Ginocchio, Meredith Giordan, Tamryn Glaser, Paula Glass, Melanie Glemser, Larry Glock, Molly Glock, Kevin Gocoran, Paul Goebel, Mike Goehrig, Norman Goldman, Evelynn Goldner, Irma Gomez, Kathy Goodkin, Mario Goodson, Cindi Gordon, Nancy Gottardi, Jonathan Grabis, John Grady, Chris Graham, Susan Gramea, Adam Gramty, Cyndi Grant, Rich Grant, April Graves, Julie Gray, Bob Green, James Green, Selene Green, Jason Greene, Justin Greene, Francisco Gregory, Steve Gresson, James Griffin, Sean Grimes, Leo Grody, Molly Groome, Dustin Gruss, Sandy Gruszynski, Carole Guerra, Rae Guerrieri, Brannon Gullatt, Elizabeth Gunn, Richard Gurley, Barb Gurtor, Susan Gusho, Eduardo Gutierrez, Anne H., Lisa Hailes, Mary Haina, Anne Hall, Denis Haly, Barbara Hames, Louis Hanemaun, Tonya Hanigan, Michael Hargett, Emily Harkins, Michael Harkins, Paul Harkins, Scott Harkins, Kim Harmon, Betty Harrigan, Liz Harrington, Charity Harris, Cheryl Harris, J. Scooter Harris, Jackie Harris, Kim Harris, Woody Harris, Doug Hart, Jennifer Hart, Danielle Hartle, Phil Hartman,

Linda Hartung, Bob Haslett, Brandi Hasting, Kim Hatcher, Michael Hatton, Jessie Hausmann, Janice Hawkins, Chelly Haycraft, Tim Hayes, Stephanie Hazeelrig, Janice Hecht, Stuart Hecht, Jason Heflin, Christina Heid, Maryann Heide, Knut Heimer, Joe Helfand, Judy Helie, Maria Helms, Barbara Henderson, Clyde M. Hennessey, Marc Hennessey, Ann Hennessy, Jennifer Henry, Samantha Hepburn, Fred Herbst, Gloria Hernon, Michele Herrmann, Tina Hessen, Kay Hessman, Linda Hetz, Tavia Highsmith, Lisa Hilgenberg, Andrew Hill, Susan Hillman, Carmaletta Hilton, Daniel Ho, Jonathan Hobgood, Dan Hochman, Riett Hoffmann, Jennifer Hogge, Annie Holden, Carol Holko, Pat Holland, Kat Horace, Jay Horgan, Melissa Horn, Katie Hosie, Ralph Houch, Ralph Houck, Beth-Ann House, Melissa Hovis, Bruce Howard, Michael Howard, Jim Huang, Bonnie Hudson, Lindsay Huff, Mary Hugger, Ashley Hughes, Marie Hughes, Beverly Humphrey, Eddie Humphrey, Hugo Huns, Daniel Hunt, Sarah Iddings, Toni Imhoet, Edie Indrisk, Mike Infonte, Mike Jackman, Carolyn Jackson, Jacquelyn Jackson, C. Aimee Jacobs, Marla Jacobson, Bill Jankowski, Julie Jawor, Jason Jefferies, Steven Jensen, Brittany Jobe, Gordon Jochem, Paul Johnsen, Andrea Johnson, Bronwyn Johnson, Diane Johnson, Edie Johnson, George T. Johnson, John Johnson, Karen Johnson, Kim Johnson, Rozanne Johnson, Sean Johnson, Toni Johnson, Robert Johnstone, Bev Jones, Cheryl A. Jones, Jessica R. Jones, Kee Jones, Michele Jones, Sheena Jones, Sue Jones, Jeanie Joran, Alise Jordan, Chris Jordan, Jeffrey Joseph, John Jowle, Benjamin Juares,

Steve Jurczyk, Kelly Justice, Jeff Kalina, Shannon Kane, Mitchell Kaplan, Ty Karnitz, Richard Katz, George Henry Keen, Linda Keller, Robyn Kellison, Jennifer Kelly, Jodi Kelly, Jacki Kendall, Craig Kennedy, Stormy Lee Kennedy, Lucelle Kenny, Alex Kerr, Kenya Kidder, Joe Kill, Mike Kilroyne, Christine King, Barbara A. Kiser, Paul R. Klein, Karen Knopp, James Knowles, Kim Knowlton, Jennifer Knox, Pam Knudtzon, Connie Kocian, Crissy Kokes, Brent Koontz, Thea Kotroba, Barb Kovacs, Pam S. Kowalski, Greg Kozatek, Kelly Kramer, Lynn Kramer, Emily Krasner, Asya Krasteva, Roger Krause, Roberta Krinsky, Linda Krumrai, Vicky Kugler, Kitty Kunkel, Kim Laime, Kathy Lajoie, Lianne Lajoie, Cathy Lakin, Heather Lamothe, Paul Landry, Phillip Landry, Maria Landsberg, Helen Langelier, Rebecca Langley, Sue Lanham, Matt Lappa, Ananne Lara, Michelle LaRose, Emma Larson, Dee Laskoars, Rebecca Lasky, Michele Lauber, Lisa Lauerman, Tim Lause, Rand Laverty, Jennifer Lavuie, Vicki Lawrence, Clare Lazarek, J. Lea, Laura Lee, Brianna Leech, Ms. Kirby Vi Leeds, Amanda Lemco, Tracy Lemmo, Charlie Lemoine, Kim Leonard, Jesse Levi, Beth Lewis, Kristyn Lier, Keller Lindsay, Ron Lindsey, Michale Link, Sue Little, Laura Loeb, Jeri Loebach, Juli Loker, Joni London, Don Longmuir, Jenn Longmuir, Teresa Lopez, Robin Lubnow, Jamie Lucas, Jim Lucas, Richard Lum, Robert Luna, Kimberly Luthin, Patricia Lynch, Jeff Macanovich, Kevin Macey, Scott Machennan, Andrew Mack, Daniel J. Madison, Tom Madden, Jaret M. Maloney, Steve Maloney, Joedan Maltin, Darlene Manchester, Yolanda

Mangham, Blake Mann, Michael Marino, Kay Marlin, Lauren Marques, Brenda Marrujo, Tony Marshall, Ashley Martin, Cassandra Martin, Miranda Martin, Jason Martinek, Celia Martiniez, Joseph Masella, Heather Massie, Tammy Mathews, Steve Matson, Drew Matthews, Michael Mattox, Lisa Maye, Matt Maye, Emily Mayer, Melanie Maynard, Greg Mayyou, Nicole Mazzone, Mike McBride, Billy McCall, Gary McCammon, Kermit McCarther, Alice McConekey, Ollie McCullom, Audrey McCune, Debbie McDonald, Kelly McElligott, Ruth McElwain, Vicki McFiggen, Fran McGeever, Bill McGhee, Brenda McGhee, Kathie McGrath, Erin McGuire, Venus McKinley, Lisa McKown, Sarah McLaughlin, Theresa McNaughton, Tracy McPeck, Julie McPhail, Brian McTague, Rob Mellen, Gail Meno, Andi Mercier, Joy Merdan, Mary Metz, Kari Meutsch, Jeni Meyer, Sue Michael, Debbie Miksch, Georgia Milionis, Barb Miller, Joanne Miller, Judy Miller, Sheila Miller, Philip Millies, Jason Milligan, Elisha Minsal, Rich Mirabelle, Jennifer Miron, Carolyn Mitchell, Jo Ellen Mitchell, Katricia Mitchell, Matt Mitchell, Raymond Mixon, Christopher Mize, Derek Moady, Maggie Moeller, Kelly Molloy, Laura Monegan, Chatham Monk, Fabian Montano, Renee Montgomery, Nancy Moore, Loana Morales, Laura Morefield, Teresa Moreno, John Mori, Karen Morin, Angela Morris, Cori Morrison, Brian Morrissey, Jim Morton, Theresa Mowry, Ian Moyer, Matthew Moyer, Sean Mulligan, Mary Murch, Elizabeth Murphy, Ann Murray, Heather Musilca, Dave Musto, Matthew Nace, Sandy Nagle, Irene Natoli, Margo

Naus, Andrew Neci, Cindy Needham, Justin Neese, Anne Nelson, David Nelson, Lance Nelson, Stacy Nelson, Danielle Neuffer, Alison Newman, Amani Newton, Tracy Nicholas, Kimberly Nicholson, Mike Nieken, Mary Ann Nilsson, Jessica Norton, Susan Novtny, Marni Ockene, Tory O'Connor, Jen Odon, Dienne Ogletree, Amber O'Kelly, Carolyn Oliver, Gunda Olsen, Jessica O'Malley, Matt O'Neill, Scott Orman, Jose Ornelas, Jessie Oulahan, Rusty Page, Alyssa Paglione, Kendrah Palk, Traci Paquin, Doreen Parish, Stephen Parisi, Arlene Parker, Melissa Parks, Jenn Pasquinelli, Bill Payton, Constance Pearce, Toi Pearson, Ryan Peel, Angelina Perdomo, Michael Perkins, Rich Perrin, Paul Pessolano, Barbara Peters, Mike Pettier, Charlotte Philips, Emily Phillinger, Cindy Phillips, Jennifer Phillips, Tess Phillips, Jane Pickering, Mike Pieczynski, David Pildner, Heather Planert, Charlie Podell, Tom Polakowski, Kathy Policicchio, Heather Polk, Michael Pollard, Kerri Pomfret, Taura Pool, Paige Poores, Jodi Pope, Josh Pope, Mark Porter, Sherry Potter, Damien Power, Carole Pozmanter, Brian Prater, Shawna Prested, Dan Preston, Mary Prfhoda, Adam Price, Margaret Price, Vivian Priest, Dawn Prudenti, Jeff Putnam, Wink Qursgard, Josh Rachlin, April Rager, Jenna Raich, Rosemary Rambo, Keith Ranalli, Tammy Randolph, Bill Rankin, Bob Rathbun, April Ray, Sara Rebennack, Jean Recapet, Cindy Reid, Kristin Reis, Debbie Repass, Kathy Rettinger, Jimmy Rholerson, Rich J. Rhymbant Jr., Jody Rice Kirby, Leah Richey, Johnathan Richez, Clinton Rickards, MK Riddell, Kathie Riddle, Amber Ridinger, Sherri Riffel, Heather M. Riley, Christine Rillo, Crystal

Rinehart, Margie Ringel, Richard Rivellese, Sherise Rivera, Terry Robare, Amy Deming Robb, Stanley Roberson, Darcy Roberts, Him Robins, Jacob Robinson, Roger Rodriguez, Linda Roe, Linda Roebuck, James M. Roemele, Charli Rogers, Kathy Rogers, Jessica Roland, LeAnne Rollins, Michelle Romano, Jennifer Romesburg, Patricia Rooney, Michael Rosczak, Michelle Rose, Theresa Rosinski, Chad Rouch, Jayne Rowsam, Alexis Roy, Catherine Rozmarynowycz, Harley Ruda, Bob Rudman, Jessica Russler, Louis Russo, Bob Ryan, Christopher Ryan, Mart Sadler, Sage, Melinda Salonga, Patricia Sanders, Carrie Sasville, Cale Satterlee, Natalie Sawyer, Dolores Scanio, Christina Scatchell, Erin Schaeffer, Alisa Schnaars, Fred Schodey, Fred Schooley, Marya Schrier, Brian Schropp, Carol Schubert, Joseph Schutz, Eric Schwendeman, Phil Scopa, George Scott, Robin Scott, Joyce Sebek, Bob Seibel, Brad T. Seibel, Larry Seigel, Jane Selavka, Angelica Serrano, Pete Sesko, Susan Sewell, Jeremy Seybert, Sara Shaffer, Glori Shanda, Sharron Shannon, Razra Shariff, Jonathan Shaver, Kelly Shaw, Rachel Shaw, Peter Sherman, Patrick Shingleton, Penny Shipley, Jim Shoaf, Kim Shoop, Sally Shrago, Kim Shriver, John Shurtleff, Christine Siegrist, Matt Silver, Jason Simon, Jessic Simon, Tina Simone, Carol Simpson, Joanne Sinchuk, Marcy Singer, Bob Siwiecki, Marggie Skinner, Greg Skipworth, Paul Skotarski, Anne Smiley, Adam N. Smith, Alisha Smith "Amarie," Edward Smith, Karen Smith, Kathy Smith, Kimber Smith, Marlin Smith, Matthew Dow Smith, Melissa Smith, Peggy Smith, Robert T. Smith, Sandra Smith, Stephanie Smith, Terri

Smith, Ruth Smyrl, Elaine Smyser, Julie Snow, Karenne Snow, Marion Sokolowski, Carlos Solorzano, Robert Sommerville, Sarah Sonnett, Adlinmarie Soto, Kendra Soule, Jamey Sovey, Eric Sroka, Grag Stahl, Mike Stancombe, Michael Staples, Pamela Starkovich, Frank Staseik, Eileen Stauffer, Megan Steele, Chad Stegmiller, Ulrike Steiert, Brian Stepanic, Paul Sternburgh, Catherine Stevens, Jodie Stevenson, Paula Stewart, Ellen Stewert, Kathleen Stilwell, Jennifer Stone, Andrea Storiale, Brenda Strong, Jim Stroup, Mike Stuart, Stephanie Suer, Irene Sullivan, Mike Sumser, Greg Swanson, Melissa Swart, Patti Swift, Stephanie Swisher, Shelle Takacs, Angela Tarbett, Mary Tatz, Kelly Taylor, Lelia Taylor, Moe Taylor, Susan M. Taylor, Derek Teixeira, Patts Templeton, Lee Anne Test, Melissa Theel, Joanna Thomas, Kate Thomas, Shumara Thomas, Ryan Thomley, Evelyn Thompson, Bonnie Jeanne Tibbetts, Anne Tingo, Andrew Todd, Chris Tokar, Anne Tokos, Christina Tomaselli, Lorenz Tomassi, Jennifer Tomczak-Moore, Shalor Toncray, Brian Torbert, Jessica Torres, Rich Torres, Janis Torzillo, Amanda Toth, Tina Trevaskis, Erie Trevina, Tom Trotter, Monica Tsuneishi, Freeman Turley, Tegan Twedt, Jeannie Tyler, Kurt Van Buren, Pat Van Deusen, Fred Van Patten, Jan Van Skiver, Karen Vanan, Doug VanderSys, Pat Vann, Daniele "Danni" Vargas, Ann Varwig, Isabel Vasallo, Kimberly Vater, Kristrin Vates, Jessica Vera, Tracie Vettel, Linda Vetter, Vince Vieceli, Christina Villa, Carol Villaverde, Steven Viola, Margia Wagner, Sue Wakeman, Brian Walker, Katherine Wall, Karen Wallace, Harold Waller, Brandon Walsh, Lisa

Walston, Abby Walters, Drew Watson, Hazel Watson, George Way, Susan Weaver, Cari Webb, Joolee Webb, Matthew Weeks, Brad Wees, Darlene Weir, Jeff Welch, Debbie Wells, Kristen Wells, Matt Welsh, Eleanor Wenger, Beth Wentworth, Bill West, Sue Westmeyer, Amy Wheeler, Barbara Whetstone, Ann White, Ron White, Dale Whitham, Brad Whitmire, Alan Whitson, Megan Whitt, William Wildly, Denise K. Williams, Joe Williams, Kelly Williams, Kim Williams, Sandra Williams, Tabbetha Williams, Rhonda Williams-Snell, Matt Wilson, Meredith Wilson, Jeannette Wilson-Bell, Jason Wingate, Pat Winter, Hal Wishman, Flo Witalka, Chris Wolak, Jay Wolferman, Kathi Wolff, Debbie Wood, Rob Wood, Rushton Woodside, Wendy Worth, Mary Wright, Nancy Bass Wyden, Pat Wynn, John Yezzi, Corryn Young, Rosemary Young, Ted Zabawski, Sherry Zabikow, Yassar Zacks, Elisabeth Zak, Scot Zellman, Paul Ziebarth, Dan Zimmeran, Gina Ziria, and Henry Zook.

There were also many folks who helped me out by inviting me into their homes, helping me tour their cities, or buying me food.

Huge thanks to the following:

Paul Abruzzi, Tasha Alexander, Wayne Thomas Batson, Bill Blume, John Bodnar, James O. Born, Stacey Cochran, Jim Coursey, Linda Darter, Charlie Davidson, Karen Dionne, Rebecca Drake, Moni Draper, Jane Dystel, Barry Eisler, David Ellis, JT Ellison, Miriam Goderich, Lynne

Hansen, Sean Hicks, Adam Hurtubise, Bill Johnson, Cynthia Johnson, Elizabeth Krecker, Rhonda Lukac, Steve Lukac, Terrie Moran, Bob Morris, Karen E. Olsen, Barbara Parker, PJ Parrish, MJ Rose, Tom Schreck, Steve Schwinder, Jason Sizemore, Alexandra Sokoloff, Jeff Strand, M.G. Tarquini, Robert W. Walker, Leslie Wells, James R. Winter, Becky Zander, and Rick Zander.

And also, big thanks to the fans. Without you, Jack and I wouldn't have this incredible career. You folks are the best!

If you loved

DIRTY MARTINI,

be sure to catch

FUZZY NAVEL,

J. A. Konrath's latest

Jacqueline "Jack" Daniels Mystery,

coming in July 2008 from Hyperion.

An excerpt, chapters 1 and 2, follows.

KORK

IT'S QUIET IN THE SUBURBS. The only sound is from the cab that has dropped me off, making a U-turn at the dead end, then heading back down the quiet, winding road. Its taillights quickly disappear, swallowed up by the multitude of trees.

I walk up the driveway and look at the house. It's a ranch, laid out in the shape of an L, occupying half an acre of green lawn speckled with fallen leaves. There's a double-car garage, the door closed. I see Mom through the front bay window. She's sitting in a rocking chair and reading a book—how much more stereotypical elderly can you get? I check the front door, and as expected it is locked.

I walk around the side of the house, running my hand along the brown brick, passing windows that should probably be washed. This is a big departure from the Chicago apartment. A lot more space. A lot more privacy. I've discovered that privacy is important. No neighbors for more than a quarter mile is a good thing. With all of the tree coverage, it's like being in the middle of the woods, rather than only five miles away from O'Hare Airport.

I stop at the back porch—a slab of concrete with the obligatory lawn chairs, a wrought iron sun table, and a veranda—and I close my eyes, breathing in the cool autumn air. Somewhere, someone is burning leaves. I haven't smelled that since my youth. I fill my lungs with the scent and smile. It smells like freedom.

The sliding glass patio door is open, and I decide to give Mom a lecture about that. Just because the suburbs are safer than the city doesn't mean that all of the doors shouldn't be locked.

I walk into the kitchen, catch the odor of home cooking. A pot is on the stove. I check the contents. Stew. I pick up the spoon, give it a stir, take a little bite of potato. Delicious.

Mom yells, "Jacqueline?"

I consider answering her, but decide a surprise is in order instead. I take out my gun and tiptoe into the hallway.

"Jacqueline? Is that you?"

I look left, then right, scanning for the psychotic cat that lives here. He isn't around.

"Jacqueline, you're frightening me."

That's the point, Mom.

I peek around the corner and see that Mom is standing up. She's in her seventies, short hair more gray than brown, her back bent with age. She's wearing a housedress, something plaid and shapeless. Mom's eyes dart this way and that way. They settle on me, and she gasps.

"Oh my God," she says.

"Did I scare you? You shouldn't leave the back door open, Mom. God only knows what kind of weirdos can get in."

Mom's chest flutters, and she says in a small voice, "I know who you are. My daughter told me all about you."

She reaches for the phone, but I'm on her in three steps, giving her a firm slap across her wrinkled face.

"I'm going to ask you this one time, and one time only. And then I'm going to start hurting you."

I smile, knowing how it makes the scar tissue covering most of my face turn bright pink, knowing how horrifying it looks.

"Where's Jack?"

MUNCHEL

THE TARGET IS two hundred and eighty-three yards away. James Michael Munchel knows all about mil dots, and how to calculate distance with the reticle, but he's using a laser measuring unit instead. This isn't cheating. A sniper can and should use every bit of technology available to him in the field, whether he's on a roof in Dhi Qar, Iraq, or crouching behind some shrubs in the Chicago neighborhood of Ravenswood.

Munchel is sitting on the lawn, legs crossed, the tip of his Unique Alpine TPG-1 rifle peeking out through the leafy green dogwood. He arrived here two hours ago, but had selected this spot three weeks earlier. The house is unoccupied, and Munchel has pulled the For Sale sign out of the lawn and set it facedown. Realtors probably won't stop by this late. If one does . . . well, too bad for her.

Munchel is wearing a camouflage jacket, leggings, and black steel-toed boots he bought at the army/navy surplus store on Lincoln Avenue. He can't be seen from the sidewalk fifteen feet away. Munchel knows this for a fact, because he's done several dry runs prior to today.

He's practically invisible, even if someone is staring right at him.

To avoid arousing suspicion, Munchel didn't walk here in full camo. He came in street clothes—jeans and a blue shirt—and awkwardly changed while crouching behind the dogwood, putting his civvies in the black two-wheeled suitcase he towed along.

Munchel scratches his stubble, then peers through the Leupold scope, which has been zeroed out at two hundred yards. The crosshair is slightly above and to the right of the target's head, to adjust for the wind and the bullet drop. He'll never admit it, but he doesn't understand how to determine MOA—minute-of-angle. He can fake it online, while posting on the sniper message boards, but he doesn't really know how to calculate the actual degrees. In the forest preserve near his house, Munchel can hit a target from five hundred yards and keep the grouping within a four-inch radius. Who cares what the MOA is? It's good shooting no matter how you calculate it.

The target has his back to Munchel. He's in his living room, on the first floor of the two-flat, sitting at the computer. Just like he is every day at this time.

Predictability is a killer.

The blinds hanging in the large, three-section bay window are open, and Munchel can see straight down the hallway, all the way to the back of the house. He nudges the rifle slightly, to check what the target is surfing.

Pornography. Some weird shit with chicks wearing rubber aprons and wielding whips.

Freak, Munchel thinks. *Deserves everything he's about to get.*

Munchel glances at his watch, a Luminox 3007, the same kind that Navy SEALs use. Less than a minute left. Munchel's hands start to shake, and he realizes he's breathing heavy. Not from fear. From excitement. All the training, all the planning, it all comes down to this moment.

The butt plate is snug against his armpit, his face is tight against the cheek pad, the safety is off. The aluminum gun chassis is on the concrete planter behind the dogwood, a hard surface that ensures the gun will stay steady. Munchel takes a deep breath, lets it out through his teeth. His ears tell him there is no traffic coming, which is essential because he's shooting across the street—it would be bad if a car entered his line of fire at the moment of truth.

The target stands up, walks toward the window, seems to look right at him. Impossible, of course. He's much too far away, too well hidden. But it's still unnerving. Munchel chews his lower lip, begins the countdown.

The target turns. Munchel completely empties his lungs and waits . . . waits . . . waits . . . then squeezes the trigger with the ball of his finger, trying to time it between heartbeats like he's read about online.

There's a loud *CRACK*. The target's head explodes, and he pitches forward.

Munchel sucks in some air and lets it out as a laugh. *How ridiculously easy.* He checks to see if anyone around him noticed the gunfire. The sidewalks are clear. No one opens a door and sticks their head out. Everything is completely normal, just an average fall day in the city.

He reaches for his canteen—also an army/navy store purchase—and slurps down some purple Gatorade. His untraceable prepaid cell phone vibrates, and he stares at the number. It's Swanson. Anxious to see how it went, to meet at the rendezvous point and brag over beer and chicken wings.

Munchel ignores the call. He has other ideas of how to celebrate.

A streetlight comes on, its sensor activated by a timer. Munchel loads a round, aims, and takes it out. That's two shots now. Still, no one seems to notice. How disappointing.

He takes out his phone and dials 911.

"I was walking down Leavitt and heard someone shooting. I think my neighbor has been killed."

"What is your name, sir?"

"He's at forty-six fifty-two. I think someone shot him."

"Can you give me your name?"

Munchel hangs up, sips more Gatorade, and hunkers down to wait for the police to arrive.